MW01146933

Forever

Quail Crossings

By Jennifer McMurrain

Forever Quail Crossings
By Jennifer McMurrain

©2017 by Jennifer McMurrain
All rights reserved.
This book or parts thereof may not be reproduced in any form, stored in or introduced into a retrieval system, or transmitted, in any form, or by any means (electronic, mechanical, photocopying, recording, or otherwise) without prior written permission of the copyright owner and/or publisher of this book, except as provided by United States of America copyright law.

This book is a work of fiction. Names, characters, places, and incidents are a product of the author's imagination or are used fictitiously. Any resemblance to actual events, locales, or persons, living or dead, is coincidental.

Cover Design: Brandy Walker
www.SisterSparrowGraphicDesign.com
Interior Design: Jennifer McMurrain
www.LilyBearHouse.com

Published by LilyBear House, LLC
www.LilyBearHouse.com

ISBN-13: 978-1974269808
ISBN-10: 1974269809

Also available in eBook publication

PRINTED IN THE UNITED STATES OF AMERICA

Dedication

To my baby girl, Annaley ... know you always have a forever place.

Chapter One

May 6, 1950

Alice Brewer pulled her truck over just before the driveway that led to Quail Crossings and took a deep breath. It was her first visit home since her winter break from West Texas State College, and even though she knew she had missed her home, she hadn't realized how much until she saw the two-story brown house.

"So this is it," she said.

Alice looked at the man sitting on her right, Walter Jefferson. He was tall with short dark hair, had a scrawny build, and deemed himself Alice's sweetheart. Alice enjoyed his company but had never encouraged the title of sweetheart. He had been her best friend throughout her college career, so when Walter asked if he could work at Quail Crossings for the summer, the thought didn't bother Alice one bit. She immediately asked her brother, Bill, and gained his approval.

With all the other men in her family having successful businesses, Bill was going to have to hire on help for the first time since coming to Quail Crossings. He had done right by the place, making it one of the most successful farms in the county, but couldn't do it on his own any longer. The other men helped when they could, but Bill was quick to jump on Walter's offer to work the farm through harvest before taking on a teaching job as an agriculture instructor.

"Do you think you can handle it?" asked Alice with a playful smile. "It's a big farm and Bill's done wonders with the new milo fields. It's tough work, especially for a city boy."

"You underestimate us city boys," said Walter, giving her a wink. "We're tougher than we look." He eyed Quail Crossings again. "Any last words of advice?"

"Yeah," said Alice as she put the truck in gear. "Watch out for the goose."

"The goose?" Walter questioned as he looked out the window.

Alice pulled back onto the road, before turning into the drive. "Yes, Norman. He's older than Moses and crankier than a badger. He'll leave you be, once you've been around a while, but don't turn your back to him."

"Okay," said Walter. "Don't trust the goose."

Alice pulled into the driveway as Dovie Pearce and her husband, Gabe, burst through the back door to greet them as soon as the exited the truck..

"I'm so glad you're home," said Dovie. "What took you so long? I expected you here by noon and here we are going on two o'clock. I swear I've been waiting a month of Sundays."

"I'm afraid that was my fault," said Walter, stretching out his hand to greet Dovie. "I over packed, and we had to spend time sorting out what I really needed to bring."

"You should have seen it, Momma Dovie! He had three trunks of clothes," laughed Alice.

Remembering her manners, Alice made introductions, "Dovie Pearce, I'd like you to meet Walter Jefferson. Walter, this is the one and only Momma Dovie."

"It's very nice to meet you, Mrs. Pearce," said Walter.

Dovie shook his hand. "Please call me Dovie. We aren't too formal around here."

Walter smiled. "Alice has told me a lot about you."

Dovie pulled the man standing next to her close. "And this is my husband, Gabe."

"You're the pilot," said Walter, shaking Gabe's hand.

"I am," said Gabe as Alice noticed his chest puff up a little bit.

"Wow, I don't know how you do it," said Walter. "I can't even get on a Ferris wheel without trembling like a coward."

"You either love it or hate it," explained Gabe, "but flying is different than a creaky ol' Ferris wheel. Dovie here didn't think she'd like it either until I took her up for the first time. Now, she flies every chance she gets. I'll take you for a ride sometime, and you can decide which party you're in."

"Sounds like an amazing opportunity," said Walter with a chuckle. "If I can find the courage."

Alice's younger sister, Ellie, gave them a finger wave from the back porch stoop.

"Ellie Brewer, you get over here and hug me," said Alice. "Walter won't bite."

"She's the one …?" Walter whispered, trailing off before having to say the unspeakable.

Alice nodded and whispered back. "And she doesn't talk much because of it, so don't push her."

Ellie ran over and gave Alice a tight hug.

"How have you been Ellie?" asked Alice.

Ellie gave Alice a big smile and then hugged her again.

"Good," said Alice, "Ellie, this is my friend, Walter."

"Hi Ellie," said Walter loudly.

"She's not deaf, silly," teased Alice.

"Um ... sorry, Ellie," stumbled Walter. "I am very pleased to meet you."

Ellie gave him a nod and a smile before returning back into the house.

"Dollars to donuts, Ellie's gonna be done peeling those potatoes by the time we get inside," said Dovie. She looked at Walter. "She likes to stay busy, so don't be surprised if you wake up to find all your clothes washed and your shoes shined. She's made me into a lazy mule since she's come to live with us."

"Where is everyone, Momma Dovie?" asked Alice. "I expected a whole slew of family to come and waylay Walter."

Dovie shaded her eyes and looked towards the field. "Well, I see Bill, Lou Anne, and the kids walking through the pasture now. Everyone else will be here for supper. We didn't want to *waylay* poor Walter, so I asked them to wait until evening to come. Alice, you know this bunch is more overwhelming than a swarm of wasps when someone new comes into the fold."

"The perks of having a big family I'd guess," said Walter.

"Come on in and I'll show you where you're staying," said Dovie. "Gabe, honey, will you help Walter with his things? I'll introduce you to Dad, and then you can meet Bill and his family."

"I can manage, but thanks" said Walter, walking to the far side of Alice's truck to gather his suitcases.

"So Walter, you mentioned the perks of a big family, do you come from one?" asked Gabe from the far side of the truck.

"Actually, no," said Walter, "I'm an only child, and my parents were only children, too. So, it's just me, my parents, and my paternal grandfather."

Alice laughed. "I tried to tell him he was in for a shoc …"

"Aagh!" Walter cried before Alice could finish.

Alice raced to his side, just in time to see a large grey and white goose flee the scene.

"That goose bit me!" yelled Walter. "He bit me right on the rear!"

"And that would be Norman. Remember the last thing I told you in the truck?" said Alice.

Walter nodded. "Watch out for the goose. I've got it now."

"I'm sure you do," said Alice, with a wink. "As well as a nice bruise on your behind."

"Don't worry," chuckled Dovie. "That just means you're a part of the family now."

"I'm not sure Mr. Norman thinks that," Alice said with a nervous laugh, "but it is kind of a rite of passage here at Quail Crossings. We've all been nipped by him once or twice."

"Except for Alice," corrected Dovie. "Those two took together like ducks to water."

"Well he is my bestest friend," said Alice with a smile. "Just don't turn your back to Mr. Norman."

"Also, make sure there's a stick, broom handle, or branch in the bed of any truck you drive," said Gabe. "Norman likes to trap the men in this family in the back of the truck bed ... usually on a hot day when you've got no water."

"Sounds like nothing but trouble," said Walter. "Why would you keep a fowl like that around?"

"Well," said Dovie, "besides the fact I haven't lost a single chicken to fox, coyotes, or coons since Norman hatched, he's not only Alice's *bestest friend*, he's her own personal body guard."

Alice gave him a huge smile. "So you better be nice."

"Noted," Walter said, as he glanced over his shoulder and gave Norman a weary look.

"Let's go on in," Gabe said, grabbing Walter's bags.

Dovie and Gabe started toward the back door. As Alice started to follow, Walter gently grabbed her hand and pulled her back towards him. He gave her hand a gentle squeeze.

"Since you've got me, maybe you don't need a goose as your personal bodyguard anymore?"

Alice gave him a playful smile, "Oh Walter, try as you might, you'll never replace Mr. Norman."

Chapter Two

"Mr. James, it is so good to see you," said Alice after getting Walter settled in an upstairs bedroom. "This is my good friend, Walter Jefferson."

Using a wooden cane, James stood and shook Walter's hand. About that time, a boy of nine and a girl of seven came running into the room and latched onto James's waist.

"Whoa, now," he said playfully as he fell back into his trusty soft brown chair. The two children climbed onto his lap, followed by a third girl who looked to be around three or four. James playfully frowned at the older children. "Now, Dean and Annabelle, did you just leave little Rosey behind like a lost sheep?"

"She can't keep up." Annabelle giggled. "We're too fast."

"Well, she's only four," said Bill, walking hand in hand into the parlor with his wife, Lou Anne.

"Watcha got for us, Papa James?" asked Dean.

"Well, he won't have anything for you, if you don't turn around and greet your Aunt Alice and her friend, Mr. Jefferson," scolded Dovie.

Annabelle was the first to scurry over to Alice. "Auntie! I missed you."

She gave Alice a kiss on the cheek.

Rosey and Dean quickly followed, giving Alice enthusiastic hugs.

"I missed you all, too," said Alice. She pointed to Walter. "This is my friend, Walter. Walter this is Dean, Annabelle, and Rosey. They belong to Bill, who you spoke with on the phone, and his wife, Lou Anne."

The kids gave a little finger wave to Walter, and Alice could see he wasn't sure how to greet the kids. He placed his hands behind his back, bent over a bit, and said, "Pleased to meet you."

Bill stepped forward and offered his hand. "Glad to have you on board."

Walter stood tall and shook it. "Thanks for having me. I really appreciate the opportunity."

"Dean," said Lou Anne, "take your sisters and go play outside until dinner is ready."

"Wait," said James as he pulled three peppermints from his pocket. "Have a little something to tide you over until dinner."

"Thank you, Papa James," the kids sang as they grabbed their peppermints and ran toward the door.

"Stay away from the pond and the creek," Bill shouted after them.

"Everybody take a seat," said Dovie. "The roast is roasting, the beans are simmering, and Ellie's working on her special potato salad. She won't share the recipe with anyone, doesn't even let me watch, so let's sit a spell."

"Mr. Jefferson," said James, "tell us a little bit about your farm experience."

"Please, everyone call me Walter, and like I told Bill on the phone, I just received my teaching degree in agriculture management. So I have a lot of knowledge, but I've never actually worked on a farm before."

Alice could feel the room go cold and instantly wanted to make it warm again. "Tell them why you want to teach Ag," she encouraged.

"I was pretty young during the Depression," Walter started. "My family had oil money and saved wisely. To me the effect of the Depression was the fact that instead of having three-course meals three times a day, we had eggs and toast for breakfast, supper leftovers for lunch, and then a three course dinner. Through the Depression, my parents continued to employ a full-time cook, gardener, and a house maid. I still went to the same private school, and my friends were in the same boat I was in. We just didn't understand it. I'd look at those pictures in *Life Magazine,* and it was as if I was reading about some impoverished foreign country, not the very state I lived in just a few counties away. The fascination with it continued through college."

"Well, ain't that something," said Dovie. "During the Depression, I couldn't imagine anyone not hurting in one way or another." She gave an awkward chuckle. "Hope you don't mind leftovers, because we eat them daily here."

Walter blushed. "I must sound like a privileged brat."

James shook his head. "The Depression hit everyone differently. I'm sure your family helped out however they could. We were better off than a lot of people. I was happy to be able to help others out."

"Like giving Bill a job," said Alice, beaming.

"I can't say what my parents did to help others. If my father gave to the less fortunate, it either happened when I was too young to understand it or not around to witness it. Because of my fascination with the Great Depression, I stayed near Amarillo, choosing West Texas State College back when it was West Texas Teachers College, even though I was accepted into the University of Texas's law program."

"I still can't believe he picked West Texas State College over the University of Texas," said Alice shaking her head.

He looked at her. "But then I wouldn't have met you."

Alice felt her cheeks run hot.

"Alice told me all about how your parents abandoned you all for California and how you, Bill, struggled to keep them fed until you found Quail Crossings," continued Walter. "I read stories like yours growing up, but then one day I found I was actually talking to someone who had lived it. It's an amazing tale."

"You make it sound like an adventure out of one of Alice's books," said Bill. "I assure you, if it weren't for James and Dovie, it wouldn't have had a happy ending."

"For either family," added Dovie with a sad smile. "You all helped us just as much as we helped you."

"So there you go. Look how far everyone in this room has come since then," said Walter, gesturing around the room. He pointed at Bill. "You went from orphan to managing a very successful farm. So, after hearing your story first hand from Alice and stories about other farmers that never quit during some of the worst times this country has ever faced, I decided I wanted to be a part of that spirit and strength. I wanted to discover the true meaning of strength and perseverance."

"Well, you can't say he's not enthusiastic," said Gabe, with a smile.

14

"And what do your parents think of your decision to teach agriculture?" asked Dovie.

Walter chuckled. "They think I'm nuttier than peanut butter, but as long as I'm working towards a goal and not just living off family money, they are supportive. To be honest, my dad thinks this is a phase, and that I'll be running home to get my degree in law once it has passed."

"Well," said Bill, "as long as that phase doesn't pass before this harvest is up, you're good to go. We'll teach you everything we can, but I'm not gonna lie, it's hard work, long hours, and a lot of sore muscles at the end of the day."

"I'm not afraid of hard work," said Walter.

"I'm sure that enthusiasm will only grow as you learn how a farm and ranch really work," said James with a smile. "Welcome to Quail Crossings."

"Thank you," said Walter. He looked at Gabe. "Do you work on the farm as well?"

Gabe shook his head. "I help out all I can when I'm here, but I stay pretty busy with my flying."

"Gabe runs his own transportation business," explained Dovie. "He flies everything from wheat seed to people from here to New York, Los Angeles, and even to Canada sometimes."

"Sounds exciting," said Walter.

"It can be," said Gabe as he looked towards the back door. "But not as exciting as the crew that's coming in the back door right now. Batten down the hatches, the twins are here."

Dovie stood, grabbed her basket of yarn and hurried to her bedroom.

"The last time the twins were here," said Gabe, "they unwound all of Dovie's yarn balls and strung them through the house. It was like a crazy maze of color and yarn. It took us hours to unstring and unknot all the yarn and even longer for Dovie and Ellie to twist it back into balls."

"They didn't," gasped Alice. "How did that even happen? It's hard to get a moment alone in this house, much less time to make that kind of mess."

"Dovie and Ellie had gone into town to do the market shopping, I was on a flight, and Evalyn had come over to stay with James while they were gone. But he was napping," explained Gabe as Dovie came back into the room.

"Evalyn swears she just stepped outside for a minute to settle an argument between Joy and Caleb, but when she came back in, it was like a yarn spider had webbed the house," said Gabe.

"I can't imagine," said Walter.

"I couldn't either," said Dovie. "But when Ellie and I returned home, there was Evie practically wrapped in a cocoon of yarn trying to clean up the mess. Bless her heart. She's really got her hands full with those girls."

The screen door creaked as everyone but Walter sucked in a breath.

Chapter Three

As if waiting for some unknown terror to walk into the room, every pair of eyes watched the doorway from the kitchen to the parlor.

"Hey girls," said Dovie as the twins toddled into the living room like two angels from Heaven with their shiny blonde hair full of curls and their bright green eyes. "Come say hello to Mr. Jefferson. Walter this is Bonnie and Beverly."

"I'm Bonnie," said the girl Dovie had introduced as Beverly. "Beverly is my sister."

Alice shook her head. "You can't fool me. I know you're Beverly. Do you know how I know?"

The girl shook her head.

"Because you have a faint freckle right above your eyebrow like I do." Alice pointed above her own eyebrow and then looked at Bonnie. "Which makes you Bonnie." She tweaked the little girl's nose and everyone laughed. "So don't you try to pull anything over on your Auntie Alice."

"Oh, thank goodness, reinforcements," said Evalyn walking into the room. She had bags under her eyes and her hair, which usually sat on the back of her head in a neat bun, was stringy and wild. She walked over to Walter. "Hi, I'm Evalyn, Alice's older and very tired sister."

After shaking Walter's hand, Evalyn walked to the sofa and plopped down. "You know I had to make two more pies this morning? I woke up and the girls each had their hands in an apple pie and were just munching away without a care in the world."

Evalyn sighed heavily. "I even put a chair in front of their door so I could hear it scrap across the floor and know they were awake and about, but those sneaky little devils are just too quiet. I still don't know how they moved that chair without me hearing it. So no pie for them after lunch." She looked at James. "I mean it, Papa James. Don't be sneaking them any bites."

Walter leaned towards Alice. "How old are they?"

"Three and a half," said Alice.

"They look so innocent, I can't imagine them being such a handful."

Alice laughed quietly. "Remind me and I'll tell you some stories about Evie's troublemakin' when she was younger. Every frazzled hair she's getting now, she gave the same amount to Momma Dovie when we got here."

"Thanks a lot, sis," said Evalyn.

"Momma, we brought in the pies and put them on the table," said a young girl as she walked into the room, followed by her younger brother.

They made their way to Alice, and gave her a hug. "Joy and Caleb, this is my friend Mr. Jefferson."

Joy and Caleb said their hellos before bouncing to Papa James for hugs and peppermints.

"Joy, why don't you take your siblings outside," said Dovie.

18

"Not the girls," said Evalyn. "They are not leaving my sight today because I am not in the mood to clean another mess."

"Where's Robert?" asked Alice.

"He had to take a couple of pigs to Elmer," said Evalyn. "I'm sure they'll all be here once they get that taken care of, and then my *sweet lil' darlings* can spend some time with their daddy."

By five that evening, Walter had been introduced to every family member. Alice's brother, Elmer, his wife, Tiny, and their two children, Benjamin and Sophie, Evalyn's husband, Robert, and an ol' family friend named Jacob. They had all come throughout the day so as not to overwhelm Walter, but Alice knew his mind must be whirling with names and which kids belonged to whom. She had to admit, her family was big and loud and absolutely wonderful.

"Are you doing okay?" Alice asked Walter as they carried food out to the three large picnic tables sitting behind the house.

"It's a lot, but I'm really enjoying myself," said Walter. "I've never experienced anything like this chaos that is also full of love and support. The older kids watch the younger kids and everybody helps out cooking and setting up, and then there's Jacob who eats at your table like a member of the family. It's so progressive."

"Because he is a member of our family," corrected Alice. "Jacob came to live at Quail Crossings when he was just sixteen. His family had too many mouths to feed, and, as I told you, some of our townsfolks didn't like that Jacob decided to travel through Knollwood looking for work. Of course, he spent a few years away from us, but, like everyone else in this family, he found his way back." Alice looked around the farm and gave a happy sigh.

"It seems odd to me that I come from a city like Amarillo and never once spoke to a colored person. Even the people we employ to tend the lawn and house are white, except for our cook, Lupita. She's Mexican and makes the best tamales." He closed his eyes. "I do miss her tamales. Now here I am sharing a table with a colored man."

Alice stopped and looked at Walter. "He is a person, just like you and me. Don't start treating us like a social experiment. There's nothing different about him except the color of his skin."

"Of course," said Walter. "I didn't mean to imply otherwise. I'm just very excited about all the opportunities. I'm going to be working on a real farm with your sister, Ellie, who has endured travesties I can't even begin to relate to, watch how twins function between themselves and others, and get to know a person I probably wouldn't have bothered to talk to on the street. Not to mention I'm getting to spend copious amounts of time with you."

Alice laughed, then continued to the table and put the beans down. "You'd think we were all movie stars."

Walter looked at all the people gathering around the picnic tables. "No, I've met movie stars. I much prefer your family."

"Let me know if you still feel that way in a week when all the politeness has worn off and the hard work has begun," said Alice with a wink.

Alice took the platter of roast beef from Walter and placed it on the table. "So, here's how our big family dinners work. The kids go through the line first, with the women making plates for the younger ones, and then the kids go sit at the far end of the table. After the kids, the men fix their plates, and they fill up the middle table and talk farming. After they get through, we ladies fix our plates and sit at this table with the food."

"Well, that doesn't seem fair," said Walter. "Why should you eat last, especially since you all went to the trouble of cooking it all?"

"Honestly, we don't mind," said Alice. "Having the men closer to the kids means they can deal with the squabbles, and we women can talk about anything but farming. Plus, it's nice to be close to the food when there's only one chicken leg left, and you see your brother eyeing it from other the end of the table. Guess who gets to it first?"

"Sounds like I should sit with the ladies," said Walter with a lopsided grin.

Dovie rang the dinner bell and got everyone's attention before moving to stand beside Alice and Bill. "All right y'all, you know how this works. But first bow your heads and Papa James will say grace."

Everyone stopped where they were and complied as James started. "Dear Heavenly Father, Thank you for this glorious day. It's so nice to hear the birds chirping and feel the sun shining after such a long winter. Thank you for bringing us a new friend in Walter and for allowing us to stay close to our old friends. Thank you for the bountiful feast we are about to eat and bless the hands that prepared it as well as the hands that raised it. Help us to be conscious of

your word as we go through our daily lives. In your name
...."

A loud honking interrupted the expected simultaneous amen causing everyone to look up as a cherry red Packard convertible raced into the driveway. Alice finished her prayer with thankful praise that none of the kids were playing in the road.

Everyone stared as a young man got out brandishing a huge smile. "Hey now, I wasn't expecting a welcome party, but I'll take it!"

"Who is that?" asked Walter. "Another brother?"

Alice shook her head. "I don't know. I've never seen him before."

Mumbled whispers started as the family tried to figure out who this person was and who should greet him, when James hobbled over with his cane and gave the young man a huge hug.

"I can't believe it," cried James. "I never thought I'd see you again."

James looked to Dovie. "Dovie, hon, it's June's boy, Nicholas, your nephew."

Chapter Four

"Nicholas?" Dovie's hand flew to her mouth as she froze in disbelief. She was sure the entire family was staring at her to see what she was going to do next.

Bill leaned over to Alice. "Nicholas? Isn't that June's boy?"

"You mean Dovie's sister?" Alice's eyes widened. "The sister that disowned the entire family? I've only heard James and Dovie talk about them a handful of times, but it must be. James said it was Dovie's nephew, unless Simon had a brother or sister."

Regaining her senses, Dovie ran to Nicholas. "Oh, my dear boy, let me look at you." Tears formed in her eyes. "You look just like my sister." She gave him a hug. "Have you eaten? Come on over here and get you a plate. Did you drive all the way here from New York? You must be more tired than a fly at a feedlot."

Nicholas laughed. "My mother always said you had the silliest sayings. Guess that's something I better get used to, huh, Aunt Dovie?"

"Guess so. How long you stayin'?" asked Dovie.

"Well," said Nicholas, "I guess that depends on how long you think forever is?"

"I don't understand." Dovie replied shaking her head.

Nicholas looked around Quail Crossings. "Well, I figured if this is going to be mine one day, then I ought to come and learn the family business."

"Yours?" Alice stepped forward. "Why on Earth do you think Quail Crossings is going to be yours? Mr. James and Momma Dovie own this place. Bill has been running it since the war and making it thrive, I might add."

Nicholas laughed and took a step toward Alice. "You must be Cousin Helen."

Everyone standing in the yard gasped except for Walter, who wore a look of utter confusion. Nicholas's smile faded as he stopped and turned back toward Dovie.

"Didn't your Momma tell you?" Dovie asked as Gabe rushed to her side to wrap a protective arm around her. Dovie turned and buried her head in Gabe's shoulder.

"Tell me what? What did I say?" asked Nicholas. He extended his hand to Gabe. "You must be Uncle Simon."

"Nicholas," Gabe said firmly, ignoring Nicholas's outstretched hand. "I'm Gabe Pearce, Dovie's second husband, Simon and Helen passed in a car accident in 1934."

Nicholas rubbed his hand over his face and looked around at everyone staring at him. "I'm so sorry. I didn't know."

"I don't understand," said James. "I can't imagine why June wouldn't tell you about your uncle and cousin."

Dovie picked up her head and dabbed at her eyes with the corner of her apron. "Nicholas, if I remember right, you're what, twenty-two? Twenty-three?"

"Yes ma'am, twenty-three," answered Nicholas.

"Well, it makes sense," said Dovie. "You were just a child when Helen and Simon passed. I'm sure your momma just didn't want to burden you with such horrible news, especially since we don't talk much. After she didn't have the decency to come to Mom's funeral, we communicate only at Christmastime."

Dovie wrapped Nicholas in another hug. "It's just so good to see you and to hear that we'll be getting to know you, too." She looked around the lawn, where everyone still stood staring with their mouths open. "Come on, let's eat. Food's getting cold."

She guided Nicholas to the table as Evalyn, Tiny, and Lou Anne started making plates for their children. "Everyone, this is Nicholas Banner, he belongs to my sister, June, who lives in New York."

Everyone started to approach and introduce themselves as Dovie held up her hand. "Y'all, go ahead and get your food. After we eat, you can introduce yourselves. Lord knows the food would spoil by the time we got through everyone."

Once all the kids were seated, Dovie looked at Walter and Nicholas, "You two boys go ahead. You are our guests after all. Sit anywhere at the middle table." She looked at Gabe who was still standing close by. "Gabe, please help us get started. Go on, now that the kids are done."

As Gabe and Nicholas left to fill their plates, the other men followed suit. Alice leaned toward Dovie. "You okay?"

Dovie wrapped her arm around Alice. "You're sweet to ask, and yes I am."

"Why do you think he's here?" asked Alice as she looked at Nicholas, sitting across from Walter. Both men were sitting as far as they could from the table of rowdy children.

"I wouldn't worry about that right now," said Dovie. "I'm just glad he's here. I never thought I'd get to see any of June's children. Go ahead and fix your plate so you can sit by your friend. He's looking a bit lost."

Alice let out a chuckle. "I think we all are."

Dovie watched Alice start making her plate and then saw Bill take a seat beside Nicholas as he introduced himself. Alice had been right to ask about Nicholas. His visitation was more out of the blue than a snake in the winter.

Dovie shook her thoughts away as she fixed her own plate and sat in the empty seat beside Nicholas.

"We left that for you," said Lou Anne, regarding the spot. "We figured you'd want to sit by your nephew."

"Thank you," said Dovie. "I do." She turned to Nicholas. "How are your brother and sister?"

"They're great, David is a milkman, and Sally married a nice fellow by the name of Henry a few years back and now has three boys," said Nicholas swallowing a bite of beans. "Lordy, Aunt Dovie, did you make these baked beans? They are the best I've ever eaten and this potato salad … damn."

The whole table let out an audible gasp and Dovie watched color flood Nicholas's cheeks. "Nicholas, honey, we don't use that kind of language, especially around the children."

"Sorry, I just got carried away," said Nicholas. "We don't eat like this in New York. I don't think my belly's ever been this happy."

"Glad to hear it," said Dovie as everyone returned to their conversations. "I did make the beans and," she pointed to Ellie, who sat at the end of the table, "Ellie, made the potato salad."

Nicholas lifted his fork in a salute to Ellie. "It's mighty good, Ellie."

Ellie narrowed her eyes at Nicholas and then looked away.

"Okay," Nicholas said slowly.

"Don't mind, Ellie," said Dovie. "She doesn't like strangers and is very protective of me. She'll warm up to you, I'm sure."

"Aunt Dovie, who are all these people?" Nicholas asked in a whisper. "I really thought it was just your family and Grandpa living at Quail Crossings."

"Well, about six months after Simon and Helen passed …"

"And I'm real sorry about that," Nicholas interrupted. "I honestly had no idea. I didn't mean to bring up bad memories."

"I know you didn't. Please don't give it a second thought," said Dovie. "As I was sayin', about six months after they passed, Dad was at the Knollwood Café in town and saw the Brewers, well everyone but Ellie. He knew they needed help. It was a hard time for everyone back then, but these kids were living out of a truck at the time. Anyway, Dad hired Bill, and we took them all in. Here we are sixteen years later," she said, as she gestured around the table.

"So they're basically hired hands," said Nicholas.

"We're family," snapped Alice.

"Alice," said Bill, giving her a warning look. "But she's not wrong, Dovie and James became our family when we needed one the most, and I'd like to think we did the same for them."

"You did," said Dovie. "And Nicholas, you might not have had a Quail Crossings to come to had it not been for Bill. He kept this place running and profitable during the war."

"Did you serve?" asked Elmer as he cut some of his son's roast into small bites.

Nicholas shook his head. "My brother and brother-in-law did, but I wasn't drafted."

"You didn't enlist?" asked Alice, her eyes wide.

"I wanted to and headed out the door the minute I turned eighteen," said Nicholas. "But my Ma begged me not to because both David and Henry were over there. My sister and her kids lived with us throughout the war, and I was the only one making any money to support the household stateside. So I didn't. How about you guys?"

"I served, joined when I turned sixteen," said Elmer, then he pointed to Gabe, Robert, and Jacob. "They did too."

"Guess you couldn't serve on account of your eye," said Nicholas, referencing Bill's left eye patch. "How'd it happen? I figured during the war until now."

"You'd guess right," said Bill, a hint of annoyance in his voice. "I was kicked in the head by a horse during a tornado a few months before Pearl Harbor. I wanted to join, not sure even Lou Anne could have stopped me, had the Army seen me fit."

"Well now," said James, "that's enough about the war. Today is a day of celebration. Walter and Nicholas have found their way to our table, and I'm sure we can think of a lot better things to talk about. Nicholas, you said you were working, what did you used to do?"

Nicholas pointed to his car. "I sold cars, just like that."

Robert whistled between his teeth. "Sure is fancy."

With that, the conversation between the men turned to cars, and Evalyn started talking about the wedding dress she was making for a local girl's upcoming nuptials. Soon all the tables buzzed with their normal, friendly conversations.

Dovie glanced at her father and noticed James looked happier than he had in a long time. She hoped that James's smile remained when Nicholas explained further his initial comment about taking over Quail Crossings. Nicholas may be their family by blood, but the Brewers had become their family by love.

Chapter Five

Alice carried a plate of apple pie over to Tiny who was sitting on the back stoop trying to get baby Sophie to drink a bottle of goat's milk.

"Hey Tiny, want some pie?" asked Alice.

Tiny shook her head as Alice sat beside her. "No thanks, I'm not hungry."

Alice put the plate down and reached her arms out for Sophie. "Mind if I try? I haven't seen little Sophie since she was born."

"Sure, it's not like I can get her to eat anything I offer. She wouldn't drink from me, and now she won't drink from a bottle," said Tiny. She handed her to Alice which caused Alice to smile a mile wide.

"She is so gorgeous," said Alice as she gazed down at her baby niece.

Tiny didn't respond, so Alice placed the three-month-old baby in the crook of her elbow and gently placed the nipple of the bottle in Sophie's mouth. The child took it instantly, and Alice heard Tiny's exasperated sigh.

"Everything okay, Tiny?" asked Alice.

"I'm just tired," said Tiny. "Do you mind if I go for a walk while you feed her?"

"Not at all," said Alice.

Tiny got up and ambled toward the orchard. As Alice watched her sister-in-law walk away, she couldn't help but notice the drastic difference in both Tiny's stature and demeanor. Once full of life and always ready for a laugh, Alice hadn't seen Tiny crack a smile all day, and, although Tiny had always been on the slender side, she now looked too skinny. Alice couldn't figure out how anyone could be too skinny at Quail Crossings. If Dovie wasn't trying to feed you, Ellie was.

Elmer sat beside Alice breaking her from her thoughts.

"I see you got Sophie to eat," said Elmer. "Thanks."

"You know me, I'm always happy to help my brother when I can," said Alice. She tipped her head in Tiny's direction. "Is she okay?"

Elmer shrugged. "Honestly, I don't know. She hasn't been herself since Sophie was born. Dovie said sometimes women go through this after they have a child. She just needs time, but I'd be lying if I said I wasn't worried about her."

"Is she home alone all day with Benny and Sophie?" asked Alice.

"Usually," said Elmer. "She doesn't feel like going anywhere, not even here."

"Well," said Alice, "I'll try to stop in and check on her while I'm here. Maybe all she needs is a friend."

Elmer wrapped his arm around Alice and gave her a gentle hug, careful not to jostle Sophie and her bottle. "Thanks sis, I'd appreciate that."

"How's the butcher shop?" asked Alice.

"Great," said Elmer. "Jacob practically runs the front of the shop now, and I tend to the back."

Alice smiled. She knew her brother worked hard to grow his butchery after the war and was pleased to hear it was still doing well. Knowing that most of the town now accepted Jacob as one of their own also warmed her heart. He had had some rough years between being on his own at sixteen, then losing a leg in the war, as well as his wife leaving him.

Alice glanced at Nicholas who was still sitting at the picnic table with James, eating his third slice of pie. "What do you think about him?"

"Nicholas?" Elmer cocked his head. "I think it's gotta be hard to come here thinking you're walking into one thing, only to find out it's something else."

"What do you mean?" asked Alice.

"Nicholas probably thought he was coming to help Dovie and James out," explained Elmer. "I'm sure he had it in his mind that Helen was the only one left to run Quail Crossings, and they'd need someone young to take over. And he's not wrong, Alice. Remember, they did need someone young to come in and help. It just happened to be Bill."

"I just don't trust him," said Alice.

"Now Alice, I've never known you not to give someone the benefit of the doubt," Elmer said.

"I don't know," said Alice. "He just doesn't sit right."

"Well," said Elmer standing, "if you don't want to give him the benefit of the doubt, give it to James and Dovie. They've always done right by us. Can't see them stopping now."

Ellie walked up and sat by her sister.

"Ellie, what do you think of Nicholas?" asked Alice.

Ellie wrinkled her nose and shook her head.

"See," said Alice. "I'm not the only one, and Ellie is a good judge of character."

"Right," said Elmer. "Remember when Ellie first saw Jacob and thought he was going to murder you all in your sleep?"

Ellie turned a bright red and shrugged her shoulders.

"That's different," said Alice. "Jacob startled her and Nicholas, well ..."

"He's bossy," said Ellie.

Both Alice and Elmer couldn't help but giggle. Ellie had come to live at Quail Crossings just five short years ago, and she already ran the roost. If you didn't have your chores done in what Ellie believed to be an acceptable amount of time, she'd do them for you. Then you'd get *the look*. She rarely had to say a word to make a person feel like they were lazier than a box of rocks.

"Ellie, do you mind finishing up with Sophie?" asked Alice. "I think I want to hear what Mr. James and Nicholas are talking about."

Ellie nodded, and Alice handed the baby over to her. Sophie let out a squeak of a burp, causing everyone to smile. Alice hated to leave her new niece, but she couldn't shake the feeling Nicholas was up to no good. She mosied over to the table, trying to look nonchalant.

"Well, Nicholas," said James, "I think you could learn a lot from working here at Quail Crossings. You'll have to share a room with Walter, though. We've hired him on for the summer."

"So, he can stay in the bunkhouse," said Nicholas. "Wouldn't that be customary?"

"How about you stay in the bunkhouse," said Alice.

"Nobody is staying in the bunkhouse. We've been using it for storage for decades, so it ain't fit for a dog to sleep in, much less a person," said James. "There's plenty of room in the second upstairs bedroom. Bill, do you think you can find enough work for both Walter and Nicholas?"

Bill gave them a smile. "I don't think that will be a problem."

"Great, we'll start at eight," Nicholas said standing to grab another piece of apple pie.

Bill shook his head. "No, we start at sun up."

"Well, what time is that?" asked Nicholas.

"When the rooster crows," said James. "We rise when the sun rises and sleep when the sun sets. It's the life of a farmer and, Nicholas, Bill is in charge. You will learn a lot by listening to him."

"Absolutely," said Nicholas. "Can I get someone to show me my bunk? I'm worn out."

"You bet," said Bill. "I'll show you."

Alice waited until Nicholas had retrieved his bag from his car and went inside the house before she looked at James.

"How are you feeling about all this?" Alice asked.

James sighed. "I'm glad he's here. I never thought I'd get the opportunity to know any of my grandchildren."

"Mr. James, you have a whole gaggle of kids running around who adore you and see you as their grandfather."

"Yes, and I love you all dearly," said James. "I know you were young, but do you remember how it felt when you found out your parents had abandoned you for California?"

"Kinda," said Alice with a shrug.

"Well, I felt absolutely heartbroken when June ran off with David Banner to New York and got married. I was even more devastated when she didn't come to the funeral of her own momma. It was like she had abandoned us. Even when I went to New York to make amends, she slammed the door in my face and told her children I was just a stranger. My biggest regret was giving my daughter an ultimatum that made her feel like she could never return home to her family. I feel like God's giving me a second chance with Nicholas."

"I understand that now," said Alice, "because from the very first day we came to Quail Crossings, I felt God had given us a second chance to have a family."

Chapter Six

Walter walked into the barn just as the sun started to rise over the horizon. He hadn't bothered to wake Nicholas when the rooster crowed, after all, it wasn't his responsibility to make sure Nicholas was to work on time.

Alice confided in him the night before as they walked through the orchard. She was concerned Nicholas didn't have honest motives and that his mother might want a piece of the pie known as Quail Crossings. She admitted they were blood family and might even deserve a portion, but her main worry was that her family would be pushed off the land and be cast out of a family they loved.

He tried to assure her that everything would be okay, while at the same time, silently vowing not to let the Yankee outwork him. He didn't want Alice to worry about Nicholas. The city boy would see soon enough how hard farm life could be. Walter chuckled to himself. He was going to be learning that lesson himself, but he wanted to impress Alice. The first step was outworking Nicholas.

Walter couldn't help but feel nervous as he approached Bill, who was brushing down a beautiful white and brown horse. Walter reached up slowly, letting the horse smell his hand, before gently petting its muzzle.

"This is Pronto," said Bill. He pointed to the solid brown horse in the next stall. "That ol' boy is Tex." He continued pointing across the barn to two cows. One stood in a stall while Ellie milked the other. "Ellie is milking Marigold, and Poppy is the other milk cow. We need to muck their stalls. Have you seen Nicholas?"

"He was still asleep when I came down," said Walter.

"You didn't wake him?" asked Bill.

Walter shook his head. "I thought that would be awkward, since I barely know him."

Bill nodded. "I can see that. Grab a pitchfork and get busy."

"Doing what, exactly?" asked Walter, scratching his head.

"So you've never mucked out a stall?" asked Bill.

"Afraid not," said Walter.

"There's not much to it," said Bill as he grabbed a pitchfork and started to demonstrate in Marigold's empty stall. "Scoop out all the old hay, throw it in the wheelbarrow, and when the wheelbarrow is full, dump it out in the big pile behind the barn. Once you've gotten rid of the manure, grab hay from the clean pile and replace what you've mucked out." He handed the pitchfork to Walter. "When you hear the dinner bell, that means Dovie has breakfast ready. Just make sure all the animals are secure and wash up at the pump over yonder. There won't be room in the kitchen for you to wash up there. One more thing ..."

Bill motioned for Walter to follow him to the last stall.

"This is Bolt," Bill said, pointing to a beautiful white stallion who had a single black mark on his hindquarter resembling a lightning bolt. "He will eventually take Tex's

place as a ranch horse, but he's not broken. Do not muck
this stall. Leave it to me. Bolt has a temper."

"I'm an accomplished rider," said Walter. "My parents
made sure I had lessons. Horses are probably the one thing
I'm comfortable around on the farm."

"Have you ever broken a horse?" asked Bill.

"Can't say that I have," said Walter, "But I wouldn't
mind giving it a try."

Bill let out a low chuckle as he handed the pitchfork to
Walter. "Easy to say when you've never been on the
backside of a wild horse, but we'll see. For now, just muck
the stalls. I'll be over at the pig barn. It's just on the other
side of the small pasture behind the barn." Bill started out
the back of the barn, then paused. "If Nicholas ever shows
up, tell him to put on a pair of those muck boots and come
help me with the pigs."

"Yes, sir," said Walter. He turned to the stall and tried
to scoop the hay with the fork, but most of the hay fell
through the spaces between the fork spikes. He tried again,
resulting in the same effect.

Walter shook his head and looked at Ellie who was
unhooking Marigold from the milking station. "Bill made it
look so easy. At this rate I'll be at it all day."

Ellie gave Marigold a little pat on the rump sending the
cow into the outside corral, then walked over, grabbed the
pitchfork, and stabbed it into the hay. "Stab, stab, stab, then
quickly into the barrel."

She demonstrated, handed the pitchfork back to
Walter, grabbed her bucket of milk, and walked out of the
barn without another word.

"She is an odd duck," said Walter, before turning back
to the stall. He stabbed the hay and pulled up just a little as

he had seen Ellie do and repeated the motion three times. After getting a large mound of tangled hay on his fork he quickly dumped it into the wheelbarrow.

Walter let out a laugh of triumph. "She might be an odd duck, but she's a clever odd duck."

Walter worked hard to finish the stalls quickly, yet efficiently. A sharp pain stabbed between his shoulders as his muscles grew more tired, but he was determined to finish all the stalls and help Bill in the pig barn before breakfast and especially before Nicholas awoke.

After the last stall was cleaned and all the animals were secured, Walter quickly put on a pair of muck boots and headed toward the pig barn. As he passed Bolt's stall, he paused.

"I'll clean Bolt's stall, then Bill will see how good I am with horses," muttered Walter. He grabbed the pitchfork and wheelbarrow, then hurried back to Bolt's stall.

"How about you and I become friends?" he said to the horse, "Help me earn some good points with Bill?"

Bolt snorted and turned his back to Walter.

"I guess that's a no," said Walter as he started to unlock the stall.

"I wouldn't do that," came a voice from the doorway. Walter quickly jumped back and let out a little laugh as he saw a young boy scooping chicken feed into a bucket.

"Dean, right?" said Walter scratching his head.

"Yes, sir," said Dean, "and Daddy don't like anyone messin' with Bolt. Not even Uncle Elmer gets to mess with him."

Bolt kicked the stall door as if to emphasize the point.

Dean pointed to the wheelbarrow. "You done with that? I need it to clean the chicken coop."

"Yeah," said Walter. "Here's the pitchfork, too."

Dean wrinkled his nose at Walter. "You don't use a pitchfork to clean a chicken coop, you use a rake."

"Okay, then," said Walter putting the pitchfork by the back door while trying to hide his embarrassment, "I'll just go see if your father needs any help with the pigs."

Walter walked toward the pig barn and tried to regain his confidence. He knew when he asked for a job at Quail Crossings, he had a lot to learn. He tried to convince himself he shouldn't feel embarrassed that Dean knew more about what needed to be done than he did. The boy had grown up on the farm, so of course he would know the routine by heart by the time he was nine.

As Walter crossed the small pasture that housed the mother cows and small calves, he reminded himself that it was still his first day working and only his second full day on a farm at all. He visited farms during his studies but only for short periods of time. He had never done a real day's work in his life.

It was going to be difficult to keep up with Bill, but Walter was determined to do so. At any rate, he was already doing miles better than Nicholas, who was probably still in bed.

Approaching the pig barn, Walter slowed as Norman the goose waddled between him and the door. Alice's words, "Watch out for the goose," ran through his head.

"Hey there, Norman," said Walter, trying to keep his voice low and steady. The bite Norman gave him the previous day throbbed at the sight of the bird. "Just going to help Bill out. Gonna let me by?"

Norman raised his wings and hissed.

"Now, Norman, there's no reason to act like that." Walter found himself taking a step back, but then he stopped himself. He could not be scared of a goose. What would Bill say if he said he couldn't help him with the pigs because a bird was blocking the door?

Norman lowered his head and hissed again, taking a step toward Walter.

Walter again found himself backing up. Stopping himself, he firmly planted his feet. "I'm not scared of you, Norman. You're a bird, practically dinner."

Norman let out a ferocious honk before taking flight and heading straight for Walter. Forgetting his need to be brave, Walter backed up quickly, throwing his hands up to ward off the goose. The heel of his muck boot hit a yucca plant, the tips of the plant stabbing his calves through his jeans. Losing his balance, he fell flat on his back hearing an uncanny *splat* as he hit the ground.

Walter expected Norman to continue his attack, but, as he looked around, the bird was standing beside him letting out a low series of honks that sounded a bit like laughing.

Seeing the danger was gone, Walter sat up and tried to steady his nerves, when the strong smell of grass and manure started to assault his nose. Walter remembered the odd noise that came from his fall, a *splat*, instead of a *thud*.

"Oh no," sighed Walter. He reached around and felt a wet, mud-like substance on the back of his shirt. He brought his hand around and sniffed, confirming his suspicion. Quickly getting to his feet, Walter saw he had fallen right in the middle of a large, fresh cow patty.

Anger started at his toes and rushed through his body. "Norman!"

Chapter Seven

Walter ran across the pasture back to the barn and grabbed the pitchfork he had left by the door. He swung it madly in the air as he started after Norman who had followed him at a leisurely pace. "I'm gonna make you dinner!"

Norman honked wildly as he ran toward the pig barn.

"Get back here, you flea-bit monstrous fowl!"

Norman flapped his wings and hurried away from Walter, all the while honking at a deafening level. Seeing he wasn't going to catch the bird, Walter launched the pitchfork at Norman, barely missing him.

"Walter!" called Bill, "What in tarnation is goin' on?"

"That bird made me fall in a pile of cow …"

Bill held up his hands. "Walter, I know Norman is not innocent in all this, but trust me when I say this, if you want to stay in good graces with Alice, you'll make your peace with Norman. You might need to carry a broom around with you until he gets used to you, but Walter, we aren't in the business of throwing pitchforks at our livestock, no matter what."

Walter bowed his head. "I'm sorry. I lost my temper."

"Easy to do with Norman," said Bill. "Now, come over here, and we'll get you washed off. You can't go into breakfast like that. While you were chasing Norman around the pasture, Dovie rang the bell."

Dovie heard the commotion in the pasture behind the barn, thought about checking it out, but then changed her mind. Bill was more than capable of running Quail Crossings as he had proven more than enough times. She took a moment and wondered where Quail Crossings would be if Bill had gone off to fight during World War II.

As much as he hated staying stateside due to losing all sight in his left eye, it really was a godsend after all. When over half the men in Knollwood, Texas, the town Quail Crossings was closest to, were gone fighting the war against the Nazis, Bill became the go-to guy. Not only had he kept Quail Crossings going, he mended countless fences, found lost dogs, took care of thieving coyotes, and even rounded up a group of people to help when a large herd of cattle broke out of Mrs. Tuttle's pasture causing havoc on Knollwood's Main Street. If anyone had a problem or needed an extra pair of hands, they turned to Bill.

She remembered back to the time when the scrawny young man walked into Quail Crossings with a humble heart and three siblings to feed. She didn't want to think of what would've happened to all the Brewer children had James not been in the café and offered Bill a job.

"Momma Dovie, everything okay?" asked Alice, snapping Dovie out of her thoughts.

"Oh yeah," said Dovie. She came in off the back stoop and started to move the freshly baked biscuits from the baking sheet to a bowl lined with a tea towel. "Sometimes my mind wanders off like a pup who's caught a scent."

"Do I smell bacon?" asked Nicholas, coming down the stairs, his light blue eyes heavy with sleep.

Alice put her hands on her hips. "Well, look who's just rolling out of bed. Bill and Walter have been working for over an hour now."

"What?" Nicholas ran a hand through his wild blonde hair. "But we haven't even had breakfast yet."

"That's how it works around here," said Dovie. "Everyone gets up when the rooster crows and starts tending to their chores until breakfast is ready."

"That's insane," said Nicholas. "We've got the whole day to work. Why start before breakfast?"

"Oh, you'll have plenty to keep you busy all day," said Dovie. "That's why we start at dawn."

"Well, damn," said Nicholas, causing everyone to stop in their tracks. He looked at all their shocked faces. "What? The little ones aren't here."

"We don't cuss," said Alice. "Can't you think of any other words to use?"

"What, like golly jeepers or dagnabit?" Nicholas said with a wink.

"Tiny already says jeepers," said Ellie, placing a large plate on the table piled high with bacon.

Alice folded her arms and smirked at Nicholas. "Guess that means you're stuck with dagnabit."

Nicholas returned her smirk, but Dovie could see there was more humor in his than hers. "Guess I am."

Dovie turned to Ellie and tried to change the subject, "Thanks for cooking the bacon, Sweetie."

"You're welcome, Momma Dovie," said Ellie as she turned and walked toward the indoor bathroom which had been added on the year before. Dovie still couldn't believe they had an indoor toilet and now that she had one, she wondered why they had waited so long to add it on, even though they had been one of the first country houses to get one.

"I can't help but be surprised every time she cooks bacon," said Alice, turning her back on Nicholas.

"Why?" asked Nicholas as he walked over to the table to grab a piece of bacon.

Alice slapped his hand. "We wait for everyone, and we say grace first."

Nicholas held up his hands in a peaceful gesture. "Okay, I'll wait. Now, why would it be a big deal for Ellie to cook bacon?"

"It's a long story," said Dovie, "but the short of it is she burned her hand very badly cooking bacon about five years back."

Just then, James came in the back door with Dean at his side, and caught the end of the conversation.

"That was a dark day," he said, placing his hat on the peg by the door.

"What happened?" asked Nicholas.

"We don't talk about it," said Dean.

"Dean, hon," said Dovie, as Ellie came back into the kitchen, "are your momma and sisters coming over for breakfast?"

Dean shook his head. "Rosey's got an earache, so they're staying home this morning. Annabelle will come over for lunch though so she can help Aunt Ellie with bread afterwards. Momma said to tell you she was cookin' dinner for us, but we'll be back over after since Daddy said we'll all need to help with the garden."

"Your daddy's right. We have to weed," said Dovie. "Our garden is three times bigger than it was last year, trying to keep everyone fed, but if we all go out there, it'll take no time."

"Isn't that farmhand stuff?" ask Nicholas.

Alice rolled her eyes. "It's anybody-who-wants-to-eat stuff. If we don't garden, we don't eat in the winter. Of course, you'll probably be gone by then, so it doesn't matter if you help."

Bill came strolling in the back door, a big grin on his face, followed by a wet Walter wearing only his white undershirt and jeans.

"Walter, what happened?" asked Alice, hurrying to his side.

"And where's your shirt?" asked Nicholas biting back a laugh.

Bill shook his head. "Norman got him."

"Again?" asked Alice. "But how did he get you all wet?"

"Remember when Norman had me swimming in the pond in March," interrupted James with a laugh.

"I thought that was Alice's fault," said Bill, taking a seat at the table.

"Really? I didn't think Alice was capable of having faults," said Nicholas with a wicked grin.

"I was six-years-old," said Alice. "Everyone has faults at six-years-old. I was trying to get weeds out of the pond so Mr. Norman would have more room to swim. There was about half as much water in there than there is now, and I got the hoe stuck."

James laughed. "Ol' Norman jumped on my back while I was trying to retrieve it, and I fell right in that freezing cold water,"

"You weren't laughing then," Dovie said, placing a big pan of scrambled eggs on the table.

"But how did Norman, who is a bird if I remember correctly, get you all wet Walter?" asked Nicholas.

"He didn't," answered Bill. "Let's just say we had to hose him off after Norman got through with him."

"Ha!" Nicholas slapped his knee. "You fell in a pile of sh-..."

"You hush now," snapped Alice. "Why are you even here? Just go home."

Nicholas shook his head, his smile remaining. "Oh no, I'm not going anywhere. My ma told me stories about this place, and, so far, she hasn't exaggerated. I'm really beginning to like it here."

"All right, everyone," said Dovie. "Nicholas, sit down. Walter, run upstairs and find a shirt. We'll hold breakfast for you. Alice, would you help me in the parlor please?"

"Of course, Momma Dovie," said Alice throwing a glare at Nicholas as Walter hurried up the stairs.

Alice followed Dovie into the parlor.

"How can I help?" asked Alice as she stood by the fire place.

"Alice, honey, why are you being so hard on Nicholas?" asked Dovie.

Alice folded her arms. "I don't like the way he's come in here actin' like he owns the joint. I'm worried about his intentions."

"I think it's sweet that you're looking out for us, but remember, he is family and right now you're being pricklier than a cactus. You need to cut him some slack and get to know him."

"But Momma Dovie, he's just so arrogant. It's really getting under my skin," stated Alice.

Dovie frowned at Alice. "Bottom line, we don't treat people so rudely in our home, no matter how arrogant you think he's being. You know that. I'm ashamed of you, Alice."

Alice dropped her arms. "I'm sorry, Momma Dovie. I'll try to be nicer."

"That's all I ask," said Dovie. "I hear Walter comin' down the stairs. Let's go eat before it gets cold. I don't know about you, but I have a feeling if we don't get our bacon first, between these fellas, we might not get any."

Alice laughed, just as Dovie hoped she would. As they made their way back into the kitchen, Dovie said a small prayer for patience.

Chapter Eight

The breakfast prayer said, the table began to buzz with conversation as plates were filled. Alice was quick to grab the plate piled with bacon, taking a few pieces for herself before handing it to Dovie, a knowing smile passing between them.

"Where's Gabe off to today?" asked Bill.

"He flew to Wichita before the sun was even up, had a delivery to pick up," said Dovie, as she took the bowl of biscuits from Alice. "How's your momma?"

"Ma? She's doing all right," answered Nicholas. "Works for Macy's, this huge department store in the city, in women's apparel now. She worked her way up from the perfume counter."

"Oh, that's great," said Dovie. "She always did love fashion. I bet she's really good at her job."

"She does okay," said Nicholas.

"So she's getting by with David gone?" asked James.

"Truth be told, Grandpa, it's hard living," confessed Nicholas. "That's why I'm here."

"I knew it," Alice whispered, causing Dovie to give her a nudge.

"How's that?" asked Bill.

"Honestly, I'm not very good at selling cars," said Nicholas. "I thought I'd come out here to Quail Crossings and help make it successful. That way I can send Ma money to help her out."

"So, you can't sell cars, but you think you can farm?" asked Walter, an eyebrow raised.

"I think it's very noble," said James before Nicholas could answer. "I'm just not sure why you'd think Quail Crossings wasn't already successful."

"Well, it was something Ma said after Pop died about you guys possibly sending her some money to help with expenses, but since you never did, I assumed the farm wasn't doing so well and you guys couldn't afford to." Nicholas grabbed a biscuit before passing the pan to James.

"We never knew there was a problem," said Dovie, spooning herself some scrambled eggs. "Had she written to us, we would've helped where we could. Do you think she'll come visit now that you're here? It would be nice to see her."

"She was probably too proud to ask outright for money. One thing about my ma, she assumes people can read her mind. I don't know how many times I got into trouble for not doing something she thought I should do but never asked me to," said Nicholas, as he tore his biscuit in two. "I doubt she'll come though. She's pretty upset that no one came to Pop's funeral."

Dovie's mouth dropped open. "She's upset that no one came to David's funeral?"

Nicholas nodded as he buttered his biscuit. "She said you guys knew, but none of you showed up."

"That's rich," said Dovie, swallowing hard. "She didn't seem to find it necessary to come to her own mother's funeral, nor did she acknowledge the death of both my husband and child. Yet she's upset that we didn't come to David's funeral or send her money?" Dovie's voice rose with anger as she stood. "It's just as well she stays away."

Alice watched as Dovie stormed out of the kitchen and headed to her room.

Nicholas raced after her. "Aunt Dovie, I'm so…"

He was blocked by Ellie as his sentence was lost in the slamming of Dovie's bedroom door. He turned, shook his head slowly, and looked at the table as Alice folded her arms. In the span of two days, he had managed to bring Dovie to tears, twice.

James cleared his throat. "Nicholas, son, come on over and sit down."

Nicholas did as he was told. "I'm sorry, Grandpa, I really keep putting my foot in it with her."

"See how easy it is to step in sh-…."

"Alice!" Bill snapped, stopping her sentence.

Alice bowed her head in shame, thankful Bill had stopped her from cussing. She had just promised Dovie that she'd cut Nicholas some slack, and she was already breaking that promise. Besides, she would not stoop to Nicholas's level and start using foul language for the sake of making a point. She was a college educated woman who could, and would, do better.

Nicholas sat, and James patted the back of his hand. "None of us have done right in this situation. We should have come to your father's funeral, just as y'all should've come to your grandmother's funeral, not to mention Simon's and Helen's."

"Ma really never told us," said Nicholas softly as his face dropped. "I'm not here to cause trouble. If the farm is already doing well, then put me to work so I can send some money to Ma. That's all I really want to do."

For a second Alice felt badly for him. They had gone through so much in years past. Without all the information it would be easy to say the wrong thing.

"Well," she said, clearing her throat, "We should finish our breakfast. Then Ellie and I will tend to the kitchen, and, I'm sure, given some time, Momma Dovie will come back out and join us."

"You can say your apology then," added James. "But Alice is right, it's time to get to work."

"Daddy!" cried Benny.

Elmer sprung out of bed and wrapped up his son. "What's wrong?"

Elmer blinked hard trying to get his mind to focus on where he was and what was going on. He had been dreaming of the war, surrounded by the smell of smoke, gunfire, and the sounds of his fellow soldiers falling.

As his bedroom came into focus, the sunlight streaming through the windows told him he had overslept. He focused his attention on Benny who was still whimpering on his shoulder. "Son, what's goin' on?"

"Momma and Sissy," said Benny softly. "They cryin'."

Elmer nodded and sat his three-year-old son on the bed. He quickly got dressed and mentally prepared himself for what he needed to do. It wasn't the first time Benny had woken him up because Tiny was crying over one thing or another. Elmer wished Tiny would've woke him at his regular time, but he wasn't surprised that she decided to let him sleep. She knew better than anyone that he still carried the heavy burden of war. As much as he appreciated the extra sleep, he knew she was going through a war of her own that he didn't quite understand.

Elmer got dressed, grabbed Benny and hurried out of the room, hoping Tiny had regained her composure.

Hearing Tiny's sobs and Sophie's wailing from the hallway, Elmer quickened his pace and raced to the kitchen. There sat Tiny, with Sophie on her lap, both crying uncontrollably.

"Mary, sweetie," Elmer called out Tiny's given name softly as he walked over to her, "what's wrong?"

"She won't stop cryin'," Tiny said through hiccups. "It doesn't matter what I do, she won't stop. Then Benny started to cry because Sophie was cryin' and … Elm, I just can't take it."

"It's okay," said Elmer, he looked at Benjamin. "Benny, son, I want you to go to your room and get your boots on. We're gonna go see Momma Dovie and Papa James."

The little boy nodded as Elmer put him down and did as he was told. With his hands now free, Elmer reached out and took Sophie from Tiny's arms. He bounced the baby up and down on his shoulder, and soon Sophie's wail turned into a soft cry followed by the soft breathing of light sleep.

Tiny threw her hands up in disgust. "My daughter hates me! All she does is cry when I hold her. I might as well not even be here."

"Now, don't say that," said Elmer. "We all need you, and Sophie and Benny love you. You're their momma. Did you get any sleep?"

Tiny shook her head. "Between your nightmares and Sophie needin' to feed, not a lick."

"Go to bed," said Elmer. "I'll take the kids to Quail Crossings. I'm sure Alice would love to spend more time with them since she just got back from college. You get some rest."

With a nod and a sniffle, Tiny got up and shuffled toward the bedroom just as Benjamin waddled back in the kitchen, boots on the wrong feet.

"Hey buddy," said Elmer, patting the chair. "Why don't you switch those boots around, and we'll get going. Did you eat anything?"

Benjamin shook his head as he crawled up on the chair and pulled off his boots. "Is Momma gonna be okay?"

"Yes," said Elmer, struggling to help with the boots while trying not to jostle Sophie. "She's just tired."

Benjamin bowed his head. "Why doesn't Momma love me?"

Elmer thought his heart was going to break into a million pieces. "Aww, Benny, your momma's love for you is bigger than the state of Texas. Don't you ever think your momma or me don't love you, 'cause we do."

"Why she act like that then?" asked Benjamin, trying to pull his boot on the right foot.

Elmer sighed. "Like I said, Benny, she's just tired, and when people get tired, they get cranky. Come on, we'll go down the road, get some food, and when we come home, Momma will feel all better."

As Elmer helped his son put on his last boot, he prayed he was telling him the truth.

Chapter Nine

Ellie had just handed Alice the last pan to dry when Elmer popped through the door, kids in tow. He gave her an apologetic smile.

"Hey, Sis, Mary's not feeling too good this morning. Any breakfast left for Benny and your favorite brother?"

Alice wiped her hands on a towel before placing them on her hips. She gave him an ornery smile. "Well, for my nephew, I bet we can find something, but I'm pretty sure Bill already ate." She gave him a wink. "But I can whip up some eggs for my second favorite brother I guess."

"Leftovers are fine," said Elmer. "Don't go to any trouble. I need to be getting to the butcher shop." He bit his lip. "Would y'all mind watching the kids today?"

"Not at all," said Alice as she opened the ice box. "I can make you a fried egg sandwich for the road. Will that work?"

"That would be great," said Elmer, his stomach growling as if to second the appreciation.

"What's wrong with Tiny?" asked Dovie as she walked into the kitchen. Alice could see her eyes were still red from crying over Nicholas's statement at breakfast and hoped Elmer wouldn't ask why.

Elmer shook his head. "I honestly don't know."

Ellie, having just finished cleaning the sink and drying her hands, walked over and gently took the still sleeping Sophie from Elmer. "I'll put her down in Dovie's room."

"Thanks," said Elmer, giving little Sophie a soft kiss on her forehead.

"Well, does she have a fever, stomach trouble, headache?" Dovie asked Elmer, grabbing the tin of biscuits and handing one to Benny. "Should I go over there?"

"I really wish I had an answer for you," said Elmer. "She just gets this way from time to time."

"What way?" asked Dovie.

Alice gave Elmer a knowing look hoping he would tell Dovie everything, before cracking an egg into the hot frying pan. "Benny, you want an egg too?"

"Yes, ma'am," said the little boy, around a mouthful of biscuit.

Elmer rubbed his hand over his head. "She just cries, and I can't make out the reason for it."

"She don't like me," said Benny into his biscuit.

"Nonsense," said Dovie, wrapping an arm around the little boy. "She'd be a fool not to love you, and your momma ain't no fool." Dovie pursed her lips. "Benny, what I'm about to say is hard for a grown man to understand, much less a little boy, but sometimes mommas get out of sorts after having a baby. It'll pass in time but know it's not your fault, and it's not Sophie's fault. It's just something that happens."

"So how do you treat it?" asked Elmer.

"With patience," said Dovie, giving Benny another squeeze. "Try to get her outside, doing the things she enjoys doing."

"Like knitting," said Ellie, coming back into the kitchen. "Didn't she knit us a whole mess of sweaters when she was stuck in bed waiting for Benny to arrive?"

Elmer nodded. "She did, but I haven't seen her pick up the needles since."

"Well, who has time to knit when you're a new momma," said Dovie. "I still remember when Helen was born. I was at my wits' end. She was a good baby in many ways, but she did not like to sleep through the night. I was more tired than a mule trying to run the Pony Express. I kept making silly mistakes like bringing the rake into the house. One time, I hung the dirty laundry out to dry before I had even washed it."

"Did she get this way after Benny was born?" asked Alice, sliding a fried egg on a plate and handing it to Dovie to be cut up for Benny.

Elmer shook his head. "Not that I recall, but I wasn't fully myself then either. I was getting the butcher shop up and running, not to mention trying to get my own mind right after the war."

Nicholas popped his head in the back door, saw Dovie, and came all the way inside taking off his hat and holding it in his hands. "Aunt Dovie, good you're up."

"We're kinda in the middle of something here," snapped Ellie, folding her arms. "Go milk the goat and then come back. We'll need it for Sophie."

Alice felt a laugh rise to her throat and choked it back. She had never heard Ellie tell anyone what to do so bluntly before. Nicholas looked from face to face and then tapped the door frame.

"You want me to milk a ...." Nicholas swallowed hard. "... goat?"

58

"What? You said you wanted to help," said Alice, trying not to laugh at the beads of sweat dripping off Nicholas's forehead. "Is that too much to ask?"

"Um ...." Nicholas scratched his head. "No, not at all. Happy to help, but please, Aunt Dovie, a moment of your time after I finish milking the goat?"

"Absolutely, Nicholas," said Dovie.

As Nicholas retreated outside, Alice let her laugh loose. "Well, Ellie, I never thought I'd see the day when you bossed anyone around."

"So what do I do?" Elmer asked Dovie, bringing the subject back to Tiny. "I hate seeing her like this."

"We just need to help her out until she gets rested and can get to feelin' right again," said Dovie. "Bring the kids over here in the morning. We'll get 'em fed and look after them. Go about your business and let her rest as much as possible. I'll go over and talk to her later, but for now, you better take your sandwich and get to movin'. Jacob will be wondering where you are."

It wasn't that Jacob couldn't handle the morning business. Elmer might be the owner, but Jacob was definitely the one who managed the place. When Elmer had first bought the butcher shop, everyone thought Tiny would be the one to work up front and tend to the customers, but by the time he opened, Tiny was pregnant with Benjamin and couldn't stand the smell of the raw meat. Fortunately, Jacob had come back to Knollwood and needed a job. The two men worked together like a well-oiled machine.

"Thanks, Dovie." He smiled as he held up the sandwich Alice made and wrapped in wax paper. "And thank you Alice. Your second favorite brother appreciates it very much."

Alice smiled back.

"We'll expect you for dinner," said Dovie as Elmer walked out the back door. "Tiny too."

"Wouldn't miss it," Elmer hollered back as he walked to his truck.

"You done eatin', Benny?" asked Dovie.

Benny nodded.

"Go play outside for a bit," said Dovie. "It's a beautiful morning, and Lord knows, it's getting hotter every day."

Alice waited until Benny was in the middle of the yard playing before she ventured her question. "What are we going to do about Tiny?"

"As I said," said Dovie, taking Benny's plate to the sink to wash, "We're going to help out as much as possible, and once she gets rested she'll be right as rain. She just needs some help is all. I'm thankful my momma was still around when I had Helen. We women think we have to do it all on our own, but the truth is, we were never meant to. That's what family is for. I reckon Tiny's sleeping now. Here in a bit, I'll go over and see to her, try to get her over here for lunch."

A small cry came from Dovie's room.

"Sounds like Sophie's awake," said Ellie, heading toward Dovie's room. "She's probably hungry."

Alice sighed. "Guess I'll go check on Nicholas and see how he's doing with the goat."

As Alice walked out the back door, Tiny's problems weighed heavily on her mind. Tiny was not only her sister-in-law, but her friend, and she wanted to help. Just hearing little Benny say his mother didn't like him broke her heart. She knew better. They all did. Tiny had a giving spirit and was usually full of pep and enthusiasm, but even Alice had to admit Tiny hadn't seemed like herself the day before at Alice's homecoming meal.

"Hey beautiful," called Walter, standing just outside the horse corral.

Alice felt her cheeks burn hot. She wasn't used to being called beautiful, especially on her family's farm.

"Hey there," she replied walking over to Walter with a smile. "Whatcha doin'?"

"Bill's going to bring Bolt out to work with him a bit before he shows me the rest of the land," explained Walter. "He thought it would be a good opportunity for me to learn how to break a horse. What are you doing out here?"

"Checking on Nicholas," said Alice. "He's supposed to be milking the goat for Sophie, and I'm fairly certain he's never done it before."

"Bolt's coming out," came Bill's voice from the barn door. "Back away just a smidge, so he doesn't kick the fence, and keep your voices low."

As Bill popped back in the barn, both Alice and Walter took a few steps back. The side door leading from the corral to the barn opened, and Bolt raced out. The stallion galloped just a few circles before realizing he had nowhere to go. He slowed his pace to a trot, and Bill entered the enclosure and secured the barn door. Bill stood very still as Bolt circled around him.

"What's he doing?" Walter asked Alice in a whisper.

"Horses are prey animals," answered Alice in her own whisper. "Bill has to get Bolt to realize he's not here to hurt him."

"You mean he doesn't just hop on his back and ride him until he stops bucking?" asked Walter.

"You've been watching too many cowboy picture shows." Alice let out a low laugh. "Breaking a horse takes a lot of patience and time. Just hopping onto a wild horse's back without building trust is a good way to get yourself hurt. People from all over the county have brought Bill their horses to break. He's good. You can learn a lot just by watching. I better go check on Nicholas, Sophie's probably throwing a fit wanting something to eat. I'll see you in a bit."

Alice gave Walter a final smile and waved to James who was coming out to watch Bill. She passed by the main barn to the smaller barn which held a half dozen goats that helped keep the weeds under control around Quail Crossings. As she stepped in the doorway, she heard Nicholas talking and paused to hear what he was saying.

"Now, listen here, goat," said Nicholas. "All I want is a little milk for that baby in there. I've already missed morning chores for sleeping in like a nitwit, and I keep putting my foot in my mouth with my aunt. So, if you could do me a little favor and stop kicking the pail every time I get milk in it, I'd very much appreciate it."

Alice heard a small grunt followed by the sound of milk splashing along the bottom of the metal pail. The pail came rolling into the doorway, stopping at Alice's feet. Alice picked it up.

"Dam ... Dagnabit!" cried Nicholas.

"Problem?" Alice asked holding up the now empty pail.

"Me and the goat are not seeing eye to eye on this situation," explained Nicholas. "I've begged, pleaded, and even threatened, but nothing works with her. I get one squirt in, and then she kicks the bucket across the barn."

"Show me," said Alice with a smirk as she handed the bucket out to Nicholas. "Not the begging and pleading part, just the milking part."

Nicholas took the bucket, sat down on the stool, and yanked on the goat's teat. Again, the milk came shooting out and, again, the goat belted and kicked the bucket.

"You're hurting her," said Alice calmly as she picked up the bucket. "That's why she's kicking the bucket."

"Hurting her?" Nicholas raised both hands in disbelief. "How? I tried barely squeezing and nothing came out."

"You just have to find the right amount of pressure," said Alice. "Move over or Sophie will never get to eat."

Nicholas did as he was told and moved off the stool. "You've got to be both gentle and firm," Alice said as she took his place beside the goat.

The small barn filled with music of milk splashing into the metal pail. Alice tried to concentrate on the job at hand and not the fact that Nicholas was watching her so intently. She was not good at being the center of attention, whether it was someone calling her beautiful or doing an everyday chore such as milking a goat.

"You did do one thing right," said Alice as she stood with the finished bucket of milk.

"Oh yeah?" Nicholas leaned forward in anticipation.

"Talking to the goats helps," said Alice. "It calms them. I'll take this on up to the house. Put this goat up and get the other nanny goat. Milk her, then bring that up. Sounds like Sophie will be staying with us all day, so we'll need it. I'll be back in a bit to check your progress, but remember, if she kicks the bucket, you're trying too hard."

"Sounds like my life right now," mumbled Nicholas.

"How's that?" asked Alice.

"Just trying too hard," explained Nicholas. "Seems the more I try to fit in here, the more I end up saying the wrong things."

Alice sighed, acknowledging to herself she hadn't helped Nicholas feel at ease. "Look, we're a tightknit group, and we've been through a lot together, none of which you could've known without your ma letting you in on what's been going on around here. It's easy for us to get protective of each other."

"That's what I like about Quail Crossings," said Nicholas. "And that's why I'm gonna stay, no matter what."

Chapter Ten

Nicholas could hardly hide the skip in his step as he walked back toward the house after finishing milking the second nanny goat. He followed Alice's advice and got more milk than Alice had out of the first goat. It felt good to be useful.

He looked over and saw Walter and James watching Bill in the corral as he worked with the beautiful white stallion and was glad they hadn't left yet for a tour of the grounds. He wanted nothing more than to continue watching Bill gaining the horses's trust, but he remained focused on his current task of getting the goat's milk to little Sophie.

As he hopped up the back steps, the door swung open and Ellie held out her hand for the pail. Nicholas hesitated. "I was hoping to talk to Aunt Dovie for a minute."

Ellie shook her head. "She's busy. Give me the pail, and I'll see to the milk."

Nicholas sighed. "Look, Ellie, I know I really put my foot in it this morning … and well … a lot of other times since I've been here, which hasn't been long … and I know you're just trying to protect her, which I appreciate, but," he continued, "all I want to do is apologize. Won't you give me the opportunity to make it right?"

"Ellie, let the boy in," said Dovie as she walked up to the door. "Good gracious, you both are standing in the doorway chattering like chickens and letting a whole flock of flies in."

"I'm sorry, Momma Dovie," said Ellie, stepping to the side so Nicholas could pass into the kitchen with the milk. "I just don't want to see you cry anymore."

Dovie smiled and gave Ellie a kiss on the forehead. "And God love you for trying to protect me, but I don't need protection from Nicholas."

The women allowed Nicholas inside. He sat the pail in the sink and turned to face Dovie. "Aunt Dovie, I'm very sorry I've continued to hurt you with my callous remarks. It's not my intention, I assure you, but regardless of my intentions, I know I've upset you. Again, I'm sorry."

"Thank you for the apology, Nicholas," said Dovie. "Sit for a minute."

"I'd love to Aunt Dovie, but I don't want to miss going out with Bill to get the lay of the land," said Nicholas.

Dovie looked at Ellie, who was hovering by her side. "Ellie, hon, go on out and ask Bill to wait on Nicholas, as a favor to me. Thanks."

Ellie hurried out the back door to do what she was told. Nicholas reckoned she would hurry back just as fast to make sure he didn't hurt Dovie again.

"Aunt Dovie," said Nicholas, "I just don't understand why Ma would keep stuff from me. She acted like you guys didn't care. Had I known …."

Dovie reached out and patted his hand, letting him know she understood. "Nicholas, it really is okay. I'm sure your Ma didn't tell you half the stuff that's gone on here … for that matter, I'm not sure I've told her. I write your mother once a year, and the last thing I want to do is fill it with the unpleasant things that have happened over the years."

"But why do you only write her once a year?" asked Nicholas.

Dovie pursed her lips. "Well, I guess I should just leave it at the fact that hurt runs deep sometimes. No matter how much we want to forgive, some hurt just buries itself in our core."

"So why did Ma leave Quail Crossings in the first place?" asked Nicholas. "This place is great."

Dovie let out a short chuckle. "I wish your mother would've seen Quail Crossings with your eyes. Some people are drawn to country life while others are not."

"Let me guess," said Nicholas. "Ma was not."

Shaking her head, Dovie smiled. "She definitely was not. Me and my folks could sit around the table and talk about Quail Crossings for hours. Even as a young girl, I was interested in everything from chickens to cattle, and I loved baking and helping Mother prepare meals. Getting my hands dirty wasn't just a way of life, it was a passion. June, on the other hand, wanted something more refined than what Quail Crossings had to offer. She couldn't understand why we gave so much away instead of keeping it all for ourselves."

Now it was Nicholas's turn to laugh. "My ma, always the generous one."

"She was generous in her own way," corrected Dovie. "Believe it or not, she was great with horses. Had she been running Quail Crossings, we would've been in the horse business instead of cattle, but she did want the finer things in life, things our parents thought were frivolous."

Dovie let out a heavy sigh. "She and Dad fought a lot. Mom used to say because they were so much alike, they could hardly stand each other. We tried to make peace, but June found salvation another way, through your dad."

"Dad, huh?" Nicholas shook his head.

"Now, Nicholas, I don't know what your father was like in New York," said Dovie. "But he got into a lot of trouble here before they eloped. The truth is, June wanted to marry your father, but Dad told her if she did, she shouldn't come back."

"Really?" Nicholas asked as he sat back in his chair.

"A statement I regret every day," said James as he walked through the back door and put his hat on the peg beside it.

"Have you told her that?" asked Nicholas.

James nodded as he sat at the kitchen table. "After your grandma died, I went to New York to make amends. You were just a baby, so I'm sure you don't remember, but your brother, David, Jr., answered the door and when your mom saw who it was, she closed the door on me. I overheard her tell y'all that I was a salesperson. I knocked again, hoping she would answer the door just enough for me to say two simple words, I'm sorry, but she never did. I sat on that stoop all day long, until the police came and told me I had to move along."

"She called the police on you?" Nicholas asked as his mouth dropped open.

"I don't know if it was June," said James, "Could've been one of the neighbors, I reckon."

"So you see, it's very complicated," interjected Dovie. "We still love June, very much, but love might not be enough."

Silence fell between them. Nicholas was having a hard time picturing his grandfather giving his mother such a drastic ultimatum, but he was sure his mother hadn't been quick to accept any form of apology, even with the grand gesture of James traveling all the way to New York. Hearing his father had been in trouble growing up wasn't a surprise either.

The sound of a truck horn broke the silence.

"That'll be Bill," said Dovie. "He's probably ready to show you and Walter around the pastures."

Nicholas rose. "It seems I've got a lot to think about."

Dovie grabbed his hand. "We're glad you're here, Nicholas. You don't need to think about that, it's a sure thing. I'm hoping you being here will mend some long broken fences with your mom."

"And Nicholas," added James, "know this place is just as much yours as it is ours."

Nicholas gave them a tight-lipped smile before heading out the door. As he walked to the truck, he couldn't help but feel angry toward his mother. The feeling surprised him since he had always been fiercely loyal to her, but it seemed to him like his loyalty was the result of many lies. He imagined his mother would say it was Aunt Dovie and Grandpa lying, but they had seemed to come forward with their part in the whole horrid mess. One thing was for sure, Nicholas would have to figure out where he fit when it came to the loyalty he felt for his mother and his longing for Quail Crossings.

Evalyn draped herself over the sofa and sighed heavily. Her back and feet hurt, and there was a throbbing in her head she was sure would last for days. The rooster crowed, and she glanced over at the clock. It was seven in the evening.

She knew she should get up and start cleaning the kitchen, but every ounce of her motivation was gone. She had barely had enough energy to fix dinner after chasing chickens around the yard.

She had sent the kids outside to play under the trees and warned them not to come inside until it was dark. A part of her felt guilty leaving Joy and Caleb to keep the twins busy and out of trouble, but she just needed a few minutes of quiet. The rooster crowed again.

Evalyn let out a groan of disgust and bit her lip to keep herself from crying from exhaustion.

"Hun?" came Robert's voice from the door. "You okay?"

"I'm fine," said Evalyn pushing herself up off the sofa, "Just needed a moment of silence."

The rooster crowed.

"What are we going to do about that?" asked Evalyn, throwing her hand up to the ceiling.

Robert shrugged. "As long as he stays put on the top of the roof, not a whole lot we can do. We'll try to get him back in the coop in the morning."

"Oh, great," mumbled Evalyn as she shuffled to the sink, "Another day of chasing chickens." She pumped water into a big tub before heaving it over to the stovetop to warm the water for washing dishes.

"Just one chicken," said Robert with a smile as the rooster crowed again.

"It shouldn't be any chickens!" Evalyn dropped her head in her hands. "How did the twins get the coop open? How do they seem to know the exact time to get into trouble? Why do they cause such mischief? Joy and Caleb are so good and then ... the girls ... I don't understand."

The rooster crowed.

"Oh, shut up!" screamed Evalyn out the kitchen window. "Just shut up, you stupid, stupid bird. It's not morning."

Robert walked across the kitchen into the parlor and turned the radio on.

"Please, Robert, not now. I just want to do the dishes in peace and quiet. The last thing I want to listen to is the news."

To Evalyn's surprise, it wasn't the grainy voice of the news anchor that came through the speakers. It was the sweet baritone of Perry Como. Robert slid up behind her and wrapped his arms around her waist. She leaned into him and rested the back of her head on his shoulder, feeling her body relax as she was engulfed in his love.

He gently turned her around and took one hand in his while resting her other hand on his shoulder. "How long has it been since we danced?"

Evalyn smiled and shook her head. "I don't even remember the last time."

He twirled her in a circle. "Well, that is far too long, Mrs. Smith."

Evalyn couldn't help but giggle. "You are correct, Mr. Smith."

He rocked her back and forth in front of the sink and stove as Perry Como's *Forever and Ever* played on. Evalyn snuggled in close, wanting to feel every ounce of him against her. As the song came to an end, Robert gently lifted her chin, placing a soft kiss on her lips.

Her heart raced as she remembered how close she had come to losing him, not once, but twice. She couldn't believe how lucky she was to have met Robert on that bus five years before, but she knew she was never letting him go again. She smiled at him.

"What's that smile for?" asked Robert.

"Because I'm happy," replied Evalyn.

The rooster crowed.

"Still happy?" asked Robert with a low chuckle.

"As soon as we have chicken for dinner," Evalyn reached up and kissed Robert again, "Absolutely."

Chapter Eleven

Jacob swept the already immaculate floor of the butcher shop. He needed something to do with his hands. Elmer was almost an hour overdue to work, and it was unlike him not to stop at Quail Crossings and use the telephone to say he'd be late.

Jacob's mind flashed back to the tornado of 1940, when he found Elmer and Tiny in the tangled mess that used to be Elmer's truck. The tornado had flipped the truck on its side, dragged it through the mud, and then flung a fence post through the driver's side of the windshield for good measure.

His mind had gone through a dozen gory scenarios of what he would find inside the truck, but, thankfully, both Elmer and Tiny had only had minor wounds. It could've been a lot worse. Jacob looked down at the wooden leg that replaced the one he had lost in the Great War. It was a constant reminder of how bad things could get.

He shook the thoughts away. His leg may be wooden, but he was still standing. Not only was he standing, he had a good job and most of the citizens of Knollwood had come to know him for the man he was instead of the color of his skin.

He laughed to himself as he took the broom to the storage closet. Elmer probably just overslept. He had done that before and confessed to Jacob that when he dreamed of the war, he had trouble getting up the next morning. Jacob understood those dreams all too well. He had them as well, always waking up and reaching for his lost leg. Funny thing, the leg was gone, but on the nights of those dreams, it still ached.

The jingle of the front door bell filled the air, and Jacob put on his biggest smile as he exited the storage closet. "Now, I know you're the boss 'round here, but you gotta call a fella when you're gonna be this late. I've been here frettin' like a hen …"

He stopped when he saw it wasn't Elmer in the doorway, but his own wife. "Blu?"

"Hi, Jacob," she said, a half smile caressing her lips.

Thoughts flooded Jacob's mind. He had dreamt of this day when he could really give Blu a piece of his mind. He was going to tell her how much of a coward she was for leaving him while he was overseas fighting for their country. He would demand to know if another man was involved. Had she taken her marriage vows to him seriously, or were those vows before God nothing but a joke to her? He had sworn an oath to her and to this day remained faithful to it.

Even with all that running through his mind all he could ask was, "What are you doin' here?"

"I need to talk to you," said Blu.

"How did you even find me?" asked Jacob. "It's been almost ten years."

"Eight years," corrected Blu. "It wasn't hard to find you. You always talked about this town like it was some place special. When the neighbor said you'd gone off with an old white man and blonde girl, I knew exactly where you was. Of course, here you are workin' for them. Bet they got you thinkin' this is your home. That little white girl, let me think, oh yes, Alice. She still makin' the doe eyes at ya? You must know better, that'll get you in trouble, even in Knollwood."

She clicked her tongue as she shook her head, looking down at him. He couldn't help but feel he was no better than dog poop on her shoe. Jacob took a step closer and swallowed hard. Anger flooded his veins. He knew exactly how Blu felt about the good folks at Quail Crossings, especially Alice. At every opportunity she'd chastised Jacob for his relationship with them, especially his writing to Alice, vowing that one day the little white girl "being sweet on him" was going to get him killed.

"You're not welcome here, Blu, so say what you came to say and then climb right back into that hole you crawled out of," snarled Jacob.

It hurt when Jacob came home to find Blu gone, but, now, as she stood in front of him, he realized the hatred that ran through her veins would've ruined them anyway. It was something she'd hid about her personality before they had married and definitely fit the "for worse" part of their vows.

As Blu stepped back and opened the front door, the jingle sounded through the air again. "Get in here."

Jacob's eyebrows rose as a boy around eight-years-old, hurried inside and stood in front of Blu. The boy's eyes remained on the floor, his hands folded in front of him.

"This here is your boy, and it's your turn," said Blu.

"My turn for what?" asked Jacob, then blinked hard. "What do you mean he's my boy?"

"I was pregnant when you left for the war," said Blu.

Jacob shook his head in disbelief. "Why didn't you tell me?"

"At first, I knew you was fighting, and I didn't want to worry you," said Blu, her eyes narrowed. "Then you sent that picture of you with them Jap girls. I met Ruben by then, so I figured Ruben and I would just raise the boy as our own. But, Ruben's gone now, and I'm tired. So it's your turn."

"I have a son?" Jacob whispered, then shook his head. He knew the picture he sent Blu of him eating coconuts with some Pacific island natives had upset her. It was an innocent enough picture though. The women ran the market and had sold him the coconut, but now he knew there was another man involved. "How do I know he ain't Ruben's?"

"Boy, look at your father," demanded Blu.

As the boy raised his head to face Jacob, it was clear who his father was. Jacob had only seen one picture of himself as a child. His mother had kept an old black and white photo of the whole family by her bed. She'd used a week's worth of pay for that single item. Before Jacob left at the age of sixteen, he'd memorized that picture because he wanted to remember what his mother, brothers, and sisters looked like. He knew it was unlikely he'd ever see any of them again. As he stared at this boy standing in front of his estranged wife, it was like looking into a living replica of that picture.

Tears formed in the corners of his eyes.

"I have a son," he whispered again, but this time it wasn't a question. He took a small step closer towards the boy. He wanted to get eye level with the child, but knew his wood leg would make him look clumsy if he tried to kneel, so he remained standing. "What's your name, son?"

The boy mumbled something, but it was less than a whisper. Before Jacob could ask him to repeat what he said, Blu slapped the boy on the back of the head. "Speak up! What have I told you about that mumbling?"

"My name's Leon, sir," the boy said quickly and clearly.

Swallowing his anger at Blu for striking the boy, Jacob stretched out his hand. "It's nice to meet you, Leon."

Leon hesitated and then shook Jacob's hand. Jacob patted the back of Leon's hand before letting go and then rubbed the back of his hand over his eyes. He looked around the butcher shop.

"Well, it'll be crowded at first," he said. "I live in a room just behind the shop, but I'm sure we can find a house soon enough."

"Do what you want," said Blu as she pushed Leon toward Jacob. "Ain't no skin off my nose."

"What do you mean?" asked Jacob. "You don't expect us to all live in one room. That would be hard for even the closest families, and we've got a lot of mending to do before we would be considered close again. But I'm willing to give it a try for Leon, if you are. I meant my vows, and, had I known about Leon, I would've come and found you after the war. Maybe we can rent you a room until we find a house. I'll help pay rent and …."

"Man, you're stupider than I remember." Blu rolled her eyes as she interrupted Jacob. "I ain't stayin', but Leon is." She snapped her fingers at Leon. "Go get your bag out of the car. Looks like this is your new home sweet home."

Leon looked around the butcher shop for a moment, and Jacob could tell that Leon wasn't too keen on living in the shop. Blu cleared her throat loudly, and the boy ran out of the door.

"Now, Blu, I don't know nothin' about that boy. You can't just leave him here alone with me. He needs both his parents, especially his momma."

Leon hurried back into the shop, a large carpet bag in his hands.

Blu sneered at Jacob. "Just take him to Quail Crossings. They take in all the strays, right? After all, they took you."

Without another word, Blu turned and walked out. Jacob stared at the door, his feet frozen in place. He wanted to run after her and tell her this was all a big mistake, but he remembered the way she slapped Leon on the back of the head. He bet his good leg that she had done a lot more than that to the boy … his son.

Jacob's eyes fell to the child. Leon was once again staring at his shoes. He sniffled, and Jacob knew he was crying. *What child wouldn't after being abandoned like that?* thought Jacob, his heart sinking.

Inching closer to Leon, he put a hand on the boy's shoulder. "I'm awfully sorry your momma did that."

Leon wiped his nose on his sleeve. Jacob grabbed his handkerchief and handed it to the boy. Leon wiped his nose and handed it back to Jacob. Jacob took it, folded it over, and delicately lifted the boy's head so he could look him in the eye.

"You eat anything this mornin'?" Jacob asked, cleaning the boy's tear-stained cheeks. Leon shook his head.

"Well, I've got some sausage and eggs in the back. Let's get you some breakfast, and then we'll work out this situation."

The front door jingled, and Jacob looked up expecting to see Blu. He didn't figure any mother would just leave her son behind, even Blu but instead, he met the light green eyes of Elmer.

"Who do we have here?" asked Elmer, softly.

Jacob stood tall and let Leon see his widest smile. "This here is my son, Leon."

Chapter Twelve

Tiny stomped around the small kitchen, each step sending a jolt through Elmer's throbbing headache. It had been a very long day, and all he wanted to do was get Tiny and go to Quail Crossings for dinner. It had been his mistake to mention the situation with Blu and Leon before they had left the house.

"I can't believe she would do that to Jacob," ranted Tiny. "I mean how could she just leave him during the war and never tell him they had a child? Jeepers, what kind of person does that? She must be out of her mind. So, what did you tell Jacob?"

Elmer shrugged. "I told him Leon was more than welcome to stay in the apartment at the butcher shop with him, but that they may want to find larger accommodations. I helped Jacob set up that ol' cot, and we hung a blanket between the two beds to give them some privacy. It'll work for now."

"You didn't tell him to go after Blu?" asked Tiny, stopping in her tracks and grabbing the back of the kitchen chair.

"Why would I?" asked Elmer. He rubbed his forehead and looked at Tiny. "Why would I want Leon to go back to a mother who thinks so little of him that she'd drop him off with a stranger? The poor kid is only eight-years-old. Had Jacob run off to get Blu, then Leon would think nobody wanted him."

"Jacob has no business taking care of a child. What does he know about it?" asked Tiny.

Elmer sighed loudly and stood. "He knows as much as any of us did when we first had babies, except Leon's no baby. They'll get by just fine. Now, could we go to Dovie's? I'm starving."

Tiny nodded and followed Elmer out to the truck.

"Speaking of Dovie, did you ask her to drop by today?" asked Tiny.

"I said you weren't feelin' well, so she said she'd check in on you," said Elmer as he opened the truck door for Tiny. She got in, and Elmer walked around to the driver's side and slid onto the bench seat.

"Next time, I'd appreciate it if you'd keep our business, our business," said Tiny as Elmer started the truck and pulled out of their driveway.

"What are you talkin' about?" asked Elmer, feeling the dread of an argument coming on.

"You told her I was sitting in the kitchen cryin' this mornin' and didn't feed my children," said Tiny, folding her arms.

"Because you were, and you didn't," countered Elmer.

"She doesn't need to know that," said Tiny. "You made me look like a bad mother."

Elmer felt the pounding in his head increase. "Don't you think you're overreacting a bit here, Mary? I took the kids to Quail Crossings for breakfast and said you weren't feeling well. Everyone was sympathetic. No one thinks you're a bad mother."

"Everyone?" Tiny gasped. "Who all did you tell?"

"Dovie, Alice, and Ellie were all in the kitchen when I got there," said Elmer.

"Great!" Tiny threw her hands up in the air. "Why not just broadcast it on the radio that I'm failing as a mother? Soon they'll all think of me like they do Blu."

"What in the …?" Elmer shook his head. "Where is all this coming from? Right now they think nothin' of Blu 'cause I ain't told them nothin', and they all adore you. They'd never put you and Blu in the same sentence."

"Just leave me alone," said Tiny as she curled up against the door of the truck. "Take me home."

Elmer pulled into the driveway of Quail Crossings.

"I can't do that, Mary," he said softly. "I'm sure they've seen us pull up, and, if I turn around now, I'll just have to explain why. Besides, I'm sure you need to eat a good meal and spend some time with Benny and Sophie. I know they've missed you today."

"I'm sure they haven't," whimpered Tiny, "and I'm not hungry."

Elmer pulled around back and put the truck in park. "Well, I'm going inside, and I hope you'll come too."

Before Elmer even turned the truck off, Tiny jerked the handle and flew out of the door. Elmer quickly cut the engine and exited his side as Benny ran up to greet his mother.

"Momma!" cried Benny. "You feelin' better?"

Tiny sidestepped her son and looked over her shoulder at Elmer as she walked up the back stoop. "I just can't right now. You deal with him."

Elmer's eyes narrowed as Tiny went inside without looking back. Benny started to cry. Taking another deep breath, Elmer forced his anger down into his gut and smiled at his son. "Hey, Benny Boy, how was your day? Did you have fun with Aunt Alice and Momma Dovie?"

Benny rubbed his eyes and nodded. "Is Momma still sick?"

Elmer nodded and then through clenched teeth said, "She's somethin'."

Alice stood by the old fence line bordering the pasture closest to the house and watched as Bill showed Walter and Nicholas the different parts of the tractor. Hearing a truck pull in the driveway, she turned and watched Tiny storm out of the passenger side. Alice let out a heavy, worried sigh. She took a step toward the house when the tractor roared to life.

Smiling, she turned around to see Walter sitting on the tractor giving her a big thumbs up. Bill was getting ready to give him a lesson on how to drive it. Since Alice and Ellie had made four loaves of bread and a mountain of biscuits that day, Dovie and Bill's wife, Lou Anne, had banned Ellie and Alice from the kitchen until dinner was ready.

Alice glanced at the house just in time to see Tiny march in the back door. She decided it might be best if she had some alone time with Dovie and Lou Anne. Tiny looked like she might need someone to talk to, and Dovie was by far the best person to get advice from, with Lou Anne being a quick second.

The tractor lurched forward and Walter let out a triumphant, "Yee-haw!"

Alice couldn't hide her laughter. She had never heard Walter say "yee-haw" since she'd known him and reckoned it was probably the first time in his life. She also couldn't help but notice Nicholas laughing too as he leaned against the barn in the shade, waiting for his turn to learn.

Elmer walked up beside Alice with Benny in his arms. "What's going on here?"

"Tractor driving lessons," answered Alice.

"Good," said Elmer.

"You okay?" asked Alice.

"Why would you ask that?" Elmer frowned.

"Come on, Elm," said Alice. "I saw what just happened between you and Tiny. So are you okay?"

Elmer shook his head. "Not really, but I'm not ready to talk about it."

"Fair enough," said Alice. She turned her attention back to Walter on the tractor.

"But, I do have somethin' I need to tell you," said Elmer.

"Okay," Alice said, bracing herself.

"Blu came by the butcher shop today to see Jacob."

"Blu? Jacob's wife?"

Elmer nodded. Alice's eyes grew wide as she looked at her brother. "What happened?"

"As far as I can tell, Jacob realized how much better off he is without her," said Elmer. "She didn't stay."

Alice shrugged. "Probably for the best. I'm sure Jacob had a few words for her. I know I do."

"There's more," said Elmer.

Alice felt her heart jump into her throat. "He didn't go with her did he? I mean, I want him to be happy, and I know they said their wedding vows, but Jacob has to know that's a horrible idea. For the love of Pete, he didn't even say good-bye …."

"Alice, stop," interrupted Elmer. "Jacob didn't leave. He found out he has a son with Blu. That's what Blu came to tell him, but she didn't just tell him he has a son. Leon is now living with Jacob."

"What?" Alice understood the words that Elmer was saying, but, for some reason, her brain was having a hard time putting them into context.

"Blu left their son with Jacob to raise," repeated Elmer. "Said she was tired and that it's Jacob's turn to do the tending to."

"Why didn't she tell him he had a son before now?" asked Alice.

"To hear Jacob tell it, Blu run off with some guy, and they planned to raise Leon as their own. Now that guy's gone, and she doesn't want to do it anymore."

"Well, I'll be," said Alice, sighing as she leaned on the fence. She looked at her brother. "Did you invite them over for dinner?"

Elmer nodded. "I did, but Jacob thought it would be better for the two of them to get to know each other first. He did ask me to spread the word so it's not so awkward when Leon comes by."

"Oh, it'll be awkward," said Alice. "Jacob, with a son. Never thought I'd see the day."

"Honestly, I'm glad," said Elmer.

Alice cocked her head at her brother.

"I've always felt bad for him staying all by himself at the butcher shop. You know, not having a family to go home to," explained Elmer.

"He has a family," stated Alice. "We're his family."

Elmer nodded. "You know I look at Jacob like a brother, but it's different. One day when you settle down with some young man, you'll understand what I'm getting' at."

Alice nodded and turned her attention back to Walter who was now driving around in circles in the small pasture. Bill and Nicholas were monitoring his progress from the shade of the barn.

Elmer gave her a playful nudge. "Maybe even some young man on a tractor."

She felt her cheeks grow hot and turned to give Elmer a playful slap when a flash of white caught her eye right in front of the tractor. She saw Walter jerk the tractor's steering wheel to the left, right before hearing Norman honking wildly.

She scaled the fence and ran out into the pasture. "Mr. Norman!"

"He came out of nowhere," said Walter, shutting the tractor down and hopping off. "I tried to miss him."

Alice cradled Norman who lay limply on the ground. Nicholas and Bill were beside her in a heartbeat.

"Why weren't you paying attention?" she yelled at Walter. "He's an old bird, he can't move as fast as he used to." Tears fell on her cheeks as she rubbed Norman's head. "Please be okay, Mr. Norman."

Norman gave her a soft honk, before jumping to his feet and shaking his feathers.

"Oh, good, he's okay," said Walter, a sigh of relief escaping from his lips as he took off his hat to scratch his head. "I didn't think I hit him, but it all happened so fast."

Norman narrowed his eyes at Walter before waddling off, favoring his right leg.

Alice stood. "You did hit him."

"I swear I didn't," said Walter holding up his hands.

"He looks fine," said Bill, "but I'll go check on his leg."

Alice watched as Bill jogged over to Norman and gently grabbed him up to inspect the leg. She turned to Walter and took a deep breath. "I'm not saying you did this on purpose, but Walter we've got all kinds of fowl, livestock, and even kids running 'round this place. People die on tractors. You've got to be careful. It ain't a toy."

"He's fine," Bill hollered, putting Norman down. "Probably, just sore."

"Look," said Walter, flinging his hand out toward Norman. "He's not even favoring the same leg."

Alice narrowed her eyes at him. "That's because you hurt both his legs by your careless driving."

"I know I didn't hit him," said Walter. "The bird is faking it to get me into trouble!"

Alice shook her head in disgust. "I'm gonna go inside. You ought to wait awhile before you do the same."

As she stormed off toward the house, she saw Walter start after her. Nicholas put a hand up on Walter's chest to stop him. She was thankful to Nicholas in that moment. The thought of losing Norman was too much for her, and she didn't want either of them to see her cry over what could've happened.

"You okay?" asked Elmer. He hadn't tried to climb the fence with Benny because, Alice suspected, he didn't want his son to see a mangled Norman, if the goose had been hit by the tractor.

Alice nodded as she scaled back over the fence. She intended to go straight into the house and up to her room where she could cry out her fear in private, but as her feet hit the ground, Elmer wrapped her up in a hug.

She wept into her brother's shoulder as her little nephew, Benny, patted her on the top of her head. After a few minutes she wiped her eyes as she stepped out of the hug. "I'm sorry. I know Mr. Norman's fine, but he's gettin' so old, and I know he's not gonna be around forever. I just can't stomach the thought of losing him."

"Never apologize for your feelings towards Norman," said Elmer. "You two have been a couple of peas in a pod since you were six years old. I'd think less of you if you weren't cryin'."

"Are you sick like Momma, Auntie Alice?" asked Benny.

Alice felt as if she was going to start crying all over again.

"Come on," said Elmer, putting an arm around her and steering her in the direction of the orchard. "I'm ready to have that talk."

Chapter Thirteen

Almost a week had gone by and Tiny still stomped around the house, exclaiming to all that would listen what a horrible mother Blu was for abandoning her child. Elmer had tried to get her to let the subject go, but Tiny seemed fixated on Blu.

"Mary," Elmer said gently, "We've got to get ready for church, or we're gonna be late picking the kids up from Sunday school."

"You go," said Tiny. "I'm in no mood for the looks today."

"What looks?" Elmer shook his head in frustration.

"Oh come on!" said Tiny, flinging her hands in the air. "Your sister is taking our kids to Sunday School instead of us, and you don't think people are gonna look at me and wonder why I'm not the one bringin' them to church. Jeepers, Elm, it's written all over their faces."

"Why in the world would you think that, especially since Alice and Ellie are working in the nursery today?" asked Elmer. "It made perfect sense for them to take the kids since they were going in early anyway."

"You just don't understand." Tiny sat in the kitchen chair and folded her arms. "I'm no better than Blu in their eyes. I might as well have abandoned my own children."

The anger that had been sitting in Elmer's gut all week exploded as he thought of the way Tiny had been sidestepping their children.

"Then maybe you should stop ignoring them and be the kind of mother you think everyone expects you to be," snapped Elmer. He tried to keep his voice even but knew the anger he felt dripped with every word.

"I don't ignore our kids." Tiny stood.

"You do," said Elmer. "Every chance you get."

"Name one time," demanded Tiny.

"How 'bout Monday when you sidestepped Benny when we got to Quail Crossings. All he was askin' was if you felt better, and you didn't even have the decency to give the boy a hug."

"'Cause I was mad at you!"

"So?" Elmer threw up his hands. "You were mad at me, not Benny. You acted like that precious little boy had yellow fever when he ran up to you. Want to know the truth? I was mad at you, too."

"Me?" Tiny pointed to herself. "What on earth for?"

"Because even when I tried to help by taking the kids to Quail Crossings for breakfast and lookin' after, since you were in no state to do it, you accused me of making you out to be a bad mother."

"You did make me out to be a bad mother," cried Tiny.

"I did no such thing," said Elmer, his voice rising. "I've never said one ill word against you, but I've got to be honest here, I don't understand what's goin' on."

"What do you mean?"

Elmer sighed and tried to lower his voice. "Mary, you aren't yourself, and you haven't been since Sophie was born. Every time I come home, you disappear in the bedroom and cry. I don't know how many mornings I've woken up to you crying in the kitchen over toast. I can't remember the last time you cooked dinner for us, and there are more times than I'd like to admit that Benny has told me he hasn't eaten all day. That's not right, Mary, and you know it's not."

"The boy's exaggerating," cried Tiny. "He's always had an active imagination."

"Is he?" Elmer shook his head. "Because I don't believe he is. I watch him eat when we're at Quail Crossings, and he acts like it'll be his last meal ever. I see the look of hunger in his eyes, and I remember what that felt like when I was little. Don't even get me started on what's going on with Sophie."

"I do everything for those kids!" yelled Tiny. "I get them up and dressed, take care of them all day while you're gone at work. So what, I want a little time to myself when you get home. Is that too much to ask?"

"It is when you spend all the time by yourself crying instead of being with family," countered Elmer. "And when we are together, all you want to do is pick a fight. Now, I'm going to church because I don't want Benny to be scared when he comes into the sanctuary from Sunday school and can't find his parents."

Tiny narrowed her eyes at Elmer. "We're not done here. Dovie will take care of him."

"Oh, I'm done," said Elmer as he walked out the door, ignoring Tiny's threatening calls from the kitchen.

Lou Anne scanned the church searching for the kids as they came into the sanctuary from Sunday School. Everyone wore their Sunday best bearing the bright colors of spring. She held Benny's and Caleb's hands lightly, letting go of Caleb's hand briefly to wave at Dean who was helping his sisters through the crowd of kids.

"Where are Bonnie and Beverly?" asked Lou Anne. Evalyn asked her to corral up all the kids since she was singing in the choir.

Dean shrugged. "Aren't they with Joy?"

"Go back and check, I'll wait here in case you miss them," said Lou Anne. She knew Dean was probably right, but with the twins, "probably" was never the answer.

The music started, signaling for everyone to take their seats just as Elmer walked up behind Lou Anne. "Thanks, Lou Anne, I'll take Benny now."

"You're welcome, Elm," said Lou Anne. "Do you mind taking the girls and Caleb with you to sit? Dean is still lookin' for the twins and Joy."

"Not a problem," said Elmer. "Come on kids. Let's go get seated."

"Save me a seat," Lou Anne hollered after Elmer, getting a thumb's up from her brother-in-law. She knew she didn't have to ask Elmer to save her a seat. The whole congregation knew the fourth and fifth center pews were for the Quail Crossings clan.

Lou Anne scanned the sanctuary and saw Dovie waving at her. Lou Anne waved back, then realized Dovie was pointing at the twins, sitting beside her. Letting out a sigh of relief, Lou Anne scanned the hallway towards the Sunday school classroom looking for Dean and Joy.

Pastor Spaulding took to the pulpit and Lou Anne hurried to sit by Bill.

"Where's Dean?" asked Bill.

"I sent him to go look for the twins, but then I saw they were sitting with Dovie. I'm sure he'll be back in a minute. I couldn't find Joy either."

"She's helping in the nursery with Alice and Ellie," said Bill. "Dean was supposed to tell you that."

Lou Anne shook her head. "I guess I was so worried about the twins, I didn't give him the opportunity."

Pastor Spaulding asked everyone to stand for the first hymn so service could begin. The congregation rose blocking Lou Anne's view of the hallway door. She was sure Dean would sneak into the sanctuary any minute. Even though she trusted her son, a ball of anxiety began to form in the pit of her stomach.

Nine-year-old Dean had checked every room of the church but still hadn't found the twins. He suspected they'd gone into the sanctuary unnoticed by his mother, but he knew better than to not turn over every rock before going back and saying he hadn't found them. If the twins got into mischief because he didn't look for them hard enough, he knew he'd be the one in a whole heap of trouble.

He quickly made his way to the back door of the church as he heard the congregation start singing the first hymn. He wanted to make sure the girls hadn't gone out to the church playground by themselves. The church had a merry-go-round, teeter totters, and a set of three swings on the property. He knew the twins loved the merry-go-round.

As he rounded the corner of the church towards the playground, two hands pushed him hard in the chest, causing him to fall into the dirt. He felt pain in his rump and looked up at his aggressor, Barry Williams.

Dean quickly got to his feet and took a step back from Barry.

"What's a matter, baby?" mocked Barry. "Did you leave your blankie outside?"

Dean took a deep breath. "Leave me alone, Barry. I'm just lookin' for my cousins."

"Of course you are," snarled Barry. "They the only friends you got."

"I've got friends!" yelled Dean. He wasn't lying; he did have friends. He couldn't help that his cousin, Joy, just happened to be his best friend. They were close in age, in the same class, and she was tougher than any of the boys in school.

"Family don't count," teased Barry.

"What 'bout all your brothers? You hang out with them all the time," accused Dean.

Everyone knew about the Williams bunch. Barry had four older brothers and two younger brothers. Their parents, Peter and Charlotte, were outnumbered and had little control over the brood. Dean remembered his dad telling him the Williams's apples didn't fall far from the tree. Their mother, Charlotte, had been a troublemaker when she was in high school. She was the cause of the big hayride wreck of 1934, having spooked the horse by throwing rocks and causing the wagon to fall on its side. Thankfully, no one had been badly hurt.

"That's different," said Barry. "They ain't girls."

"And what's the matter with girls?" asked Joy, coming out of the back door, hands on her hips.

Dean noticed Barry's face fall for an instant before he regained his snarl. "Just telling Dean what a sissy he is for hangin' out with girls, especially you."

"You take that back, Barry Williams," shouted Joy.

"Or what?" Barry folded his arms.

"Or I'll pummel you into next week," threatened Joy.

"Let's just go," said Dean, trying to pull Joy back toward the door.

"You should listen to your boyfriend," said a voice coming up behind Barry. Dean's heart dropped at the sight of all six of Barry's brothers approaching them.

"He's not my boyfriend you nose-picker," shouted Joy as Dean dragged her to the back door of the church and shoved her inside.

"What are you trying to do?" asked Dean in a pant. "Get us killed?"

Joy waved him off. "The Williams boys are like stray dogs. You bark big enough back at them and they'll run away yelping with their tails between their legs."

"Or bite you and give you rabies," said Dean, looking over his shoulder to see if the boys had followed them into the church.

"They ain't comin'," reassured Joy. "They'd probably burst into flames if they stepped foot inside a church, since they're so ornery." She threw a side glance at Dean. "Speaking of ornery, what were you doing out there when the sermon's fixin' to start?"

"Momma sent me to look for the twins," said Dean. "I thought they were with you in the nursery. Why were you out back?"

"Alice was lookin' for the twins, too," said Joy. "She asked me to check the playground."

Dean rubbed his head. "I've looked in every room. They ain't here."

"I bet they're in the sanctuary with Momma Dovie," said Joy. "You better get in there before Aunt Lou Ann has a fit."

Dean nodded and hurried back to the sanctuary as Joy went down the hall towards the nursery. He had done all he could to find the twins and was sure, had Joy not shown up, would've had more than dusty pants from Barry to show for it.

He could hear the congregation still singing and was glad for the opportunity to sneak in while everyone was standing, instead of in the middle of the sermon, when everyone would be sitting quietly to listen.

He entered the sanctuary and did a quick scan to find an open spot on their pew when movement towards the back wall caught his eye. There sitting against the wall were the twins, Bonnie and Beverly, each giggling as they tore pages out of a hymnal and ripped them into smaller pieces before shoving the strips in their dress pockets.

Dean hurried over to stop them, just as the music stopped and the deafening rip of another page filled the air.

Chapter Fourteen

Dovie felt like a little girl in primary school waiting on the principle as she sat in Pastor Spaulding's office with the twins and Evalyn. Robert offered to stay too, but Evalyn told him to go on home and tend to the pigs. Dovie knew Robert was worried about a sow that was getting ready to give birth, but she still wished he would've stayed.

"You don't have to stay," said Evalyn, breaking Dovie from her thoughts. "It's not your fault."

"Of course it is," said Dovie, releasing a large sigh. "I don't know how they got away from me. One second they were standing beside me singing, and the next they're in the back of the church vandalizing hymnals."

"I just should've known better," said Evalyn. "Guess I'll quit the choir."

"You'll do no such thing," said Dovie. "Next Sunday I'm gonna tie them to their seats. There's no reason you should quit something you love to do because your girls got into some trouble."

"But they're always getting into trouble," said Evalyn, throwing her hands in the air. She looked at Dovie. "I'm so sorry I was such an ornery girl when we first came to Quail Crossings. No, not ornery, just horrid. You didn't deserve that, and, even though I've told you I'm sorry before, I didn't fully understand how frustrating it was until now."

Dovie let out a little chuckle. "That's what we call payin' for your raisin'. But never you mind the past, Evalyn. We'll get through this, just like we got through that."

Evalyn put her head in her hands. "I don't even know how."

Pastor Spaulding walked into his office carrying the hymnal and torn pages. Both Dovie and Evalyn quickly got to their feet.

Evalyn was the first to speak. "I'm so sorry, Pastor Spaulding. Please, let me pay for the hymnal."

"No, I'm the one who should pay," countered Dovie. "It was me who let the girls out of my sight."

Pastor Spaulding held up his hand to silence the ladies. "Please sit down."

Everyone sat, and Pastor Spaulding eyed the girls who were sitting cross-legged on the floor. To Dovie, it seemed the girls weren't aware of their predicament at all.

"Pastor Spaulding," said Dovie, "as you know, Evie was in the choir singing when the incident happened. I was the one that was supposed to be lookin' after the girls. They got away from me, and for that I apologize. I will pay for the hymnal, and the girls will be given extra chores around Quail Crossings to pay me back."

Dovie looked at Evalyn, who nodded. "They will also be given extra chores at home and no dessert until they've paid Dovie back."

Pastor Spaulding pursed his lips. "That sounds fine, but I'd like to hear from the girls."

Dovie felt her throat grow tight as a lump grew. The girls were almost three years old. She knew they talked well for their age, but what worried her was what words they'd choose to use.

"Beverly. Bonnie," said Evalyn, bringing the girl's attention from their shoes to the conversation, "Stand up and face Pastor Spaulding."

The girls stood and folded their hands daintily in front of them. Dovie couldn't help but think they were the spitting image of two cherubs.

"Girls," said Pastor Spaulding, "why did you rip up the hymnal?"

Beverly looked at Bonnie before she spoke. "It was Bonnie's idea."

"Is that true?" Pastor Spaulding asked Bonnie.

Bonnie nodded with a big smile.

"Bonnie, why?" asked Evalyn with a gasp, "And knock that smile off your face, this isn't funny."

Bonnie's smile turned to a pout. "We wanted to be close to Jesus, so we put the songs in our pockets." She reached into her dress pocket and pulled out remnants of the hymnal. She held them up in her little hand. "See?"

Pastor Spaulding leaned forward and smiled. "I do see, but hon, Jesus is in our hearts all the time. We don't need ripped up pages of hymnals in our pockets for Him to be in our hearts. Understand?"

The girls nodded, all smiles again. The pastor stood, causing Dovie and Evalyn to follow suit. "You can keep this," the pastor said as he handed the torn hymnal to Evalyn.

Dovie searched in her purse for her pocketbook. "How much do I owe you?"

Pastor Spaulding shook his head and gave Dovie and Evalyn a reassuring smile. "We are in need of new hymnals anyway, so instead of having you pay for this one, I'm going to put the two of you in charge of fundraising to get them. Sound fair?"

Both ladies nodded eagerly.

Pastor Spaulding looked back down at the girls. "Now, you two, stay out of trouble, though I reckon trouble will be hard to find with all those extra chores."

Dovie let out a laugh and Evalyn shot her a look.

"Sorry," Dovie mumbled to Evalyn. Dovie knew it would take a lot more than a pastor and extra chores to keep the twins out of trouble. It would take a miracle.

Jacob looked over at Leon sopping up the last of his gravy with a piece of bread. Leon's plate looked so spotless after lunch, Jacob wasn't sure he needed to wash it. The boy hadn't left a crumb behind.

Leon had been living with Jacob for just about a week. Jacob had tried to talk Leon into going to church, but the boy seemed afraid to leave the house.

"Did you get enough to eat?" asked Jacob. "I can fry up some potatoes if you're still hungry."

"I'm okay," mumbled Leon, drinking the last of his milk.

"Are you?" asked Jacob. "It's been a pretty unusual week."

Leon shrugged. "I traveled a lot with Ma'am. She'll be back to get me in a few days. She always does come back."

Questions flooded Jacob's mind. This was the first time Leon had really said anything other than, "Yes, sir" or "No, sir", since he arrived. Jacob decided to start with the obvious question. "Who is Ma'am?"

"My mom," answered Leon.

Jacob squinted his eyes. "You call her Ma'am?"

Leon shrugged again. "She doesn't like it when I called her anything else."

"Okay," said Jacob slowly. "So y'all moved around a lot?"

Leon nodded. "After Rueben left, Ma'am and I didn't have nowhere to go. We just kind of traveled around staying with different relatives of hers ... or friends."

The word *hers* sat heavy in Jacob's mind. "Didn't they know you were her son?"

Leon shrugged his shoulders.

Jacob's heart sank. The poor boy had been with family, and none of them had cared enough to give him a stable home. "So your mom would leave you alone often?"

"Yeah," said Leon, letting his finger trace the height of his milk glass. "She'd say she was tired and needed to leave. Then she'd come back in a few days."

"How long is a few days?" asked Jacob.

Leon shrugged his shoulders again. "I never really kept track. Sometimes it was better when she was gone, but other times it wasn't."

"I wish I would've known," said Jacob.

"Why didn't you?" asked Leon.

There was an edge to Leon's voice, but when Jacob looked into the boy's eyes, all he saw was sadness.

"I went to war before you were born. When I got back your mom was gone. She didn't tell me I had a son."

"Why would she do that?" asked Leon. "Were you mean to her or somethin'? Rueben was, but she never left him."

Jacob shook his head and tried to swallow his anger. He had been true to Blu. Thinking of her and Quail Crossings was the only way he made it through the war and recovered from his injury enough to go home. Even after he stopped receiving letters from her, he remained hopeful. He knew as well as all the other soldiers. Mail got lost often, especially the letters for the colored soldiers.

"No," said Jacob with a sigh. "I was never mean to your mother."

Jacob stood and walked to the closet. He opened the door and reached for a small caedboard box on the top shelf. He wiped it off gently and took it over to the table. "When I got home from the hospital, I found these piled on the porch and another stack on the kitchen table. At least the postman had enough decency to put them under a rock so they didn't blow away, but some of them are pretty weathered. I haven't opened them, of course I know what they say 'cause I wrote them."

Leon opened the box. "You wrote all these?"

"I did," said Jacob with a nod. "I wrote your mother every day I had the strength to hold a pencil, both before and after I lost my leg."

"But they ain't open," said Leon, looking an envelope.

Jacob nodded. "I know. Your mother never opened them. I don't know why. But you asked if I was ever mean to Blu. You'll find the answers in these letters. I wish she would've read them. Maybe she would've found a reason to stay."

Jacob felt a sting in his heart, which surprised him. He'd thought he was over Blu, but as he looked at the letters he had written with such hope for their future, his feelings for her returned and hit him like a sledgehammer. He had wanted his wife, a family, and a home, but Blu had disappeared into the wind.

Chapter Fifteen

Sweat collected on Alice's brow as she shoved the tip of the shovel into the dirt. It wasn't even mid-morning, but the day was already growing unnaturally hot for May.

Alice wiped her forehead quickly before stepping on the shovel again to shove it further into the dirt. The sooner she got the soil turned, the sooner she'd be done with this backbreaking work. With the additions of Walter and Nicholas eating with them throughout the summer, Dovie was concerned they wouldn't have enough food to can. She decided to add another row of green beans, zucchini squash, and cucumbers to their already large garden. Alice knew Dovie was determined not to leave a single empty space on any pantry shelf come winter.

"What are you doing?" asked Nicholas, sauntering up from the barn.

Alice turned the soil over, and then paused to rest on the shovel handle. "Well, being that you're from the big city, I can see why turning soil, not to mention manual labor in general, would be a foreign concept to you."

Nicholas laughed. "Manual labor, huh? Sounds like work for a man, not a little girl."

Alice gritted her teeth and tried to swallow her anger. She had been turning soil since she was ten-years-old.

Nicholas had probably never even held a shovel until he arrived at Quail Crossings. She smiled and pointed the shovel handle in his direction. "Feel free, big shot."

Nicholas grabbed the shovel as Bill and Walter came over, each carrying their own shovels.

"We were just comin' over to help," said Bill. "Dovie said she wanted six new rows?"

Alice nodded and then jerked her head at Nicholas. "Big shot here said the job was perfect for a man, so he probably won't need your help."

"That's not what I said," argued Nicholas.

Bill gave Alice a knowing smile. "Well, that was mighty nice of him. Guess he can show us how it's done."

Everyone turned and looked at Nicholas. He shrugged. "What's all the fuss about? It's just shoveling dirt."

Nicholas exchanged places with Alice, and she walked over and stood by Bill to watch. He drove the shovel straight down. Alice was sure she saw his whole body reverberate as the shovel bounced off the hard ground.

Nicholas grabbed his hand and let out a loud, "Dagnabit!"

"You've got to go at more of an angle," said Alice, trying to make her voice sound helpful. For a second, Alice felt badly for not warning Nicholas about how hard the Texas Panhandle ground got when the rain had been scarce, and lately, it had been very scarce.

"I know," snapped Nicholas.

Alice held her hands up in a peaceful gesture as her guilt faded away. Nicholas raised the shovel again and drove it into the ground, this time at an angle. Without kicking it further into the dirt, he turned the soil exposing grass roots still tangled within.

"I'm afraid that ain't deep enough," said Bill, walking over. "We've got to get past all those grass roots and into the soil that hasn't had anything growing in it. That's the best stuff."

"This soil must be good for something," said Nicholas with a slight pant. "The grass is growing in it."

"Yeah," said Bill, nodding, "it's good for growing Buffalo Grass and that's about it. Your hole needs to be as deep as Alice's are, the deeper the better."

Alice saw Nicholas's cheeks turn bright red as he slammed the shovel into the ground and kicked it hard with his boot.

"That's it," encouraged Bill. He looked over his shoulder. "Come on Walter, between the three of us, we'll have this done in no time. Alice grab that hoe and start breaking up the large clumps to even out the ground."

Alice did as she was told and grabbed the hoe leaning against the nearby tree. She started breaking up the large clumps in the row she'd turned minutes earlier, letting the men get a head start so she could follow behind.

She had just started on a new row when Nicholas let out a cry of disgust. She looked up just in time to see him throw his shovel to the ground.

"This is stupid," he said.

He rolled his shoulders back and rubbed his neck. Alice could tell the little time Nicholas had spent shoveling had already made him sore. Walter also took the moment to pause and rub his own neck. She remembered feeling the same way the first time she helped turn soil. She also remembered not quitting or complaining until the job was done.

The garden kept their family fed through the hard winter months without the expense of having to buy canned goods from the market. The work had to be done, and no amount of complaining was going to change that.

"You'll be okay," encouraged Bill. "We don't lack that much. Everybody eats, so everybody helps with the garden. Rest for a minute, and then get back to work."

Nicholas shook his head. "This is work for a hired hand. Walter can do it."

Bill stopped and rested his hands on the top of his shovel handle. He looked thoughtfully to the sky, and Alice knew he was choosing his words carefully.

"The thing about owning a farm like Quail Crossings is that all the work is your work. Hired hands or not. If the farm fails, you fail, and that means your family goes without food. A true farmer has his hand in every aspect of the work, even work deemed for the help. Something you ought to consider, since you want to run the place."

"So that's it, isn't it?" spat Nicholas. "The truth comes out."

Bill shot a confused look at Alice. She shrugged. She had no idea what Nicholas was talking about either.

"What?" asked Bill.

"You're upset because I've come home to claim ownership of Quail Crossings when you thought it was all yours after Grandpa passes. Now, you think by working harder than me and making me look bad that Grandpa won't give me what's rightfully mine. You don't like me because you know I have the right to be here, and you don't. You and your family are nothing but a bunch of squatters."

"How dare you!" cried Alice, but held back the rest of her outrage as Bill lifted his hand. Walter quickly walked over to Alice's side and put his arm around her. She wasn't sure if he was trying to comfort her, or if he was afraid she'd try to rip Nicholas's throat out like a rabid dog.

"You know why I work hard on this farm?" Bill asked Nicholas, but he didn't wait for an answer. "I work hard on this farm because when I had no place to go and nothing to feed my family, your grandpa and aunt took us in. They gave us a home and made us feel more loved than our parents ever did. I was an eighteen-year-old kid with no clue what to do next, watching my brother and sisters starve to death before my very eyes. I vowed I would repay their debt of kindness with my hard work on this farm. That debt won't be repaid until I take my dying breath because that's how grateful I am to them for saving our lives."

Bill took a moment and Alice could tell he was composing himself. He cleared his throat, "I may not be the flesh and blood of the Murphy's, and I may never own Quail Crossings proper, but you can bet your last dollar that I love James and Dovie like family and would walk to the end of the world for them. Now, either pick up that shovel and do your part or hit the road."

Bill grabbed his shovel and began to turn soil. Walter gave Alice a quick squeeze before hurrying over to help Bill. Alice narrowed her eyes and narrowed her eyes at Nicholas. To her surprise he wasn't glaring at Bill, but instead he was staring down at the soil. She watched as he took a deep breath and bent over to pick up his shovel.

Feeling tears start to form, Alice knew she needed to get away from the garden for a minute. She knew how much Bill had sacrificed for the family, but to hear him voice it stirred her emotions to the surface.

"I'll be right back," she called out hoping her voice wouldn't quiver and give her away. Not waiting for a response she hurried behind the nearest tree and bumped straight into James.

"How much of that did you hear?" Alice asked softly, looking into his icy blue eyes.

"Enough," whispered James.

"Do you think Bill saw you?" asked Alice.

James shook his head. "No, he was pretty focused on Nicholas, and I think Walter was blocking Bill's view of me anyway. Give me a few minutes to make it to the barn, and then tell Bill you hear me callin' for him, okay?"

"Yes, sir," said Alice. She turned to go back to work, then stopped and turned around to give a big hug to James. James tightly wrapped his arms around her as Alice fought to keep her eyes dry.

Chapter Sixteen

James ran his hand through his gray hair as he waited for Bill to come to the barn. Feeling his knees grow weak, he was thankful for the stacked hay bales beside him. He gingerly lowered himself down and took a seat.

He looked at the ceiling and thought about his wife, Sylvia. She had passed on in 1932 after a nasty round of influenza swept through the town. The irony, that Sylvia had contracted the disease while helping others mend from it, wasn't lost on James. Of course, he knew Sylvia wouldn't have had it any other way. Helping people was her purpose in life, and James knew she hadn't regretted it, not even in the end.

Funny how the end made him think of the beginning. James remembered the first time he saw Sylvia. His parents had made him attend Christmas service, even though James claimed he was much too busy tending to the livestock with a winter storm blowing in. They hadn't been inside the church building more than a minute when he spotted her. She wore her hair in a classic bun, curls escaping where they could. Her hazel eyes sparkled in the candlelight against her dark blue high-collared dress.

She caught him looking at her and gave him a big smile, as if they were longtime friends seeing each other after a long absence. James couldn't remember a single word that was said during that Christmas sermon, but he never missed another church service after that.

"James," said Bill, breaking James out of his memory, "Alice thought she heard you callin' for me."

James nodded. "I was, well kind of. I told her to have you meet me here after I heard what you said in the garden."

Bill's cheeks turned red. "Oh, you heard that."

"I did," said James, "and you've got nothing to feel embarrassed about. You might not have said those exact words to me, but it's nothing you haven't shown in your work at Quail Crossings, not to mention your commitment to Dovie and me."

Bill held up his hands. "Now I feel like I've put you on the spot, you know, regarding Nicholas."

James pursed his lips. "Well, that's why I wanted to talk to you privately."

"Quail Crossings is yours and Dovie's," said Bill. "I've never entertained the notion of you passing it on to me or my family. You've given us a home, and I wouldn't ask for anything more."

James patted the hay bale next to him. "Come here and have a seat."

Bill did as he was told.

"It's no secret that when y'all came to Quail Crossings, we were all a bit lost," said James. "Losing Simon and Helen was almost more than our family could take. Sure, we went through the motions of living, but our souls were wandering. I think it's always been clear that y'all coming here saved Dovie from a life full of heartache, but what might not be so clear is how much y'all saved me."

"James," Bill whispered.

The older man held up a hand and swallowed down the lump in his throat. "I always wanted a son. God blessed me with two daughters, one of which I managed to totally mess things up with, but good daughters none the less. Then Simon came along and became the son I never had. He was not only good to Dovie and Helen, he was good to me. Helen, well, she filled our world with laughter. When they passed on, I kept myself together for Dovie, but I was hangin' on by a thread ... that is until you came along."

James felt the lump return and worked hard to clear his throat. He placed his hand on Bill's shoulder. "What I'm trying to say, Bill, is you're like a son to me. Now, I don't know what I'm going to do about Nicholas. He's the only connection to my daughter, June, that I have left, but I can promise you this, I will do right by you and your family. You are just as much family as Nicholas is."

Bill nodded and reached out to shake James's hand.

"Thank you James, but don't worry about us. You've already given me five acres, and that is more than I ever dreamed of owning. Elm has the ol' Clark place, Evie has Rockwood, and we'll make sure Ellie and Alice always have a place. So, you do what's right for you, James. You've been doing what's right for us for a long time."

Dovie snuggled into the crook of Gabe's shoulder and released a contented sigh as they sat on the old bench in the orchard. "You know, we should really be helping with the garden."

Gabe hugged her tightly. "There will still be plenty of work once we get done here. I just want to spend a quiet moment with my wife. It feels like it's been forever since I've seen you and you weren't sleeping."

"Being busy with your business is a good problem to have," said Dovie. "Besides, if you spend too much time with this old woman, you might decide to fly away and never come back."

"Never," said Gabe, before kissing her forehead. "You know all I think about when I'm up in the sky is how I'd rather be down on the ground with you."

"You better be thinking about keeping that contraption up in the air," teased Dovie.

He gave her a playful squeeze. "Seriously though, Dovie, why don't you come fly with me? I can teach you how to be my co-pilot. Think about it, we can spend the night together in exotic locations instead of me rushing back here every night."

"Since when is Wichita, Kansas, an exotic location?" Dovie laughed. She turned herself to look at Gabe. "Oh, honey, I'd love nothing more than to be in the sky with you."

"But?" Gabe gave her a knowing smile.

Dovie huffed, hating how well he knew her. "But, I'm needed here, Tiny just having Sophie, Alice just getting home from college, Evie with the twins, and let's not forget about Ellie ..."

"All of which will do just fine without you every once and a while," said Gabe. "Look, I'm not asking you to make every trip with me, but Tiny, Alice and Evalyn are all grown, and even though I know you hate to admit it, Ellie pretty much runs this place. Quail Crossings will not tumble to the ground if you're not here for a few days."

"Dad," Dovie whispered, feeling her throat grow tight, "I have to be here for him. I can see him getting weaker every day, and he's not eating like he used to. It's just that I'll never forgive myself if he …"

Dovie buried her head in Gabe's shoulder, and he kissed the top of her head once again. "Oh, honey, I didn't mean to upset you. I just want to spend more time with you, that is all. Of course you want to stay here with James, I understand that, and when you're ready to go flying with me, there will be a seat waiting for you."

Dovie looked up at Gabe as he smiled down at her.

"How'd I get so lucky to have married you?" asked Dovie.

"I'm the lucky one," said Gabe as he leaned down and kissed her. Dovie may not have been in an airplane, but she felt her heart soar.

Gabe released the kiss, causing Dovie to playfully pout. "Just what do you think you're doin', mister. That kiss was far too short for as long as you've been gone."

Gabe gave her a wink. "I completely agree, but here comes your nephew."

Dovie felt her cheeks run hot as she straightened herself up on the bench and started to fidget with her clothes.

Laughing, Gabe grabbed her hands. "Keep doing that and he's going to think we were out here doing a lot more than kissing."

Dovie didn't know if her cheeks got any redder, but it certainly felt as if they had. She took a deep breath and tried to steady herself.

"Hi, Nicholas, whatcha doin' out here?" Dovie hated the way her voice sounded more accusatory than curious.

"What? Now I can't even walk right?" snapped Nicholas.

"Hey now," said Gabe firmly and Dovie could feel his shoulders stiffen, "I can tell you're upset about something, but don't take it out on your aunt."

Nicholas let out a huff as he rammed his hands through his hair. "Sorry, Aunt Dovie, Uncle Gabe is right. I'm not mad at you."

"Then who are you mad at?" asked Dovie.

Nicholas looked at the sky, before letting out a slow breath. "Myself, mostly."

"Want to talk about it?" asked Dovie.

Nicholas shook his head. "Not really, seems the more I talk, the more I put my foot in it."

Gabe and Dovie exchanged looks. Even though the Brewers were quick to lend a helping hand or even give you the shirts off their back, it could be hard to break into their tight family unit.

"Just give it time," advised Gabe. "I wasn't always a welcome sight either, but give them enough time to get used to you, and they'll be welcoming you right into the family as they've done me."

"But, I'm already family," said Nicholas. "That's the frustrating part."

"Family is a lot more than blood," said Dovie.

"Oh great, another lecture." Nicholas rolled his eyes. "I'm sorry to be disrespectful, Aunt Dovie, but I've had all the lecturing I can take for one morning."

As Nicholas walked toward the north pasture, Gabe whispered in Dovie's ear. "Are you sure you don't want to fly away with me?"

Dovie looked up and gave him a wink. "Only if we can take Dad."

Gabe laughed as he wrapped Dovie up in another hug. "Always the romantic."

Chapter Seventeen

Lou Anne walked out of the market and looked down the street for Dean. She had sent him down to her brother-in-law's butcher shop for their meat order while she did the rest of the shopping. She was surprised to see he hadn't returned to the '47 Buick.

She looked down at her girls, each holding a shopping bag. "Come on girls, let's load the car, and then we'll drive down to Uncle Elm's and see where your brother is."

"You should've sent me to get the order," said Annabelle. "I'm old enough."

"Of course you are," said Lou Anne as she smiled down at her seven-year-old, "But you know how Dean hates to grocery shop, and you're such good help keeping Rosey's little hands busy so she doesn't knock stuff off the shelves. I couldn't do it without you, Annabelle."

The little girl's cheeks flushed pink at her mother's compliment.

"Do you want me to go find Dean?" asked Annabelle.

Lou Anne opened the back door to her car and shook her head. "We'll just all drive down there." She sat her groceries in the back seat and took the bags from the girls. "Go on and get in, and mind the groceries. I don't want the apples all brown and bruised like last time."

Annabelle and her little sister, Rose, hopped into the back seat as Lou Anne scanned the street again for Dean.

"Where in the world did he get off to?" mumbled Lou Anne as she got into the driver's seat and started the car.

"He's probably just talkin' with Jacob," said Annabelle.

"I like Jacob," said Rose. "He's funny."

Lou Anne smiled. "He really is, and Annabelle is right, Dean is probably just talkin' with Jacob and his son, Leon."

"But we haven't met Leon," said Annabelle. "Why not, Momma?"

Lou Anne bit her lip as she backed out of the parking spot and started down Main Street towards the butcher shop. "Well, it's an odd situation."

"I'll say," said Annabelle. "Seems like Jacob would want us to meet his son, so he'd have someone to play with."

Lou Anne let out a heavy sigh. "It's an odd situation because Jacob didn't live with Blu after the war and only found out about Leon recently. That's why we've been giving Jacob and Leon some time before introducing ourselves. They've got a lot of catching up to do."

"I blame the stork," said Annabelle.

Lou Anne cocked her head and glanced at her daughter in the rear-view mirror. "The stork?"

Annabelle nodded. "The stork brings babies to all the mommas and daddies. Jacob's stork must've been confused and taken the baby to the wrong place, that's why Blu hasn't been around."

Lou Anne swallowed her laugh as she pulled into a spot in front of the butcher shop. "That makes perfect sense to me. Y'all stay in the car, and I'll be right back with Dean. We've got to get home, so I can get supper started."

Lou Anne was thankful the girls didn't fuss about staying in the car. She had exaggerated their lack of time, but she had a feeling that something wasn't quite right. She entered the butcher shop and stopped short as she recognized Charlotte Williams giving Elmer her meat order at the counter.

Charlotte had always been a thorn in Lou Anne's side. When they were in high school, Charlotte was keen on Bill and didn't take too kindly when Bill picked Lou Anne over her. Here they were, long past high school, and Charlotte still didn't miss an opportunity to make Lou Anne feel inadequate.

Jacob came in from the back carrying a large tray of meat and gave Lou Anne a smile. "Why hello, Miss Lou Anne, what can I do for you?"

Charlotte looked over her shoulder and gave Lou Anne a crooked smile. "Hello, Lou Anne. I haven't seen you in ages. I'm surprised you leave the farm."

"Hello, Charlotte, yes, I do get out occasionally. Please, excuse me," said Lou Anne as she hurried over to Jacob. "Have you seen Dean? He was supposed to come and pick up my order."

"Sorry, Miss Lou Anne. I haven't seen him. I've got your order in the back. I'll get it for you real fast."

"Thanks, Jacob," said Lou Anne as he left through the door leading to the back of the store.

"Looking for your boy?" asked Charlotte, false concern dripping from her words.

Lou Anne turned to Charlotte. "I am. Have you seen him?"

"You know, I did," said Charlotte, placing her finger on the side of her cheek. "He was sneaking around behind the building. It's really too bad you don't have a son you can rely on."

"Dean's reliable," said Elmer. "I'm sure whatever's keeping him is important."

Lou Anne snapped her finger and plastered on a smile. "Oh, I remember, how silly of me. I asked him to go around back and ask Jacob if he needed any eggs. Our hens have been layin' like a hard winter is coming on. I bet he's back there now, waitin' on Jacob."

"That's mighty nice of you, Lou Anne," said Elmer. "I'm sure they just missed each other, but don't worry about Jacob, I brought him some eggs this morning. I'll go back and see what's keeping Dean."

"That's okay, Elm," said Lou Anne, letting herself behind the counter. "You have a customer. I'll go get him and grab my order from Jacob. Two birds, one stone, you know."

"Sure," said Elmer, giving Lou Anne a side look, "I'll just add this week's meat to your tab."

Lou Anne pushed through the door leading to the back of the butcher shop and rushed toward the back door. She couldn't explain it, but she knew something was wrong with Dean. He would never skirt away from doing a chore, especially something as responsible as picking up the meat order.

She threw open the back door just in time to see Barry Williams on top of Dean, pushing his face into the dirt.

"Barry Williams, you stop that this instant!" demanded Lou Anne.

Barry quickly got off Dean, and Dean hurried to his feet and started to brush his face and clothes of dirt.

"We were just horse playin'," said Barry.

"That's not what it looked like to me," said Lou Anne as she hurried to Dean's side. "You okay?"

Dean nodded.

Lou Anne marched over and grabbed Barry's arm. "Inside with you. Let's see what your mother thinks about this horse playin'." She looked over her shoulder. "Come along, Dean."

Going through the back door, she led Barry through the butcher shop and back to the lobby just in time to see Charlotte paying Elmer for her cuts of meat.

"Go on now," Lou Anne said to Barry as she pushed him gently towards his mother and out from behind the counter. "Do you want to tell your mother or do you want me to?"

"Everything okay, Lou Anne?" asked Elmer.

"What's goin' on?" asked Charlotte.

"It ain't nothin'," said Barry. "Dean and I were just messin' around, and his ma thought I was being too rough."

"I found Barry on top of Dean, shoving his face into the dirt," stated Lou Anne, willing her voice not to shake.

Charlotte looked at Lou Anne and shook her head in confusion. "And?"

"And what?" asked Lou Anne, she could feel the blood throbbing through her veins in frustration.

"Well," said Charlotte with a chuckle, "boys will be boys. Take it from me, as a mother of seven boys, they were just having fun. It'll do your boy good to get a little rough. All those women at Quail Crossings, he could use some toughing up."

"Charlotte, this is not okay," stated Lou Anne as she felt Dean tugging on her arm. "Barry is two years older than Dean and at least a foot taller."

"Mom, I'm fine," said Dean. Lou Anne's heart stung as the word "Mom" instead of "Momma" rang through her ears. "We were just playin' around."

Lou Anne looked at her son, his cheeks red with embarrassment.

"There you go," said Charlotte. "See, all this fuss for nothin'. Really Lou Anne, you've got to stop coddling the boy. Come along, Barry. Grab our order. See you next week Mr. Brewer."

Elmer gave Charlotte a nod. "Have a good day."

As soon as Charlotte exited the store, Lou Anne turned to Dean. "Are you sure that's all it was?"

"Doesn't matter," said Dean as he rushed to the car.

Lou Anne sighed and looked at Elmer. "I'm sorry. I shouldn't have caused a scene in your shop."

Elmer waved her off. "We both know those Williams boys are nothing but trouble. If they were just playin' around, then I'm a cow who hates grass."

"So what do I do?" asked Lou Anne.

Elmer twisted his mouth. "You're not going to like this, but Charlotte was right about one thing."

"You're right; I hate it already," said Lou Anne as she folded her arms.

"Boys will be boys, and Dean has to fix this himself," said Elmer. "He's gonna have to fend for himself. Having his momma fend for him will only make it worse. Have Bill talk to him."

Jacob brought out Lou Anne's meat order. "Sorry for the delay. I was goin' back through your order and realized we had missed your sausage, so I was showing Leon how to make links and got you some fresh." Jacob looked from Lou Anne to Elmer and back again. "What did I miss?"

Lou Anne sighed again, knowing Elmer was right. "Just boys being boys apparently."

Chapter Eighteen

June 1950

Elmer took a deep breath before knocking gently on the door to their bedroom. It was close to four in the afternoon, and Tiny still hadn't gotten out of bed. She had missed church, and if things continued as they had the past few weeks, she wouldn't make it over to Quail Crossings for the big family supper either. Jacob was finally bringing Leon to meet everyone, and it was important that Tiny be there.

Elmer had lost count of how many times Jacob had asked him when Tiny was coming into the butcher shop so she could meet Leon. Just about everyone from Quail Crossings came at one time or another to meet him, under the guise of buying their meat. Now that Jacob felt comfortable enough to bring Leon to the farm for dinner, Elmer wouldn't be able to make any more excuses for Tiny.

"Mary," Elmer said softly, "it's time to get ready to go to supper. I took a ham to Dovie earlier for them to cook, so you needn't worry about that. The kids are already over there playing with Bill's bunch, so we just need to get you around."

A soft whimper came from Tiny, and Elmer knew she was crying. He sat gently on the bed and placed his hand on the back of her shoulder.

"Mary? Honey, please tell me what's wrong," Elmer begged.

His plea was met with louder sobs. Elmer's heart ached at her cries. Tiny had taken to her bed almost every day for the past week. Elmer had let her be, but as each day passed, his worrying increased.

"Should I go get Dovie?" Elmer had asked this question many times over the past week but was met with the same answer of louder sobs as Tiny shook her head no.

"I'm just tired," Tiny managed to say.

"Okay then," said Elmer.

He reached down and took off his boots before sliding next to Tiny in bed. He wrapped his arms around her, and, to his surprise, Tiny snuggled her body closer to him instead of jerking away as she had done previously.

"Please tell me what's wrong," he pleaded again.

Tiny's shoulders started to shake, and Elmer squeezed her tighter.

"I don't know," Tiny whispered.

"You don't know what?" asked Elmer.

"I don't know what's the matter with me," explained Tiny. "I know I should get out of bed and tend to the kids. I hear myself snapping at you, and, even though I know I'm doin' the wrong thing, I can't seem to make myself do the right thing. I'm so sorry, Elm. You deserve so much better. You should take the kids and never look back."

Elmer kissed the top of her head. "We'll figure this all out. I'm not goin' anywhere."

Tiny grabbed his hands and squeezed, her voice thick with despair, "Don't let go, Elm. Please, don't ever let go."

"Promise," whispered Elmer.

Jacob tapped his fingers along the steering wheel of his old truck as they drove down the dirt road leading to Quail Crossings. He glanced over at Leon who was looking out the window.

"It's something, ain't it," said Jacob. "Mr. James owns everything from that fence post to way up yonder, past where the eye can see. They've got cattle, pigs, chickens ... oh, and a goose named Norman. You'll wanna look out for him. He's got a nasty side."

"Do they have any horses?" asked Leon, still looking out the window.

Jacob nodded. "They've got ol' Tex and Pronto, and Mr. Bill has a new horse named Bolt. Prettiest thing I ever did see."

"Can I ride him?" asked Leon, scooting up on his seat a little.

"You could probably ride ol' Tex," said Jacob. "Even Pronto is gentle enough, I'd reckon." Jacob looked at his son. "Have you ridden before?"

"No, but one of Ma'am's friends took me to see a picture show once. All these cowboys were riding horses and shootin' at stuff. Made me think I might like to be a cowboy someday," explained Leon.

Jacob smiled. "Well, I bet Mr. Bill will let you ride ol' Tex. What do you think about that?"

"What about Bolt? Can I ride him?" asked Leon, the corners of his mouth curling a little.

Shaking his head, Jacob sighed. "I'm afraid not. Even Mr. Bill can't ride him yet."

Jacob pulled onto the driveway that led to Quail Crossings. "Are you ready to meet all these folks?"

Leon shrugged.

"You've met most of them at the butcher shop," said Jacob. "Dean, Mr. Bill's boy, is about your age, so I imagine you two will get along just fine."

"Are these people family?" asked Leon.

"They sure are," said Jacob without hesitation.

"But they don't look like us," said Leon as Jacob pulled behind Lou Anne's car.

Jacob put the truck in park. "Family has nothin' to do with looks and everything to do with heart. Come on, you'll see soon enough."

Jacob opened the door and wasn't surprised to see Dovie was the first one out of the house, with Alice following closely behind.

"Jacob and Leon, so glad y'all could make it," said Dovie. "Jacob, it feels like it's been a month of Sundays since you've been out."

"It's been too long," said Jacob as he gave Dovie a hug. Releasing her, he turned and grabbed a big pot off the seat of his truck. "I brought the green beans."

"I'm sure they'll be wonderful," said Dovie.

"Of course they will be," said Jacob with a big smile. "They came from your garden. I did add a little bacon, but basically, I just opened the jars and put them over some heat. You sure know how to grow 'em, Miss Dovie."

Dovie waved him off before she grabbed the pot and headed into the house.

"Hey there, Jacob," said Alice as she gave him a hug. Releasing the hug, she looked around Jacob's shoulder and into the cab of the truck where Leon still sat. "Hi, Leon, remember me? I'm Alice."

Leon nodded slightly.

"Dean's down by the pond fishin'," said Alice. "I'm sure he wouldn't mind the company if you want to join him."

"He wants to ride a horse, if that's okay," said Jacob.

"Sure," said Alice, "how about you go fishin' for a bit while I get Tex saddled up for you. Then you can ride around the corral. Will that work?"

Leon produced a large smile. "Really?"

"Of course!" Alice pointed towards the pond. "Dean is just over there under the large group of cottonwoods, and he has an extra pole if you feel like fishin' or you can just watch."

"Thanks," said Leon before jumping out of the truck and heading towards Dean.

Alice looked at Jacob. "Want a glass of tea?"

Jacob wiped the sweat from his forehead with a handkerchief. "That sounds mighty nice. Warm for June, ain't it?"

"Seems we're in for a long, extra hot summer," said Alice. She bit her lip. "How's Leon doin'?"

"Alright, I reckon," said Jacob, his smile falling. "Hard to tell sometimes. He don't talk much."

"Give him time," said Alice. "Can't be easy to be dropped off by your momma like that with a stranger you just learned is your father."

Jacob nodded. "Only, he did tell me this isn't the first time he's been dropped off to stay with someone while Blu runs off and does whatever she pleases. Did I tell you Blu makes Leon call her Ma'am instead of ma?"

Alice shook her head. "That's awful, but he's here now. We'll see to it he feels loved."

Jacob's smile returned. "I'm countin' on it."

Chapter Nineteen

Evalyn scanned the yard looking for the twins. Joy was supposed to be watching them play in the yard while she made an apple cinnamon cake for the big family gathering, but to Evalyn, it was eerily quiet outside.

"Girls?" Evalyn called out. "Caleb?"

Five-year-old Caleb came scurrying out of the barn with a fluffy yellow chick in his hands. "Yes, Ma?"

"Caleb, have you seen the girls?" asked Evalyn. "It's almost time to go to Quail Crossings."

"They were playin' under the trees," answered Caleb.

"Thanks," said Evalyn. "Put that chick back and then go wash up."

Caleb hurried back to the barn as Evalyn made her way to a small patch of trees Rockwood boasted on the north side. It was supposed to be a wind break, but too many of the evergreens had died during the drought of the Depression to make it effective, letting the wind barrel through what was left of the cottonwoods. There she found Joy engrossed in a book as she leaned against the largest cottonwood tree. Bonnie and Beverly were nowhere to be seen.

"Joy!" snapped Evalyn.

Joy looked up with a start, the book falling into the dirt. She looked around with confusion and then terror. "I'm sorry Momma. I'll clean up their mess. I didn't mean to lose track of them, honest."

Evalyn felt her anger slip away as fear took its place. She tried to keep her voice steady, "Joy, honey, do you know where the girls are?"

Joy jumped to her feet. "Oh, Momma, I'm so sorry. I'll look for them."

"Go check the barn and out buildings," said Evalyn. "I'll have your brother check the sand plum thicket since he's small enough to crawl under the thorny bushes. I'll go check the pig barn. Maybe they're with your father. Ring the dinner bell if you find them."

Joy ran towards the tool shed as Evalyn dashed to the house. She found Caleb washing his hands in the sink, playing with the bubbles the soap made.

"Rinse off, Caleb, and then go look for the twins in the sand plum thicket. Ring the dinner bell if you find them."

Evalyn rushed back outside, ignoring Caleb's groan. He had definitely gotten the short stick with the sand plum thicket, but she knew the girls had hidden in the small opening between the bushes before, calling it their thorny fort.

She scanned the pasture as she made her way to the pig barn. She hoped that the girls were with Robert. Her heart raced as she thought about her three-year-olds roaming around the prairie alone. Rattlesnakes had been abundant, not to mention the coyotes, bobcats, and cougars looking for an easy meal.

She found Robert cleaning out the largest pig pen.

"Robert!" she hollered over the loud grunt of pigs.

He looked up and gave her a smile as he walked closer.

"Have you seen the girls?" asked Evalyn.

Robert's smile faded. "No, I thought they were with Joy."

"They were," said Evalyn, with a sigh, "but she was reading and ...." A sob escaped her lips.

"It'll be okay," said Robert. "We'll find them. They couldn't have gotten far. I just saw them about fifteen minutes ago. Let me get these muck boots off, and I'll check the south pasture. You go west. You know there's that little creek where we catch crawdads I bet they're there." He reached out and gave Evalyn's arm a little squeeze. "I'm sure they're fine."

He hurried back to the door leading from the pig pen into the barn as Evalyn took the opportunity to go around the corner and scan the western pasture.

"Evie," came Robert's voice from the doorway. She turned around just in time to see him come around the barn, still clad in his muck boots. He was biting his lip, but the corners of his mouth were curved upward.

"What Robert ... what is it?" asked Evalyn.

"I found the girls, and they're fine," said Robert. He bit his lip again. "But..."

"But?" asked Evalyn, dread dripping from the word.

"Well, just come and look," said Robert.

He motioned for her to follow him inside the barn. Evalyn didn't think her feet could move fast enough. She needed to see her girls with her own eyes and know they were okay. They entered the pig barn, and Robert led her to the far corner where he kept the sows and piglets.

"They wanted to see the babies," said Robert.

Evalyn stepped past him and choked back a gasp. There, in the small piglet pen, sat Beverly and Bonnie, each holding a little piglet. The girls were covered in mud, and what Evalyn suspected was pig poo. They had it on their clothes, in their hair, and on their faces.

As much as Evalyn wanted to cradle her two girls in her arms, she swallowed her smile. She'd save the tight hugs for after the bath.

She put her hands on her hips. "Girls! Do you know how worried we were? You know better than to mess with these piglets without your daddy. That sow can be meaner than a badger when you mess with her babies."

"Shhh, Momma," said Beverly, "we just got the babies to sleep."

"They were scared," whispered Bonnie.

"Daddy blocked their momma from comin' in here," said Beverly. "So we're their mommas now."

Evalyn glanced at Robert. He shrugged. "I explained to the girls yesterday that I was separating the sow from the piglets. They're old enough to be weaned."

"Regardless," said Evalyn, folding her arms, "we're due at Momma Dovie's house in half an hour, and you two are dirtier than the pigs. Come on, let's get y'all cleaned up."

The girls put down the piglets, stood, and walked past their mother. Evalyn fought the urge to hold her nose. Robert had been pig farming for the past four years, but Evalyn still wasn't used to the smell. Now her daughters were ripe with the stench.

As the girls walked toward the door, Robert threw an arm over Evalyn's shoulders. "Nothing a bath won't help."

Evalyn knocked his arm off. "They know better than to get in these pens without you around."

"No harm done," said Robert. "I'm gonna finish cleaning this pen, and then I'll be ready to go to Quail Crossings."

Evalyn watched as he walked to the door that led to the large pig pen. "You're not going to help me clean up the girls or at least say something to them about how bad this all could've been?"

"Joy will help you wash the girls," said Robert, "and I don't see the need to go hollerin' at them when they were just trying to do something nice."

Without waiting for Evalyn's reply, Robert walked through the door and back into the large pen. Evalyn let out a huff and resisted the urge to lock Robert in with the pigs.

"You must be the goose, Pa warned me about," said Leon as he looked at Norman, who stood in his path to the pond. "You don't look so bad."

Norman honked.

"I can honk, too," said Leon, before letting out a loud honk. "Ma'am said I sound just like a goose. What do you think?"

Norman cocked his head and honked again. Leon honked back. Pretty soon they were both honking at each other. All the honking gave Leon the giggles, and when he sat down Norman waddled up and sat beside him. Leon let out a long contented sigh before petting Norman's soft back feathers.

Soon Norman put his head on Leon's knee and closed his eyes. Leon knew he should go to the pond, but he didn't want to disturb the goose's nap. He looked around Quail Crossings. He had never been on a farm so big before. He wondered what it would be like to ride a horse along the prairie. He pictured himself riding a brown stallion chasing down bad guys and taking them to jail. The goose let out a soft snore.

Leon smiled at Norman. "You're not so bad."

"He can be," came a girl's voice from behind, "But he seems to like you."

Leon jumped to his feet and turned, causing Norman to let out a gruff honk. A teenage girl with red hair stood nearby, carrying a fishing pole. She smiled at Leon.

"I'm Ellie, and I was just headed to the pond to fish with Dean," said the girl. "Coming?"

Leon nodded and joined Ellie as she passed Norman.

"What's so bad about that goose?" asked Leon.

"His name is Norman, and sometimes he bites," explained Ellie, "But once you're his friend, he'll fight to the death to protect you. I've heard lots of stories. He protected Alice from a dust storm, Elm from some boys that were after your daddy, and, a few years ago, he tried to protect me from the doctor."

"You needed protectin' from a doctor?" Leon cocked his head.

"He was a mean man," said Ellie. "Very mean."

"Ma'am is mean to me sometimes," said Leon. "She hits me, sometimes harder than others. Did the doctor hit you?"

"Yes," said Ellie. "I didn't talk for a long time because of him, but this is a safe place. Your momma won't hurt you here."

"What if she comes back?" said Leon.

"I reckon everyone here will protect you like they did me," said Ellie.

"But you're family," said Leon.

Ellie stopped and looked at Leon. She gently grabbed his arm so he would stop too. Her eyes were soft and her voice tender as she said, "So are you."

Chapter Twenty

Alice walked into the barn to saddle Tex for Leon. Jacob had told her all about Leon's desire to be a cowboy, and, after everything that boy had been through, Alice was determined to get him on a horse that very afternoon.

She didn't have to worry about Leon riding Tex. He was an old horse who preferred to mosey rather than gallop. Alice's biggest worry was that once Leon started to ride, all the kids would want a turn. With one horse and eight kids, it would be hard to give any of them any type of lengthy ride. She could also saddle Pronto, but she couldn't lead both horses and everyone else was busy with dinner preparations.

She spotted Nicholas. "Would you mind saddling up Pronto? Leon wants to ride a horse today, and I'm sure once he starts to ride, all the other kids will want a turn too."

"I'm busy," said Nicholas.

"What's wrong with you?" snapped Alice, noting that Nicholas was doing nothing but leaning against the stall wall, fiddling with a piece of metal. "It's not that hard to saddle a horse."

"Of course it isn't," said Nicholas with a shrug. "But once we're done, we have to unsaddle them, cool them, and then brush them. Like I said, I'm busy, and technically, this is my day off."

Alice grabbed a saddle blanket and threw it at Nicholas. He barely caught it before it hit his face, causing a cloud of horse hair and dirt to puff up. Nicholas coughed and fanned the dust out of his face.

"Last I checked, there are no days off on the farm," said Alice. "Just saddle Pronto, I'm sure I can get Walter to help me take care of the horses after we're done, since you can't be bothered."

"Aren't you bossy," said Nicholas, throwing her a smirk.

"Aren't you lazy," countered Alice, resisting the urge to knock that smirk right off his face. She opened Tex's stall, slid the bit into his mouth before sliding the bridle up to fasten it, and then led him out into the corral, leaving Nicholas to saddle Pronto.

"Hey there, beautiful," said Walter as Alice entered the corral with Tex. "Thought maybe we could take a walk before dinner."

"I'd love to," said Alice. "Just let me finish getting Tex ready for Leon to ride."

"I can do that," said Bill, coming up behind Walter. "Y'all go enjoy this beautiful day."

"Are you sure?" asked Alice.

Bill climbed over the corral fence. "Yeah, I was coming out here to do this anyway. I overheard Jacob talking to Dovie about Leon wanting a ride and you promising him one. I'm not sure who's more excited, Jacob or Leon. Figured the other kids would like to ride too."

"I had the same thought," said Alice, "Walter and I will tend to the horses after the kids ride. That okay, Walter?"

"Sure," said Walter.

"Sounds like a deal," said Bill.

Alice tied Tex's reins to the side of the corral and walked with Bill back inside the barn to get Tex's saddle and blanket.

"Nicholas is supposed to be saddling Pronto," said Alice, but as they walked into the barn, Pronto still stood in his stall. Nicholas was nowhere to be seen. Alice felt her blood boil. "Where did he go? That boy, I swear, he's absolutely good for nothing."

Bill held up his hands. "Don't worry about it, Alice. I think I can handle saddling both Tex and Pronto."

"And what if the kids want to ride, and I'm not back?" asked Alice.

"I'm sure Elm will be here by then. He can help me or Ellie," said Bill. "There is no reason to get upset about this. Evie's bunch isn't even here yet." He patted her on the shoulder. "Now, go for your walk and relax."

Walter met her at the barn door and offered his elbow. Alice pushed her frustrations away, smiled, and looped her arm around his elbow. They started walking toward the orchard.

"I can see why you love this place," said Walter. "The air is so pure, and there's nothing like hard work to make you feel like you've actually accomplished something with your day."

"I wish everyone felt like that," said Alice. "I can't believe Nicholas would just leave, after I asked him to saddle Pronto."

"What?" Walter cocked his head.

Alice unlooped her arm from his and let out a groan of frustration as she threw her hands up in the air. "Nicholas! He's the laziest man I've ever met. I asked him to saddle

Pronto while I was saddling Tex, but he didn't want to. You should have heard him, Walter …," Alice turned her voice to a whine. "I don't want to brush them or cool them off or basically do anything other than sit on my rump."

Walter guided Alice to the orchard bench. "Don't let him get to you. We all know what he is."

"You're right," said Alice as she sat. "He's an imposter that has no right being here. How do we even know he's June's son? We don't. It's not like anyone has contacted June and asked her if Nicholas is supposed to be here. But here he is, just walking around like he owns the place." She stood and started to pace. "And he doesn't! He has no claim to a piece of property he has never ever set foot on in the twenty-three years of his life." She stopped and pointed to herself. "It was my family who came in and helped take care of this place. It was Bill, Evalyn, Elmer and I who put in the sweat and the sore muscles to make sure Quail Crossings made it from one year to the next, even during the worst of times."

"No one is disputing that," said Walter, patting the seat. "Come sit with me."

Alice ignored him and continued her rant. "If he thinks he can just waltz in here and take Quail Crossings he's got another thing coming. He hasn't earned his place here. From the sound of it, he hasn't earned his place anywhere. Just free loading from one job to the next until it becomes real work, and then he's off like a roadrunner."

Walter stood. "Alice, stop!"

Alice froze, her eyes searching the ground for a rattlesnake or other reason Walter would be yelling at her to stop.

Walter sighed. "I wanted to go on a walk with you, just like we used to at college. Where we talked about everything. I understand that technically Nicholas falls into that category, but he is definitely not what I want to talk about."

Alice's shoulders slumped as she looked at the frustration written on Walter's face. He had a right to be upset. Alice could feel her cheeks run hot and knew she was blushing. "I'm sorry, Walter; you're right. I don't know what it is about Nicholas, but he really gets under my skin."

Walter laughed as he walked over to Alice and gave her a hug. "Trust me, Alice, we all know. I think he likes getting under your skin. How about you be a royal pain in his rump and not let him be a pain in yours. That will bother him more than you getting all riled up."

Before Alice could respond, the roar of a tractor broke the silence.

"What is that?" asked Alice, breaking away from the hug.

"Sounds like a tractor," said Walter, with a bit of annoyance.

Alice shook her head. "Not our tractor. It's too loud to be our tractor."

Without another word, Alice started back down the path that led to the barn, Walter close on her heels. As she entered the clearing which led to the main property, Alice stopped dead in her tracks, causing Walter to bump into her.

"Alice, what is it?" asked Walter.

"Our old tractor," said Alice with awe in her own voice. "It hasn't run in years."

She hurried over to the tractor, and Nicholas smiled down at her from the old tractor's seat.

"I can't believe you got it to work," yelled Alice over the thumping of the old tractor's engine.

"What?" said Nicholas as he turned off the tractor.

Alice smiled. "I said, I can't believe you got this old thing to work."

He gave her a wink. "I told you I was busy."

"I know, but I didn't ...," Alice bowed her head. "I'm sorry I called you lazy."

Nicholas hopped off the tractor and put his hands on her shoulders. "Oh don't worry, I am lazy. The whole reason I wanted to fix the tractor was so it will only take half the time to plow the fields, and I won't have to sit in the sun as long."

Alice looked up into his icy blue eyes and felt as if she were swimming. There was a warmth to his features, and she knew by the way he looked back at her, he hadn't done it just to spend less time in the sun. He had done it to help Quail Crossings.

Alice heard Dovie giggle. She turned to find half of the Quail Crossings family had also gathered upon hearing the old tractor's familiar rumble. Bill cleared his throat, and Alice felt her cheeks grow hot, knowing she was standing in Nicholas's embrace in front of everyone. She quickly took a step back, just in time to see Walter storming down the path back to the orchard.

Chapter Twenty-one

Alice hurried after Walter as he marched toward the orchard bench.

"Walter, wait," Alice called after him.

Walter stopped, shoved his hands in his pockets, and looked at the ground.

"I'm sorry," said Alice.

"You have nothing to be sorry about," said Walter, shaking his head.

Alice took a step closer. "Yes, I do. All you wanted to do was to take a walk, but I ruined it by talking about Nicholas. You're my best friend, Walter." Alice thought she saw him cringe at the words "best friend" but continued. "So I guess I thought it would be okay to go on and on about how awful Nicholas is."

"You don't seem to think he's so awful now," said Walter.

"I was just surprised he actually did something on his own for the betterment of Quail Crossings and not just himself," said Alice.

Walter sat on the bench and put his head in his hands. "I don't want to be your best friend."

"What?" Alice took a step back as his words hit her in the chest like a brick.

He looked up. "I mean, I want to be your best friend, but I want to be more than that. I've never let on any differently. I was hoping this summer you would see me with your family and realize how good we are for each other. I know they mean the world to you, and I just want to mean the world to you too."

"Oh, Walter," Alice whispered.

He held up his hand. "I know, you've been really clear on not wanting a beau. That's why I've cherished and continued to cultivate our friendship. It kept me close to you, and I hoped you'd change your mind. I still do."

Alice sat beside her friend, not really knowing what to say.

"It just burns me up inside to see you looking at a man you claim to dislike the way I wish you'd look at me." Walter sat back.

"It wasn't a look of longing," Alice started, choosing her words carefully. "I think, for the first time since he's gotten here, I found a redeeming quality in him. He puts on this big show about not wanting to sit in the sun ... I saw something in his eyes that told me he wants to be a part of what we have here at Quail Crossings."

"Well, that was not how he was looking at you," said Walter. "He wanted your admiration, and I know that look well because I've given it to you many times. But never once have you looked at me like you looked at him just now."

"I'm sorry I made you feel like I like him more, but that's not even close to being the truth." Alice turned toward Walter and grabbed his hand. "I admired that he fixed the tractor for unselfish reasons, that's all."

Walter nodded, then he gave her an ornery smile. "Guess I better work on my tractor mechanics, now that I know that's where your heart is."

Alice laughed and put her hands on her chest. "Oh yes, engine repair makes my heart go all aflutter."

Walter squeezed her hand, and Alice's eyes shifted back to meet his.

"Walter," she said, "I can't promise you spending the summer here will make me feel any differently. I love that you get along so well with my family, but I don't want you to get your hopes up about me."

Walter brushed the hair gently from Alice's cheek. "Have you ever found yourself going through an old box and finding something you wanted but weren't actually looking for it at the time?"

"Yes," Alice answered.

"A day will come when you look at me and find something you want but weren't looking for, and until that day comes, I'll wait."

Leon stood just on the other side of the corral fence and listened to Bill's every word as he gave instructions on how to ride a horse.

"Now, you won't have to worry about much," said Bill. "Tex is way past his wild stallion days, which makes him a great horse to learn on. I'm just going to lead you around the corral today, and then you can have your dad or Elmer bring you out for more riding."

Leon nodded.

"All right," said Bill, "climb on top of the fence. You always want to mount your horse on the left side and never walk directly behind a horse ... even a horse as tame as Tex."

Leon did as he was told, and Bill maneuvered Tex where his left side was parallel to the fence.

"Now, when you get a little more experience, you can mount from the ground, but I want you to mount from the fence until you're strong enough to pull yourself all the way up. Now climb down until you're just below the stirrup."

Leon could feel his entire body shaking with excitement as he climbed down a few fence rungs. He couldn't believe he was actually about to ride a horse. He glanced over to his father who gave him a thumbs up. The entire family had gathered around for the event, but Leon couldn't help but wish they hadn't.

"What if I fall?" asked Leon as he turned his face back to Bill.

Bill gave him a smile. "Then you get right back on. Let me tell you a secret, all cowboys fall. What makes them a cowboy is the fact they get right back into the saddle. You ready?"

Leon nodded.

"Okay," said Bill, making a final check of the cinch to make sure the saddle was on firmly on, but not too tight. He handed the reins to Ellie, who was petting Tex's head, and then stood behind Leon to help him balance. "Take your left foot and put it in the stirrup. Grab the saddle horn with both hands if you need to."

Leon did as he was told and was glad Bill was there for support.

"Good," said Bill, "now step up with your left leg and swing your right leg over."

Leon did as instructed and, with Bill's help, found himself firmly in the saddle. His heart raced, and he could feel a laugh bubbling up from his excitement.

Jacob and the rest of the Quail Crossings gang cheered, and Leon's cheeks started to hurt from smiling so much.

"So do I say giddy-up now?" asked Leon, causing a round of light laughter from the onlookers.

"Not today," said Bill, boasting his own smile. "Today I'm going to keep hold of the reins, while you get used to the feel of the horse. Do me a favor and keep at least one hand on the horn."

Bill took the reins from Ellie, clicked his tongue, and he started to walk forward. Tex waited a beat, then followed Bill. Leon grabbed the saddle horn tighter as the horse moved forward. He had not prepared himself for it to be so bumpy or for there to be so much sway. He looked toward the ground and felt himself grow dizzy. The horse was a lot taller than it had looked on the ground.

"How you doin', Leon?" asked Bill.

"I'm okay," said Leon, barely above a whisper.

"Let your body relax a little," said Bill. "I promise ol' Tex won't bolt, and there's no reason to be lookin' at the ground below you. Always look at where you're going, so you can protect yourself and the horse."

Leon took a deep breath, lifted his gaze to the pasture just over Tex's head, and willed his body to relax a little. His dizziness left almost instantly, and he felt his body start to move with the horse.

"Ready to go a little faster?" asked Bill.

Leon nodded and tightened his grip on the saddle. Bill picked up his pace to a quick walk, and Tex followed suit. Soon Leon was bouncing along and pretending to be a cowboy moseying up to his homestead at Quail Crossings. He could feel his smile returning as he pictured himself with a silver studded hat and a fringed buck-skinned shirt, just like Clint Montgomery wore in the movie *Red River*. Without another thought, Leon placed his feet firmly in the stirrups, stood up in the saddle, and let out a whooping, "Yeee-haw!"

"What a day," Bill said to Lou Anne as he climbed into bed. "Did you see how happy Leon was to be riding Tex? I've never seen a smile so big. He was ready to gallop across the field, and probably would have, had I given him the reins. Well, Tex, wouldn't gallop if his life depended on it, lazy ol' horse, but you know what I mean."

"Uh-huh," said Lou Anne absentmindedly as she stared at her book.

Bill reached over and gently shut the book. "I know you're not reading. What's on your mind?"

Lou Anne gave Bill a small smile. "That obvious?"

"Well, between the fact that your book was upside-down and how lost you seemed during the whole family gathering, it doesn't take much to realize something is bothering you," answered Bill.

"It's the Dean and Barry thing," said Lou Anne, smoothing out the covers. "I know you said I need to let Dean take care of it on his own ...."

"Because you should," said Bill.

"Barry is two years older than Dean and a good head taller," countered Lou Anne. "It's not a fair fight."

"Not all fights are fair," said Bill. "Remember how Charlotte used her dad's friendship with James to make you think dating me would mean the end of my job at Quail Crossings? She might not have been a foot taller or two years older, but she hit you where she knew it would hurt the most. Might not be physical, but it was just as bad."

"No, it's not the same, Bill," countered Lou Anne. "There's a big difference between words and fists."

"Fine, if you'd like, I'll talk to Barry's dad," said Bill, "I don't think Dean will like that. It could become worse for him if Barry gets in trouble, but I'll talk to Peter tomorrow."

Lou Anne patted Bill's leg. "No, you're right. If Barry gets in trouble with Peter, since we know Charlotte won't punish the boy, he'll take it out on Dean. I'll do my best to stay out of the middle of things."

Bill gave her a kiss on the cheek, before putting his head on the pillow. "You're a good momma, and Dean's a smart boy because of it. He'll figure it out."

Lou Anne rolled over and switched off the lamp, silently vowing she'd find a way to fix it anyway.

Chapter Twenty-two

Walter headed to the barn to while, Bill and Nicholas were out checking fences. Bill had told Walter to find something productive to do but didn't name anything specifically.

Ever since Nicholas had fixed the old tractor, Bill had been encouraging Walter to find ways to help out on his own. Walter figured this was good experience in general, but for the life of him, he wasn't sure what needed to be done. Quail Crossings was a well-oiled machine as far as he was concerned.

He saw Alice weeding the garden and knew it was the perfect opportunity to do something productive as well as spend time with Alice without Nicholas interrupting them. He couldn't be sure, but it seemed Nicholas was always finding a reason to be with Alice lately.

Walter would take Alice for a walk, and pretty soon, Nicholas would be strolling up the same trail, always acting surprised when he stumbled upon them, but never leaving them alone. If Alice was working in the garden, or tending to the chickens, or brushing the horses, Nicholas seemed to be doing the same thing, always acting as if it were a coincidence.

What felt even worse to Walter, was that Alice wasn't bothered by all the time Nicholas was spending around her. The two actually had lively conversations and made each other laugh. If Walter didn't know better, he'd say Alice now enjoyed having Nicholas around.

Nicholas might have pulled one over on Alice, but Walter wasn't fooled. Something had changed between them during their exchange by the tractor, and Walter wasn't going to let some Yankee swoop in and steal his girl.

Walter thought about Alice and smiled. He had met her on her very first day of college. She was bogged down with books from the library, and he rushed over to help her with them. Her pale blonde hair was pulled up into a ponytail and tied back with a bright green bow that matched not only her dress, but her eyes.

"Here, please, allow me," he had said.

"Thank you," said Alice, handing over a portion of the books to Walter. He tried to carry all her books, but Alice insisted that she carry some.

"Have you been to the library?" Alice asked after they introduced themselves. "I've never seen so many books in one place, both fiction and nonfiction. I think I've died and gone to Heaven."

Walter couldn't help but laugh. "I've been there a time or two, but you might not feel the same way after you've spent hours in there doing research for a paper. It does get tiresome."

"I can't imagine ever getting tired of being in a library or doing research for that matter," said Alice. "There's so much to learn, and I just want to know it all, but I guess...." She glanced at the stacks of books they carried. "... trying to learn it all at one time is a lot like trying to do laundry while washing a pig, doesn't work out too well."

Walter laughed way too hard at her country saying and almost dropped her books, which had caused her to start laughing even harder. Soon they were sitting in the grass, talking about their school plans and their lives before college. They sat there for almost two hours until Alice's stomach started to growl and Walter realized it was dinner time at the cafeteria. He helped her to her dormitory and waited outside for her to put her books away, so they could go dine together. They had been practically inseparable ever since.

As he entered the barn to get a hoe, he paused so his eyes could adjust to the lack of light. Norman came flying down from the rafters and landed on Walter's face, causing him to crash to the ground.

Walter batted the goose away. "Dammit!"

"Dammit!" came two little voices behind him.

Walter froze when he heard his cuss word repeated and prayed he heard wrong. He slowly turned just in time to see Beverly and Bonnie run toward the house.

Evalyn sauntered up the hill, a quilt draped over one arm and a wicker basket on the other, to where she knew Robert was resting. He had taken a break from tending to the pigs to read in the shade of the old cottonwood trees. Robert had always been a lover of books, especially westerns, and more times than Evalyn liked, Robert would grab his lunch to go, so he could read in the peace of the cottonwoods instead of the chaos of the kitchen table with four children.

Today, when he hadn't come in at all for lunch, Evalyn decided to take lunch to him. The kids were all at Quail Crossings playing with their cousins, and Evalyn was going to take advantage of a homestead absent of kids.

"Hey there," she said as she approached the little grove of cottonwoods, "mind if I join you? I brought lunch."

Evalyn held up her basket as if she needed to tantalize Robert into letting her stay. He instantly put down his book.

"Please do," said Robert, "I was going to come inside in a minute, but I just got to the really good part, so I wanted to read it first."

"What are you reading?" asked Evalyn.

Robert held up the copy of *Shane* by Jack Schaefer that he had borrowed from the library. "It's really good."

"I'll have to borrow it when you're finished," said Evalyn. "Can you pull yourself away from it long enough to eat? Since the kids are gone, I thought we'd have a picnic."

"Of course I can," said Robert. "I'd much rather spend time with you than any ol' book anyway."

Evalyn set the basket down and spread the quilt over a large grassy patch between two trees. Robert kicked off his dirty boots and maneuvered himself onto the quilt.

"I'm starving," he said.

"Then you should've come in for lunch," Evalyn teased. She sat down and started to unload the basket. "Nothing fancy I'm afraid. We've got some sandwiches made from last night's roast, some carrots, sliced apples, and the rest of the banana cake."

"Sounds like a feast to me," said Robert, taking a sandwich from Evalyn. "I'm surprised there's any cake left."

Evalyn gave him a sly smile. "I hid it from the kids or they probably would have eaten it for breakfast. According to Joy, it's basically a banana flapjack in cake form."

They both laughed and sat in silence as they ate.

"Sure is quiet around here without the kids," said Robert.

"I love our kids," said Evalyn, grabbing an apple slice, "but I'm not exactly missing the noise or having to worry about what trouble the twins are getting in."

"They are a handful," said Robert.

"As was I," Evalyn admitted. "So I guess, as Dovie suggested, I'm paying for my raisin'. In my defense, I was sassy, not messy. I swear I spend half my day cleanin' messes those two girls make. I try to keep an eagle eye on them, but they seem to find the time to make a mess anyway. What about you, did you wreak havoc on your poor parents?"

Robert shook his head. "I was a pretty good kid. Since I was an only child, it was hard to get into too much trouble by myself. Once though, when I was about six or seven, I shot a skunk and thought my parents would be really proud of me for bringing meat home for dinner. Unfortunately, the skunk wasn't quite dead when I brought it inside, and it ended up spraying everything in the kitchen and parlor, including us, before my father killed it."

"What a mess," said Evalyn with a chuckle. She quickly dropped her sandwich on her plate and folded her hands together in prayer. "Dear Lord, please, please, please don't let Bonnie or Beverly bring a skunk into the house, ever. Amen."

Robert laughed at her. "Yeah, it was just as bad as it sounds. Ma left the windows open for weeks after that, and

I don't know how many times she scrubbed the floor and furniture trying to get the smell out. She had a very firm rule about no skunks in the house, alive or dead, after that." Robert shook his head and smiled. "We told that story every year at Thanksgiving. Ma would put the turkey on the table and say she was thankful it wasn't skunk. My father was good about inviting a family of lesser means to dinner every year, so every year Ma said what she said and every year we'd have to explain it."

"I wish I could've met your folks," said Evalyn.

"Me too," said Robert. "You remind me a lot of my ma, especially how you are with the kids."

"Really?" Evalyn felt a rush in her stomach. She knew Robert was paying her a very high compliment. "How so?"

"Well, you're always finding ways for them to have fun, even when it's rainy outside ... drawing pictures or putting on a play. I could never think up those things like you. I would probably just tell them to shut their traps and read a book every day. Our kids are always laughing and smiling, and I know it has nothing to do with me since I'm always farming. Then there's Joy."

"What about Joy?" asked Evalyn, not sure she wanted to hear Robert's answer.

"The way you took her in when she needed it and called her your own, knowing it was going to cause a firestorm." Robert grabbed Evalyn's hand. "You took in little Joy without a second thought because you knew she would pay the price if you didn't. You had nothing to your name but a few dollars for a bus ticket back home, yet you put her first."

Evalyn thought about Joy's real mother, Harriet. When Evalyn moved to California after finishing high school,

Harriet Wheaton had joined her. They had great jobs making clothes for Hollywood movies until Harriet got pregnant. Once baby Joy was born, Harriet wouldn't have anything to do with her, leaving Joy with Evalyn for weeks at a time.

Evalyn was unable to keep her job because she couldn't afford child care and couldn't leave Joy alone. So Evalyn did the only thing she felt she could do; she brought Joy home to Quail Crossings. It had been divine intervention that Robert had been on the same bus and hatched the plan that they get married secretly and call Joy their own.

Harriet had perished during a tornado that took out half of Knollwood later that year, and no one knew where Joy's real father was. Robert's and Evalyn's claims were never questioned. No one had any reason to. Even the few people who knew rarely mentioned it and Joy was none the wiser.

Robert gave Evalyn a smile. "I probably don't say it enough, but I'm very thankful for that stinky old bus."

Evalyn felt her cheeks warm as Robert leaned over and kissed her. Dropping her sandwich, Evalyn wrapped her arms around her husband's neck and returned his passion.

If someone had told her eleven years ago that she would be madly in love with her husband of convenience, whom she met at a bus stop after a vile man tried to attack her, she would have balked at such notions. This day, she couldn't begin to imagine a life without him.

Chapter Twenty-three

Ellie hung the laundry on the line as a breeze sent the sheet billowing upward. She giggled a little as the wet fabric tickled her cheek. She was glad for this breeze, instead of the usual Texas Panhandle gale. It was just enough to keep the afternoon from being unbearably hot, and she was thankful it didn't get her sheet dirty with dust.

She looked up, hoping to see clouds, but was met with only blue sky. Ellie frowned. It didn't take working on a farm to know they needed rain. Even though it was only early June, most days had a mid-July heat to them.

Walking over to her basket, Ellie grabbed another sheet and said a silent thank you to God for the invention of the electric washing machine. Dovie had bought one just the year before and the contraption, although intimidating at first, was a huge time saver. Ellie used to have to scrub all the laundry by hand, and then put it through the wringer before hanging it up to dry.

She was never one to shy away from hard work, but washing clothes was still her least favorite chore because the soap always left her skin dry and cracked. Now the machine did the washing part, then Dovie would roll it through the wringer, and Ellie would take it outside and hang it on the line.

She pinned the sheet to the line as she watched Nicholas stroll up the hill. He was sweaty and dirty from his ride in the pasture. As he approached her basket, he took his shirt off and threw it on top of her clean white sheets.

"Ellie, be a doll and wash that for me please," said Nicholas. "It's so dirty, I think it might just grow legs and walk out of here."

He gave her a smile before starting toward the house. Hands full, Ellie quickly pinned her sheet and hurried to her basket. As she removed the dirty shirt, her heart sank. The clean sheets were now soiled with the grime from Nicholas's shirt. They would have to be washed again.

Letting out a loud whistle to get Nicholas's attention, she picked up the basket along with the dirty shirt and marched toward him. As he turned, she shoved the basket and shirt into his arms.

"You can do your own laundry from now on," said Ellie, "and you can rewash those sheets."

Anger coursing through her veins, she brushed past a speechless Nicholas and marched toward the pond. As much as she wanted to go inside and tell Dovie, she wanted Nicholas to explain it himself. Ellie paused at the barn long enough to grab her fishing pole. Now that Nicholas was going to be busy with the laundry, she might as well enjoy an hour of fishing under the shade of the cottonwoods.

Nicholas turned to apologize to Ellie and was surprised to see she was already gone. He wasn't sure how he had made her so mad.

"Well, that was awful," Alice said walking up to Nicholas with Walter at her side.

"What did I do?" Nicholas asked, looking down at the laundry. He sighed as the realization hit him. "Aww, man, I thought they were dirty."

Alice cocked her head. "Why would Ellie be hanging dirty sheets on the line?"

Nicholas shook his head. "My mom didn't always wash the sheets. Sometimes she just put them on the line to air out. I wasn't thinking."

"That is apparent," said Walter.

"So what do I do?" asked Nicholas, ignoring Walter and looking at Alice.

"You rewash the sheets," Alice said with a shrug.

"I know that," said Nicholas, "but how do I get into Ellie's good graces. She was just starting to tolerate me, and now I've gone and messed that up."

"Ellie is impressed most by hard work," said Alice. "Apologize, of course, and then pick up some of her chores, not because you want to get into her good graces, but because you want to help her out."

"Thanks, Alice," said Nicholas. She gave him a small nod as she and Walter started to the house. "Alice, one more thing …."

"What's that?" asked Alice turning around.

Nicholas gestured to the basket. "Can you show me how to use the washing machine? I've never done laundry before, and I don't want to ask Aunt Dovie. I have a feeling she'll just do it for me."

"Sure," said Alice, her smile stating that Nicholas was right about Dovie doing it herself. Alice glanced up at Walter with an ornery smile. "Guess we'll see how good of a teacher I've become since going to college. This could be a challenge."

Nicholas felt a breath of relief escape. He wanted to do right by Ellie, but he didn't want to break Dovie's beloved washing machine in the process and find himself in hotter water than his shirts.

"This is great," said Walter. "It'll give me a chance to learn too. I'm embarrassed to say, I've been using a service at college. My folks always had a maid, so I never gave it much thought until I was on my own."

"I'm not sure I would justify your college or current living situation as on your own," said Nicholas.

"What would you know about it?" snarled Walter.

"I know that being on your own with a silver spoon in your mouth, means you still have a silver spoon," said Nicholas. "What I don't know is what you're doing here? You'd last two minutes on a farm alone, and I know Alice has no plans to leave this place. So, what's your plan?"

"Knock it off, Nicholas," snapped Alice, before Walter could say anything. "If you want to learn how to use the washing machine, you'll stop running your mouth. You want to know why Ellie can hardly tolerate you? It's because you don't think before you talk. So for once, shut your trap and listen or you're on your own."

"You're right," said Nicholas, "I do have a habit of putting my foot in it. I will keep my mouth shut and listen."

"I'm gonna hold you to that," said Alice.

Nicholas followed Alice and Walter to the house. He watched as Walter gently put his arm around Alice's shoulders before sending a smirk back to him. The pit of Nicholas's stomach burned. He tried to brush the feeling

160

away, but as Walter's hand squeezed Alice's shoulder playfully, the burning intensified.

"Get yourself together," Nicholas whispered to himself, "You cannot be jealous of Alice and Walter. You barely like her."

"What's that?" asked Alice as they reached the stoop leading to the back door.

"Just giving myself a little pep talk," said Nicholas.

Alice laughed as she walked up the steps. "Oh, it's not even that hard now that we have the electric washer. Now, had you done this before we got it, you'd have something to complain about."

Alice opened the back door and then let out a gasp. "What in the world is going on in here?"

Walter let out a low whistle as Nicholas put the basket of laundry down and hurried up the steps.

As he looked over Alice and Walter's shoulders, he saw Beverly and Bonnie running around the kitchen both with a bowl of flour in their hands, throwing it up in the air while gleefully shouting, "Dammit. Dammit. Dammit."

Alice looked at Nicholas, her mouth open wide. He quickly held up both his hands. "It wasn't me. I haven't said that word since you told me to stop. I promise!"

"Oh my goodness! Girls, you stop it right now!" came a voice from the parlor.

The twins froze in place as Nicholas and Alice's heads both shot towards the parlor doorway where Dovie stood, covered in flour from head to toe. Nicholas felt his own mouth drop open at the sight of his aunt.

"I thought you were watching them," said Alice, carefully entering the kitchen.

"I fell asleep like an old woman and I know better," cried Dovie, throwing her hands up in the air in frustration, causing a cloud of flour to form around her. "It's in the parlor, too. What a mess!"

Nicholas stepped in front of Alice. He grabbed the brooms he knew Dovie kept behind the backdoor and gingerly walked across the flour-covered floor. He handed one broom to Beverly and another to Bonnie.

"I just found out the hard way," Nicholas said, "that there's a very strict rule around here about cleaning up your own messes, so you better get to it."

Beverly's lip started to pout as Bonnie said, "But we're too little."

"Big enough to make the mess," countered Nicholas, "big enough to clean it up. You girls start sweeping the flour into a neat pile." Nicholas looked at Dovie. "Do you have a couple of wash buckets in here?"

"In the closet by the stairs," said Dovie. Her eyes were wide, still in shock over the mess.

"Walter, grab the buckets, will ya? We'll get these filled, and then you can start cleaning up in the parlor while I get started in here," said Nicholas. Walter grabbed the buckets and handed them to Nicholas, who put them in the sink.

"I'll go get Ellie," said Alice. "We're going to need everyone's help."

"Let her fish," said Nicholas. "When she comes back, we'll put her to work as well as anyone else who has the bad fortune of walking in that door before we're finished. Are most of the kids still over at Bill's?"

Dovie nodded.

"Okay then," said Nicholas, "Alice, why don't you help Dovie get washed up. But you're gonna wanna go outside and brush as much of that flour off as possible first, or it'll just make a paste in the tub."

Everyone stared at Nicholas, so he clapped his hands together. "All right, you guys, let's get started."

Chapter Twenty-four

Tiny took a deep breath before she entered the butcher shop with a sleeping Sophie. She knew she should've waited for Elmer to get home to have the conversation she was there to have, but she didn't want to lose her nerve.

Pushing the door open, Elmer looked up at her as the bell above the door jingled. His smile grew as she walked in, and she couldn't help but smile back.

"Hey," said Elmer as he walked up to Tiny and gave her a small kiss on the cheek, "this is a pleasant surprise."

"Sophie's having a good day, so I thought I'd bring her by," said Tiny, knowing she was stalling. "Benny's at Quail Crossings. All the cousins are over there today, so he wanted to play."

"I'm so glad you did," said Elmer as he took Sophie from Tiny. "How are you feeling?"

"I'm okay," said Tiny slowly, "I'm actually here to talk about that. Is Jacob around?"

Elmer shook his head. "He ran over to the post office. Leon's in the back, I can have him run for Jacob if you need him."

"No," said Tiny, "I hoped we would be alone."

"So, what's going on?" asked Elmer, frowning a little.

"The truth is," said Tiny, feeling herself getting teary before she had even really started saying what she needed to say. "I don't rightfully know. What I do know is that I'm not actin' right. I love you and the kids so much, yet most of the time, I can't hardly stand being near you. So I stay in bed all day or yell at y'all for no good reason. I know these things are wrong, but I can't seem to stop myself from doin' them. It's like I'm standing outside of my body, watching myself act horribly, and I'm not able to stop."

"It's okay," said Elmer.

"No, it's not," said Tiny. "It's not okay for me to treat you so poorly when you've been so good and understanding to me."

Tiny's eyes stung as the tears came with full force. "I'm so sorry, Elm. You deserve so much better. I'm going to be better from now on. I promise."

Elmer wrapped his arm around Tiny and gave her a hug. She noticed how gentle he was being as he tried to comfort her and not wake Sophie.

"I think you should talk to Dovie," said Elmer.

Tiny felt as if she'd been slapped in the face. Here she was putting it all out there, and he wanted her to talk to Dovie.

"Do you not believe me?" asked Tiny, her voice sounding weak in her ears.

"I believe you want to be better," said Elmer. He delicately took her hand and led her to the two stools that sat behind the counter so they could sit. "You said it yourself, Mary, you see yourself doing these things you know you shouldn't, but you can't stop it. That tells me you need help, and as much as I want to be the one who helps you, I think you need someone who will be able to relate more to your situation."

"Relate more?" Tiny fought the urge to slide off the stool and storm out of the butcher shop, but she also knew that would be an over-reaction, something she had just promised she'd work at stopping. She took a deep breath. "Why in the world do you think Dovie could relate to what I'm going through? The woman has motherhood down pat. She raised the four of you with barely a hiccup while she was still grieving for her own child. She's pretty much perfect."

Elmer gave her a sad smile. "She's not perfect, and she'd be the last person to claim to be. Dovie learned a lot from her mother about healing, and all I'm suggesting is that she might know some remedies for how you're feeling. She helped you when you were going through that horrible morning sickness when you were with Benny. What will it hurt to talk to her?"

The front door bell jingled as a customer entered the butcher shop. Elmer got up and handed Sophie back to Tiny. He gave her a kiss on the cheek. "Please, just talk to her. All I want is for you to feel better."

"Whatcha doin' there, son?" asked Jacob as he spotted Leon leaning just inside the door frame leading to the front of the butcher shop.

Leon spun around as his cheeks turned red. "Mr. Elmer was talkin' to his wife, and I didn't want to interrupt them."

Jacob put his hands on his hips, the mail he had gotten at the post office still in one hand. "So you stood there and listened in?"

The boy looked at the floor. "I was gonna leave, I swear, but then Miss Tiny started to say some stuff I felt like I needed to hear."

"We don't listen to other people's private conversations, Leon," scolded Jacob. "You'll need to apologize to Mr. Elmer for stickin' your nose where it don't belong, you hear?"

"Yes, sir," said Leon, meeting Jacob's gaze. "Can I ask you somethin' first?"

Jacob nodded.

"Ms. Tiny was talking about how sometimes she's mean to her kids and Mr. Elmer. She doesn't want to be, but she can't seem to stop. Do you think that's why Ma'am was mean to me? Do you think that's why she gave me away?"

Jacob's heart sank. He felt bad for Elmer and Tiny, but his heart was breaking for Leon. He bent down, so he'd be eye-level with his son.

"I wish I could tell you why your mother did what she did, but I can't speak for another person's actions. I can tell you, I choose to believe she loves you so much. She knew she was doing wrong by you and hoped I'd do better. If I don't let myself believe that, then I'll be angry. I don't know about you, Leon, but I'd rather believe in love than be angry."

"Me too," said Leon, tears falling on his cheeks.

"Hey, how 'bout we go down to the market and get an ice cream sandwich?"

Leon smiled as he wiped his eyes and nodded. "What about me apologizing to Mr. Elmer?"

"Ice cream, then apology," said Jacob. "I bet if we bring Mr. Elmer an ice cream sandwich, he won't mind the apology comes second."

James sat in the Knollwood Café and sipped his coffee. He was very thankful to Bill for allowing him to tag along during the feed runs. While Bill went to the feed shop, James would sit at the café, talk to the other farmers taking a break, and catch up on all that was happening in Knollwood.

Having a late morning chat with his farming buddies used to be a daily thing, and he had missed it since having a stroke five years before. He couldn't remember a time since the stroke when he woke to greet the day without his body aching or making it through the day without a nap or two. He had gone from riding Tex across the pastures to check on the stock, to sleeping and listening to the radio all day.

The door opened, and James looked up to see his longtime friend, George Wheaton.

"Hi there, George," said James, lifting his mug of coffee.

"Hey James," said George as he sat down. Annette, the owner of the Knollwood Café, brought George a cup of coffee. "Thanks, Annette. I love how I don't even have to ask any more for a cup. How about some of that apple pie this morning?" He looked at James. "You want a piece?"

James smiled. "Sounds nice."

"Comin' right up," said Annette, returning his smile. "Ice cream on yours, James?"

"You betcha," said James.

"It's been a long time," said George. "Sorry I haven't gotten over to Quail Crossings to have coffee."

James waved him off. "I know you're busy. It hasn't been so long since I was in your shoes."

Annette brought the pie, and the fellas thanked her. George pointed his fork at James. "No matter how busy you got, you made time to visit. After Harriet passed during that tornado, you were out every day. I've got no excuses. I'll do better 'bout coming by. My son, Ben, practically runs our place now. He's no Bill yet, but he will be one day."

James's mind flashed back to another time they had sat in the café. Roughly fifteen years before, they had been sitting at this very table talking about the hard times of the Dust Bowl when Bill Brewer came in with his siblings half-starved.

"Yes, Bill is one of a kind," said James as he ran his fork in circles his pie. He knew Bill, and the Brewer bunch deserved to own Quail Crossings once Dovie and Gabe had passed on. Right now, James's and Dovie's wills both stated the Brewer children would all receive a fair share of the farm. James felt his face fall as he realized they had never even considered June or her children when they had made the wills after his stroke.

"What is it, James? You feelin' okay?" asked George, concern written all over his face.

"I'm fine," he replied with a shake of his head. "I was just thinking about June."

George nodded. "Have you heard from her since Nicholas came?"

"No," said James, "but Nicholas has made it clear that he thinks Quail Crossings should all go to him. He's family and, if I'm being honest, I feel I owe him something because of how things went with is mother."

George cocked his head. "Didn't you go to New York City to make amends?"

James nodded. "Yes. It didn't go very well."

Taking another bite, George paused before he spoke. "I'm gonna talk to you like one farm owner to another. If I had Bill running my farm, I'd never let him go. I'd give him whatever he wanted to make him stay, short of the entire farm, because that's Ben's."

James felt his brows furrow a little, and George held up his hand and continued speaking, "Now, I'm gonna talk to you like one father to another. Bill and Elmer have been nothing short of sons to you. Y'all are family, and Bill is a lot more than a farm manager. Nicholas might feel he has the right to the farm, but Bill and those kids have earned it. No offense to your farming skills, James, we went through some very tough times, and you know Bill has made Quail Crossings the best it's ever been. I'm sure Nicholas knows that too. Maybe he doesn't want the farm so much as just a cut in the profits. Heck, he's from New York City, and everyone knows all they care about is money."

A couple more of the neighborhood farmers walked in, causing an abrupt end to their conversation. As the other men said their hellos and sat down with them, James wondered about Nicholas. He had said he wanted to be a part of Quail Crossings, but maybe George was right. Maybe the only part of Quail Crossings he really wanted was a part of the bottom line.

Chapter Twenty-five

July, 1950

Alice took a deep breath as she walked across the pasture. It was hot and dry outside and fluffy white clouds filled the sky. Alice was sure she felt a storm on the horizon. The wind had a bit more of a burst to it, and it blew from the northwest. She hoped her intuition was right and rain was coming. It was dangerously dry.

"Hey," said Nicholas as he ran up to greet her.

"Hey," she replied, trying to keep the annoyance out of her voice, but was sure she hadn't. She had been craving a walk alone for days, but she couldn't seem to shake Walter or Nicholas to get away between chores. She was certain they were both working in the barn when she had left. She silently wished Bill would finish working with Bolt so they would have three horses to ride, instead of two, which left either Nicholas or Walter at the homestead.

"Whoa," said Nicholas, "do I detect some irritation? What did I do today?"

"No and nothing," said Alice as she continued to walk.

"Then it must be true," said Nicholas, walking with her. "I thought it was all in my imagination, but you must really hate me."

Alice stopped. "I don't hate you."

"You've been nothing short of hostile to me since I arrived," said Nicholas, also stopping his walk. "I don't think I've given you a reason really, so you must hate me."

Alice sighed and shook her head. "I don't hate you. I don't hate anyone, really."

"Then what is it?" asked Nicholas.

"So imagine this," said Alice, choosing her words carefully, "a stranger comes into your home of fifteen years, a place where you have felt love and joy in abundance, a place where you are happiest, and he tells you it's his. That you have no rights or claims to the land you love, no matter how hard you've worked to see it thrive. Did you know I came here when I was six?"

Nicholas shook his head.

"My brothers and sister and I didn't have a home during the Depression. We just bounced around from one town to another while Bill looked for work. No matter how hard he worked, he was always let go. People just didn't have any money to keep him on. We were sleeping in a truck, all four of us, literally starving. Then we arrived in Knollwood and went into the Knollwood Café to share a glass of milk because that's all we could afford. By the grace of God, Mr. James was there and bought us breakfast. It was oatmeal, but you would have thought we were eating steak and eggs. It was the first time we'd had a real meal in weeks."

Alice started to walk again and motioned for Nicholas to follow. "So Mr. James gave Bill a job and us a roof. At that time, Elm barely spoke and Evie was the burr under the saddle, getting into all kinds of trouble. But I saw Momma Dovie, and I loved her instantly. All I ever wanted was a momma who loved me. I never did feel much love from my own mother. How could she love me, yet abandon me? How could she, or my father for that matter, love any of us? So Quail Crossings became the home I never had."

She stopped in front of a gnarled old tree and pointed to the branches. "This tree is where I learned how Dovie got her name. Her momma swore she saw a white dove land on the window sill right after Dovie was born. No one else ever saw it." She pointed over toward the orchard. "Just over there is where Norman saved me from a rabid dog." She pointed toward a ditch near the pond. "That ditch is where Norman tried to fight off some boys who were out to lynch Jacob." She turned again pointed toward the northwest side of the pasture. "Just beyond that hill is an old water well. It's boarded up now, but that's where Dovie saved Ellie from a mad man who just about killed her."

"Wow," said Nicholas, as he let out a low whistle, "sounds like a lot of bad stuff has happened here in the last fifteen years."

Alice nodded. "Yes, but even with all the bad times, the best times outweighed them. In that barn loft is where I learned not only to read, but to love stories. It's also where I taught Ellie and Jacob to read. Over by the pond is where I made my very first friend, Mr. Norman the goose, and where I watched Evie and Robert vow their eternal love before God. That old cellar is where I found courage and on that old stoop, Elmer showed me what real bravery looks like. In that parlor is the first place I ever cried tears of pure happiness, and in Momma Dovie and Mr. James's arms is where I found the unconditional love I should have received from my parents but never did. Every one of those things, good and bad, have made me who I am today."

Alice swallowed hard as she thought of her life at Quail Crossings. "I love everything about this place. The way the people ask, "How are you?" with sincerity, because they really care about how you are doing. The way the wind smells of the earth and crops that keep us fed. The way the trees rustle in the wind, as if they're applauding your every move. The way the pond twinkles in the sunlight, as if always shining a spotlight on you. I love the light blue sky that seems to go on forever during the day and the millions of stars that come out at night, letting you make a million wishes. The funny thing is, I never need those wishes because I have everything I've ever wanted right here at Quail Crossings."

Alice turned and started back toward the house. She could hear Nicholas following her but appreciated that he lingered behind. She hoped she had given him a new way to think about Quail Crossings.

Walter rode up on Tex and gave her a smile before giving Nicholas a frown. "Hey there, beautiful, having a good walk?"

"Yeah," said Alice.

Nicholas walked by without saying a word to either Walter or Alice.

"Well, that was unlike him. Usually he has something smart to say," said Walter. "What were you two talking about?"

Alice gave Tex a little pat on his neck. "True love, Walter. True love."

Dovie stared at James as they sat at the kitchen table with Gabe, and wondered if her mouth had dropped to the ground and would soon start catching flies. She fumbled for the right response, not certain she was even clear on what her father was suggesting.

"So after Dovie and I pass, you want to give Quail Crossings to the Brewers like our wills state now, but change it just a bit so that Nicholas gets a yearly cut of the profits, no matter if he's working the farm?" asked Gabe, shaking his head. Dovie reckoned he was just as confused as she was.

James cleared his throat. "I'm not so much suggesting we officially change our wills, so much as I'm suggesting we let Nicholas decide if what he wants is to be here working or if he wants money. If he's just after the money, then we give him a small percentage, and he can go on his way to find his own place."

Dovie grabbed a nearby towel and twisted it, a nervous habit she knew she had, but she couldn't seem to stop herself. "I see a number of problems with this plan, Dad. First, it seems very unfair to me that Bill and everyone should work their fingers to the bone only to give a percentage away, even a small percentage. Also, and I hate even saying this, but what if Nicholas takes this deal and never comes back. I know having him here has made you happy. How will you react if he takes the money and leaves?"

James shook his head. "I'm hoping he won't do that."

"Dad, you always were too trusting," said Dovie, with a shake of her head. "I think this is a really bad idea. Doesn't it send the message we think he's greedy?"

"He hasn't shown any inclination that he is," reasoned James.

Dovie stood, walked to the kitchen sink, and looked out the window. She watched as Nicholas came in from the pasture with his head down and his hands deep in his pockets. He trudged into the barn. He looked as if he were either sulking or doing some hard thinking.

"I, for one, would be insulted," she said, turning away from the window.

"I would be as well," said Gabe. "We can't do that to Nicholas. I agree with Dovie. It sends the wrong message. So why even put this offer out there? Can't we let Nicholas show us his intentions when he's ready?"

"Because I'm torn," said James. Dovie could hear the crack in his voice.

She hurried over to him, wrapping her arms around him. "Oh, Dad."

"I know y'all don't like to talk about such things," said James, "but I've got to get my affairs in order. I'm an old man, and if I die before I've settled this, then what will Nicholas think? We didn't even think about June and her family when we made our wills."

Dovie sat back down and took both of her father's hands into hers. "First, your will states that Quail Crossings goes to Gabe and I, and we're not plannin' on making any changes to what we have going on here. So you needn't worry about how Nicholas feels. We're the ones who need to decide what happens to the farm after we're gone. The Brewers have earned it, and Nicholas needs to as well."

"Don't you think June is owed something?" asked James. "Maybe that's why Nicholas is here."

"Has she shown any interest since she left?" asked Gabe. "Asked for money or checked on how the farm is carrying on?"

"I don't think June ever wanted anything to do with the farm," answered Dovie, trying not to sound bitter. She bit her lip. She loved her sister, estranged or not. "Maybe we should ask her. Nicholas said that June knew he was here, but none of us have taken the time to write to her to see what she's wanting out of his visit, if anything."

"She doesn't want to talk to me," said James.

"What if we just give Nicholas a bit more time," said Dovie. "He's already shown some initiative by fixing the old tractor. He's been a bit difficult, but Bill says he's a pretty hard worker. This has all got to be very new to him, so let's wait until the end of the summer before we make any decisions." Dovie gave James's hand a squeeze. "While he's here, let's just enjoy having a piece of June with us and get to know him better. I'd hate to squander this opportunity to get to know Nicholas by offering him a check."

"I agree with Dovie," said Gabe. "Give him more time to see what Quail Crossings is all about. It's easy to fall in love with this place. I've traveled all over the world, but this farm is the only place I want to be. Soon, Nicholas may feel the same way, and then we'll work out what needs to be done."

"You're both right," said James. "It won't hurt anything to wait until the summer is over and see what happens. I think I'll go rest now."

Dovie leaned over and gave her father a hug. "I've got to run into town for a few things. Ellie's watching Sophie, Benny, and Leon under the cottonwoods. I'll let her know you're resting so she can keep them outside for the time being."

As James made his way back to his bedroom, Dovie grabbed her purse.

"Why are you going to town?" asked Gabe. "Did you forget something this morning when you were there?"

Dovie lowered her voice so James couldn't hear. "I'm going to send a telegram to June."

"Just call her," said Gabe, pointing to the phone.

"I don't want Dad to hear, and I don't even know if she has a phone," said Dovie. "Besides, long distance is too expensive, but I do have her address and can send a Western Union."

"I'll go with you," said Gabe as he stood and grabbed his hat. "What are you going to say?"

"I just want to know if she sent Nicholas," said Dovie. "For all I know, she doesn't even know he's here and is worried sick. I should've done this the moment he arrived, but I was too flabbergasted." She looked at Gabe. "Hon, you don't have to come. I won't be long."

"Of course I do," said Gabe. "I know how you are. You'll spend the whole drive into town thinking about how to word your telegram and have yourself in such a tizzy by the time you get there, you'll end up sending her such a long message, it'll cost more than long distance." He wrapped his arms around Dovie's waist. "Besides I have an ulterior motive."

"What's that?" asked Dovie trying not to melt into his beautiful brown eyes.

"I want to take you out to Johnson's Drug afterwards to get some ice cream," said Gabe. He kissed her cheek. "I think it's high time I took my wife out on a date."

Chapter Twenty-six

Ellie placed the faceless rag doll beside little Sophie on the large quilt and smiled. "Here you go Sophie. Lovey will keep you company."

"Why doesn't your doll have a face?" asked Benny.

Ellie smiled at the three-year-old. She knew he wasn't trying to be ugly. He was right, most dolls were made of plastic with marbled eyes and silky hair. Her little rag doll may not be much to look at, but Lovey had been Ellie's only friend for a very long time.

"She's very old," Ellie told Benny, "Besides this way I can imagine her face however I like. Maybe she's smiling, or maybe she's having a bad day and crying. The dolls you see now only have one face, but my Lovey has many."

Benny seemed to accept this answer without question and returned to playing with the wooden barnyard animals Elmer had made for him. It had become a tradition. Every year Elmer made all the kids some kind of wooden critter for Christmas. His son was no exception, having a whole collection of barnyard and wild animals.

"I had a cousin with a doll like that," said Leon. He had played with Benny a little, but now he just sat with a tattered green bag sitting on his lap. "She played with it all the time. I think it was the only doll she ever had."

"Until I came here, Lovey was my only doll," said Ellie. "She helped me through a lot of hard times. For a time, she was the only one I would talk to. I'm glad you came here, Leon. You remind me of Lovey because you're easy to talk to."

"I like it here at Quail Crossings. Even if my dad hadn't made me come, I still would have," said Leon. "He kept going on and on about how a kid my age should be playing in the grass and going on adventures."

"I was talking about coming here to Knollwood and livin' with your dad," said Ellie with a smile. "But I'm glad you like the farm, too."

"Well, it sure beats my last place," said Leon. "Ma'am dropped me off with some of her friends that lived in a run-down tenement. Bugs were everywhere. I don't mind bugs really, but these would climb in your ears at night. I watched as they pulled one out of a little girl's ear. She was about Benny's age, I guess. She just screamed and screamed until they got it out. Every time she screamed, they'd smack her, and she'd just scream some more. Took them a few days to figure out she had a bug in her ear. Some nights I still hear that screaming. After that I slept with cotton in my ears. Ain't no bugs getting in my head."

"That's awful," said Ellie. "I can't believe your mom would leave you there."

Leon looked down at his tattered canvas bag. "Ellie, do you know how to read?"

Ellie nodded. "I learned here with Alice, Evie and Dovie. The school wouldn't take me because I was too far behind. That suited me just fine. I'm not real good with people outside this family."

"Why is that?" asked Leon.

Ellie wondered just how much she should tell Leon about her past. She didn't want to scare him, but it seemed he'd understand better than anyone. "Well, like you, I lived with a bunch of different families that weren't my own before coming here. The first family was really nice. They wanted me, but we were in an accident, and they died. Some of their family members believed I caused the accident. I didn't. I was just a baby, but they thought I was the devil. They used to beat me so hard I got put in the hospital a few times. I got away, but the doctor of the family found me and put me in the hospital again. But thanks to Momma Dovie, *he* won't be finding anyone ever again."

"Did your real mother leave you with him?" asked Leon.

Ellie shook her head. "No, she left me at the hospital when I was a baby smaller than Sophie here. I was really sick, and everyone thought I died. It wasn't until later, when the lady from the state found my brothers and sisters here at Quail Crossings, that any of them knew I still lived." Ellie looked out over the farm and sighed contentedly. "Now here I am, being things I never thought I'd be. Educated, respected, but mostly loved. I never knew what love was before coming here."

Leon reached into his bag and pulled out a bundle of letters. Ellie looked over and could see they were addressed to Blu and had Jacob's return military address from the war on them.

"Do you think you could read these to me?" asked Leon.

Ellie nodded. She remembered, while growing up with the doctor's family, how much she wanted just a part of her real parents. To know them just a little bit. Now she had her siblings to tell her about their real parents, both the good and bad stuff. All Jacob had were the letters, and she wasn't about to stand in his way of getting the one thing she never had ... an inside peek.

Elmer stopped the truck and hurried around to open the passenger side door for Tiny.

"Where are we?" asked Tiny. "You've got me so turned around with all this back road driving, I'm not even sure we're in Texas any longer."

"It's a surprise," said Elmer. He closed the door after helping Tiny out and grabbed an extra-large basket from the bed of the truck.

"Jeepers, Elm, you plannin' on feeding an army?"

Elmer gave the basket a tap. "This here basket has all our needs for the day in it, not just food."

"Wow, now I'm really intrigued," said Tiny.

Elmer offered her his hand. "It's just a short walk over this hill."

Tiny took his hand, and the two made their way up the large grassy hill. As they crested it, Elmer heard Tiny inhale sharply.

"Elmer, it's beautiful," she said as they looked over a crystal clear lake surrounded by cottonwood and oak trees. "How did I never know this was here?"

"Not many people do," said Elmer. "It was private land up until recently. The Game Department bought it for regulation hunting. It's not open for hunting now, but since it's public land, anyone can use the lake for swimming and the land around it for picnicking. One of the sheriff deputies told me about it at the butcher shop last week. He said he had brought his kids and wife for a swim, and they had lots of fun."

"Oh, Elm, I haven't been swimming in ages," said Tiny. "We used to swim at the pond all the time before Benny."

"I know," said Elmer as they started down the hill. "So, now we can have a swim and have a little time to ourselves. Both are greatly overdue."

Tiny pulled him over and kissed him. Elmer had to fight for his balance, but he managed to stay upright on the side of the hill. He couldn't remember the last time Tiny had instigated a kiss. He wished his hands were free so he could wrap his arms around her.

Tiny broke their embrace and then gave him an ornery smile. "Race ya!"

She took off down the hill, leaving Elmer feeling a little stunned. He raced after her, but it was no match with him carrying such a big basket full of food, towels, and a blanket. He reached the bottom shortly after her.

She looked out over the water before turning and giving him a playful pout. "Elm, I didn't bring my swimsuit. You can't expect me to go swimming in my skivvies when just anyone could walk up."

Elmer set the basket down, opened it and pulled out Tiny's swimsuit. "I've got you covered."

Tiny squealed as she grabbed the suit and ran behind some nearby trees. As she changed, Elmer laid out the blanket and towels, so they would have a place to dry off afterwards. He took off his boots, socks and shirt. He had never owned an actual bathing suit, and his pants made a fine pair of swim trunks as far as he was concerned. Dovie had always cut off the legs of a pair of pants that were too short for him to swim in. He had stopped outgrowing his pants a while back, so he hadn't had any to sacrifice for swimwear.

Tiny came out from behind the trees, blushing in her dark blue swimsuit with halter style top. The blue of the suit made her red hair pop, and her eyes sparkled with excitement. "I can't believe this still fits, much less that you knew where to find it."

"You look amazing," said Elmer.

Tiny tossed her clothes onto the blanket and ran into the water, Elmer close on her heels. They spent the afternoon frolicking in the water and stealing kisses in between splashes.

Hours later, after they had swam and eaten, they had lain on the blanket soaking up the late afternoon sun. Tiny reached over and grabbed Elmer's hand. He gave her hand a squeeze.

"Thank you for this, Elm," said Tiny.

"No, need to thank me," said Elmer. "I'm just glad you're having a good time."

"I know I haven't been much fun lately," said Tiny.

Elmer frowned. He had hoped they wouldn't talk about all the troubles they'd been having. He really wanted the day to be something Tiny could think of when she was feeling awful.

Tiny rolled onto her side and pushed herself up on one elbow so she was looking down at Elmer. "I'm gonna do it."

"Do what?" asked Elmer, gently reaching up and brushing her hair from her face.

"Talk to Dovie," said Tiny. "I've been dragging my feet about it, but I want you to know I'm going to talk to her today. Just as soon as we get back."

"I'm really glad to hear you say that," said Elmer. "I just want you to feel better."

"This has made me feel better," she gestured to the lake and the picnic they had shared. "Spending time with you and going for a swim. I even found myself wishing the kids were here. I can't remember the last time I felt that way."

"Summer's not over," said Elmer. "We can still bring them."

"We should," said Tiny, dropping her elbow, letting her face gently land on Elmer's chest. She cocked her neck upwards and kissed Elmer's neck. He nudged his head against hers until his lips landed on hers, and they locked in a long, passionate kiss. She was acting like her old self, and Elmer couldn't help but feel something he hadn't felt in a long time ... optimism.

Chapter Twenty-seven

July 4, 1950

Alice couldn't help but smile as she walked along the rows of makeshift games and booths set up by the townspeople at the Independence Day Festival in Big Tree Park. She watched as George Wheaton sat on a board over a large stock tank and hassled people into throwing a ball at a target that, if hit, would send him into the water. George's eyes widened as his son, Ben, put down his money for a chance to dunk his father. It only took one throw, and George went swimming.

She laughed as she walked on. She waved to Elmer and Jacob who were manning a booth where spectators tried to throw a ball and knock over a stack of tin milk cans. The prizes at the festival were small, Elmer was giving out skewered sausages to the winners and bragging rights went to the folks who made George swim.

No one seemed to mind that the prizes were small or nonexistent since the money was for a good cause. Elmer and Jacob were helping to raise money for the new hymnals, while the dunking booth's funds were going to new playground equipment at Big Tree Park.

"There you are," said Walter as he ran up beside her, "I've been looking all over for you."

"I thought you were volunteering at the chicken races," said Alice. "Figured you'd be busy all day."

"I will," said Walter as he took a cigarette out of his pocket, "but we're all set up and they don't start for another half hour. I thought I'd come find you."

"Please don't light that," said Alice.

"Why not?" asked Walter, a match in his hand.

"Just seems in poor form to walk around with a small torch since we can't have the bonfire due to the drought," explained Alice. "One wrong flick of ash, and the whole park could go up."

"Nonsense," said Walter, "there's people smoking everywhere."

He lit the cigarette and took a long drag.

"Doesn't stop me from wishing you wouldn't," said Alice.

Walter let out the smoke. "I promise to be careful. I honestly don't see what the big deal is. Everyone smokes now days."

"Not everyone," said Alice.

He offered her the cigarette. "Give it a go. You might like it."

"No thanks," said Alice, "having dust pneumonia as a child really made me appreciate having only fresh air in my lungs."

Walter wiggled the cigarette at her. "Don't be such a stick in the mud. Just try it."

"I really don't want to," said Alice. "I honestly don't see the appeal."

"Because you haven't tried it," said Walter. Alice heard the annoyance creep into his voice. "You never try anything new."

Alice stopped and placed her hands on her hips. "That's not true."

Walter laughed, causing Alice's blood to boil.

"No, Alice, you don't," he said. "You have your routine, and you stick to it like glue. You should be more spontaneous like the other girls."

Walter gave a smile to a group of giggling high school girls as they threw glances his way.

Alice rolled her eyes and gestured to the giggling girls. "Walter, if you want a spontaneous girl, go for it. I'm not stopping you."

She marched off into the crowd and was partially thankful Walter didn't follow her and partially upset that he didn't. Sighing, she kept walking past the game booths and into the trees. He was right. Everyone, except her family, smoked. None of them had ever been curious enough to pick up the habit.

Her mind pricked at her until she finally admitted she was being unfair to Walter about the cigarettes.

Her mind turned to the giggling girls who were looking at him. He was a good-looking man, and she could see why they were being flirtatious. She had never been flirtatious in nature. She had a beau in high school for a while, Lawrence Dobson, but he had broken up with her stating they seemed more like friends than a couple. Even then, she hadn't been bothered when he started to date her friend Virginia. They had all remained friends, and Virginia and Lawrence were now happily married and running the Knollwood Marketplace.

Alice pursed her lips and realized all her friends were married. She had been the only one in her class to go on to college. They had all stayed back to help out with family businesses.

"A penny for your thoughts?"

Alice snapped out of her thoughts and looked up to see Nicholas sitting under a tree with a book. She tilted her head to read the cover, *The Commodore* by C. S. Forester.

"You're reading?" asked Alice in amazement.

Nicholas laughed. "I got into this series a while back, but then I started working and didn't read much. Hopped into the library this morning and saw they had part of the series I haven't read yet, so I figured why not?" He gave her a wink. "By the way, I said you'd vouch for me."

"Of course," said Alice, still hearing the surprise in her voice, "let me know if I can help."

Nicholas squinted his eyes. "Help? With reading? I've got it thanks."

Alice hurried over and sat by Nicholas. "I'm sorry, I didn't mean you can't read it on your own. I mean I can help you get books." She shook her head. "I'm sure I sounded incredibly insulting. I just love teaching people how to read and seeing people read. In fact, seeing you with the book makes me jealous I didn't bring my own."

"I figured you and Walter would be playing all the games, and he'd be winning you all sorts of prizes," said Nicholas. "Isn't that what couples do at these things? The boys prove how strong they are, and the girls get all giddy over trinkets that could be bought cheaper at Johnson's Drug."

Alice sighed. "We're not a couple."

"You should probably tell Walter that," said Nicholas.

"I have, about a hundred times," said Alice. "He doesn't seem to understand."

"Because he's a man who's used to getting what he wants," explained Nicholas, closing the book and setting it on his lap. "I bet you're the first person who has ever told him no in his life."

"Says the guy who drove up in a cherry red Packard convertible," said Alice.

Nicholas opened his book back up. "Fine, I was just trying to help."

"I know," Alice said softly. "I'm sorry. I guess I'm feeling sorry for myself because all my girlfriends from high school are married. I'm wondering if something is wrong with me because I'm not tuned into Walter's attentions. I'm a spinster."

Nicholas guffawed. "You are not a spinster! If you lived in New York City, no one would think twice about you not being married yet."

"Really?"

"Really," said Nicholas. "Answer me this, would you rather be a married, unhappy wife or a happy, unmarried spinster? Seems like an easy choice to me."

"Well, Nicholas Banner, you are smarter than you look," said Alice, giving him a playful smile.

"I have my moments," said Nicholas.

"So what are you doing out here all alone?" asked Alice.

Nicholas shrugged. "Seems this is more of a type of thing for families and couples." He gave her an ornery smile. "Besides, what would I do with all the trinkets I would win?"

"I have an idea," said Alice, "Come on."

Over the next hour, Alice and Nicholas pooled their money and played all the games, winning trinket after trinket. They had won everything from soft dolls, to wooden animals, to race cars. They sat at a picnic table where Alice spread the toys out on the table. She quickly counted, and they had just enough. She let out a happy sigh and realized her cheeks were sore from smiling so much and her sides hurt from laughing. Nicholas had been the perfect fair companion.

"You have won a trinket for every child at Quail Crossings," said Alice. "You'll be their favorite person on the farm after you hand them out."

"We," corrected Nicholas, "you helped. I couldn't, for the life of me, get that silly metal ring to loop the milk bottle. I don't know how you managed."

"It just needed a lady's finesse," said Alice.

"You mean a spinster's," joked Nicholas.

She feigned hurt feelings and then smiled. "How much money do we have left?"

Nicholas fished the remainder of their coins out of his pocket. "Fifteen cents."

"Great," said Alice, "we still have two booths left."

Quickly, she took a clean bandana from her dress pocket and carefully wrapped it around the toys, making an easy to carry bundle, then led Nicholas to the dunking booth.

"Oh no," cried George, "I just got toweled off, and now the new man in town is looking to make a splash."

"Not quite," said Alice. "I'll give you ten cents if you let Nicholas sit on that board."

"All right by me," said George, swinging his legs over to the dry side of the stock tank.

Nicholas laughed as he jogged over to the board. "It's not like I'm scared. With Alice throwing, I'm sure I'll stay nice and dry."

As Nicholas steadied himself on the board, George leaned over to talk to Alice. "Have you guys played ball out there at Quail Crossings since Nicholas came to town?"

"Nope," answered Alice with a smile.

"So he has no idea what he's getting into?" asked George.

"He does not," said Alice matter-of-factly.

George turned his attention to the crowd. "Come on over folks! See Alice the Shotgun Brewer in action! We call her the shotgun because she pitches so fast you'll never see it coming. The last man who took one of her pitches in the chest spent three days in the hospital!"

"You're laying it on a little thick," Alice whispered to George.

"All in the name of charity," said George.

"Come!" he continued. "See Alice Brewer, our hometown girl, drown the Yankee from the big city!"

"Hey now," called Nicholas from the bench. "You didn't tell me you were a ringer!"

"You didn't ask," said Alice with a smile.

She wound up the first throw and fast balled it to the center of the target. Nicholas's arms went up as he fell into the water. The crowd cheered and laughed. Nicholas bolted up.

"Dagnabit! The water's freezing!" shouted Nicholas as he righted the board and went to the side of the stock tank.

"Not so fast, young man," said George, "the lady bought two throws. She still has one more. Don't worry. I had the ice man put a block in about half an hour ago, so it'll stay nice and cool in there. It's not a lot of fun to make someone fall into a stock tank that's so warm it feels like a bath tub."

Nicholas shook his head and pointed at Alice with a smile. "You tricked me."

"Figured you'd want to cool off," said Alice with a smile. "Remember it's all for the kids."

Nicholas climbed up on the board, but before he even had a chance to get settled, Alice threw the second ball and sent Nicholas plunging back into the tank. Again the crowd cheered.

Standing, he pointed his finger at Alice. "That wasn't nice."

Alice hurried over to the stock tank as Nicholas got out.

"Where did you learn to throw like that?" asked Nicholas, grabbing a dry towel stored behind the game.

"We used to play baseball out at Quail Crossings all the time. Since there were only four of us at first, we just kind of rotated. One person in the outfield, one in the infield, one pitching, and the person at bat would also act as catcher if they missed. We swung at everything, so it really didn't matter if the pitches were good. Then one day, I was playing around, acting like I had seen the high school boys pitch at a game, and smoked one in past Bill. Papa James was acting as catcher, and I knocked him over. From that moment on, I became our pitcher at the church tournament or pickup games. It just kind of comes naturally to me."

"You should have told me that before I sat on that bench," said Nicholas with a laugh.

"Now, what fun would that be," said Alice. She looped her arm in Nicholas's. "Come on. I'll go knock over some milk cans and win you a sausage for your trouble."

Nicholas patted her hand and even though his hands were cold, his touch sent a warm sensation racing through her body.

Chapter Twenty-eight

Lou Anne looked around the fellowship hall at church and searched for Evalyn. She knew she was coming to the Ladies Circle meeting, but also knew Evalyn always ran a little late. She had to take the twins to the nursery. Ellie had offered to watch the girls, but Evalyn had refused since the flour fiasco, stating the twins needed to beconfined to a one-room nursery.

The fellowship hall was packed with twelve circular tables, each holding about a dozen women. The room buzzed with the casual conversation and laughter of the women visiting while they waited for Susan Spaulding to start the meeting. Lou Anne and Dovie were saving Evalyn a seat and hoped they could wave Evalyn over before the meeting started.

"Do you see her?" asked Dovie. "Susan's getting ready to start, and we have to give a report on the fundraising for the hymnals."

"Not yet," said Lou Anne, turning to look at Dovie, "she'll be here."

She felt someone sit next to her, turned to greet Evalyn, but was surprised to see Charlotte instead.

"Is this seat taken?" asked Charlotte, sitting without waiting for an answer.

Lou Anne wanted to say yes, but an empty seat between Dovie and Florence King remained available for Evalyn.

"You would not believe the mess that nursery is in," stated Charlotte as she fanned herself. "Unbelievable how some children act under the Lord's roof."

"Well at least they're in church," said Lou Anne, unable to hold her tongue. "Been a while since I've seen your boys attend a service. Seems so unfortunate since right here is where we all learn how to respect and care for others."

Charlotte waved her off. "My boys know all about respect. You should see how they take care of their momma. Caring is not one of their problems."

"Isn't it?" Lou Anne's eyes narrowed as she thought of the way Barry had treated Dean behind the butcher shop. "Your boys continually pick on children younger than they are, and when someone does stand up to them, they all band together like a gang of hoodlums."

Dovie put her hand on Lou Anne's shoulder to stop her, but all the anger she felt over catching Barry being nasty to Dean bubbled over her stomach and out of her mouth. "Your boys are the worst about showing anyone, including you and Peter, respect. So, until you get things controlled under your own roof, don't be complaining about the children under the Lord's because at least they're here."

Charlotte's mouth dropped open as the other ladies at the table stared at her.

"Do you all feel this way?" asked Charlotte, finding her voice.

Florence, a mother of three boys, spoke first. "Lou Anne's right, my kids won't even go into Johnson's Drug for ice cream if they see your boys in there."

"Speaking of Johnson's," another woman spoke up. "Mr. Johnson said your boys steal candy just about every day. He tried to stop them once and said you got in his way. Another time he tried to stop them, but then they broke three jars of penny candy, which you claimed to be an accident."

"It was," said Charlotte.

"No, it wasn't," said Florence. "I was inside that day buying lozenges and watched the older one pick up the jar of licorice and throw it on the ground. Then two more of your boys followed suit. There were so many boys Mr. Johnson didn't know which child to grab. Lou Anne is right, they're out of control."

Lou Anne started to feel her stomach drop as the other ladies at the table took turns chastising Charlotte for not having better control over her boys. She wanted to say something in Charlotte's defense, but knew she couldn't since she was the one who had instigated it.

"I think Charlotte has heard enough," said Dovie. "There is not one person at this table who can claim to be a perfect mother. Let us remember where we are and why we are here."

"You're right," said Florence, "this isn't the place or the time. My boys can be quite the handful sometimes. Some days, I love them more than I can stand, and other days I want to sell them at the market. I'm very sorry, Charlotte."

The other women, too, muttered apologies. Lou Anne looked at Charlotte and was surprised to see tears in her eyes. Lou Anne opened her mouth to apologize as well but had no time as Charlotte quickly got up and left the table.

Just as Charlotte left, Evalyn hurried in. She looked around the table as everyone seemed to be staring at their hands.

"What did I miss?" Evalyn asked, but before anyone could answer, Susan took to the front of the room and began speaking. Evalyn sat between Dovie and Florence.

"Settle down, ladies," said Pastor Spaulding's wife, Susan. "We've got a lot to cover today…"

Lou Anne tried to concentrate on the meeting but wasn't able. Her mind kept flashing back to what she had said to Charlotte and how the other ladies had followed her lead. They had all pounced like a fox on a rabbit. She had wanted to protect Dean and try to make Charlotte see some sense, but she realized she had gone about it the wrong way.

As Susan asked all the ladies to bow their heads in prayer as the meeting concluded. Lou Anne prayed she could find a way to get Charlotte to forgive her.

Susan finished her prayer, and a chorus of *amens* from the women in the fellowship hall followed. The women started to get up and stretch their legs, but they didn't venture too far from their tables, knowing refreshments would soon be served. Lou Anne thought she saw Evalyn cringe as Mrs. Allen, the woman who ran the nursery, walked up and whispered something in Susan's ear.

Susan turned with wide eyes to Mrs. Allen, and Lou Anne could faintly hear her say, "All of them?" to which Mrs. Allen nodded.

Susan took a deep breath and plastered on a sweet smile. She cleared her throat, and the hum of conversations stopped. "Usually this is where we enjoy conversations and refreshments. Y'all are welcome to stay as long as you'd like to visit, but I'm afraid there's been an incident with the refreshments. We will have to forego them this afternoon. I would like to thank Mrs. Walker and Mrs. King for all their hard work on the cookies. I'm sure they were wonderful. I do apologize for the situation."

Lou Anne caught sight of movement and looked at Evalyn just in time to see her drop her head into her hands, elbows propped on the table, as conversations regarding the refreshment mystery buzzed around them.

Dovie instantly turned her attention to Evalyn. "Are you okay, Evie? What's the matter? Are you hurt?"

"I'm fine," said Evalyn, her head in her hands, "don't worry about me. Just trying to hide my embarrassment, although one would think I'd be used to it by now."

Dovie looked at Lou Anne with confusion and Lou Anne shook her head.

"Evie, we don't understand," said Dovie.

"You will," said Evalyn, dropping her arms, her shoulders still slumped. "I'm sure Mrs. Spaulding and Mrs. Allen will be over here in just a few moments to let me know what the girls did to the cookies."

As if on cue, Susan and Mrs. Allen approached their table. "Evalyn, dear, may we have a word with you?"

"Just tell me," said Evalyn, looking around the table, "what did they do? Did they feed the cookies to a stray dog? Did they mash them all together to make mud pies?" Evalyn laughed hysterically, and Lou Anne was afraid her sister-in-law was about to lose her marbles. "Oh, I know, they crushed them up and put them in all the diapers."

"They ate them," said Susan bluntly. "Well, we figure they ate about twenty cookies each. The rest were on the floor."

Evalyn stopped laughing abruptly. "Twenty cookies each?"

"We had five dozen molasses cookies in the kitchen," said Mrs. Allen. "I found the girls as they were eating them. I just turned my back for a second while I was changing a diaper."

Dovie and Evalyn stood and quickly grabbed their stuff.

"Bring them to the house," said Dovie. "I've got some ipecac."

"Is that necessary?" asked Lou Anne as she stood too.

Dovie gave her a sympathetic look. "Eating that many molasses cookies, they're going to be sick regardless. Might as well get the process started, so it can end. See you at the house?"

Lou Anne nodded as Dovie and Evalyn hurried toward the kitchen with Mrs. Allen to get the girls.

"Lou Anne," said Susan gently, "I know this isn't your place, but perhaps you should suggest Evalyn leave the girls with their father during our next meeting."

"Oh, but Robert's so busy," countered Lou Anne.

"Let me explain," said Susan, "Pastor Spaulding and I are having a hard time getting people to work in the nursery due to the twins. So until things settle down, we must insist that they stay elsewhere. People will soon forget their shenanigans, and then the girls can come back."

Lou Anne felt her shoulders slump as Susan gave her a gentle pat on the arm before moving on to converse with the others in the Fellowship Hall.

"Well, I'll be," said Florence, looking aghast. "Why should you have to tell Evalyn? Susan should do that herself."

Lou Anne shook her head. "Serves me right, I'd say."

Florence cocked her head. "How so?"

Lou Anne sighed. "Here I was, the leader of the mob after Charlotte and her kids, and my two nieces get kicked out of the nursery for being ornery. Her son, Barry, has been picking on Dean, and I let my emotions get the best of me. It would serve me right if my own kids had been kicked out of the nursery."

Florence grabbed Lou Anne's hand gently and gave her a soft smile. "We may not have eaten the cookies, but none of us are innocent today. God does have a funny way of showing us that, doesn't He?"

Lou Anne gathered her things and noticed Florence's attention was taken by a young woman needing volunteer information for the Ladies Circle. Dovie and Evalyn would need someone to help watch the rest of the kids while they were dealing with the girls, so she had best get going.

She said a small prayer as she left the church. The Lord knew it was going to be a long day for all of them.

Chapter Twenty-nine

Lou Anne walked around the back of the church where she was to pick up Dean. His youth group had been meeting at the same time as her Ladies Circle. As she rounded the corner, she stopped suddenly, avoiding a collision with Charlotte.

Charlotte's eyes were red and puffy, sure signs she had been crying.

"Oh, Charlotte," said Lou Anne softly, "I am so sorry. I shouldn't have said those things about your boys. Being a momma is hard enough without other mommas ridiculing you. I was wrong and again, I'm sorry."

"No," said Charlotte, shaking her head. Lou Anne took a step back, afraid of the tongue lashing she was about to get. She fought the urge to walk away but knew she deserved anything Charlotte had to say to her.

"You're right," Charlotte continued.

Lou Anne's mouth dropped open. "What?"

"Those boys have gotten the best of Peter and me," Charlotte cried. "I wanted so badly for them to like me when they were little, I never got on to them. I gave them everything they wanted and never made them do chores. They aren't just awful around town, you should see them at home. I've stopped buying nice things because they just break anything I cherish."

"Charlotte, I had no idea," said Lou Anne.

"Of course, you don't," countered Charlotte. "I've led everyone to believe I'm perfectly fine with their behavior. You know very well, I'm the first to make excuses for it. I did it when Barry was pushing poor Dean's head in the dirt. I let my pride win over the raising of my children."

"So stop," said Lou Anne matter-of-factly.

"What?" asked Charlotte as she dabbed at her eyes with a hanky.

"Charlotte Williams, you are one of the strongest women I know," said Lou Anne, "Don't forget we grew up together, and I've seen you fight like a badger for what you want. You want your boys to behave, then make them. It's not too late."

"But it is," said Charlotte, "you've seen my boys."

Lou Anne shook her head. "The Charlotte I know will make those boys cower. You have all the power here, you just have to take it."

Charlotte gave Lou Anne a small smile. "Do you really think I can?"

"I know you can," said Lou Anne. "Now I'm afraid I have to meet Dean at the playground and get home. You come on out to coffee sometime, okay? Any time you need to talk."

Charlotte nodded. "I'll do that."

Lou Anne gave Charlotte a hug and started around the back side of the church. Again, her steps halted as she saw Barry push Dean onto the ground. Her first instinct was to run to Dean and see if he was okay, but Bill's words of letting Dean fight his own battles ran through her head.

Dean quickly got to his feet. "Knock it off!"

"What are you gonna do?" taunted Barry. "Cry like a baby? Go get your Mommy?"

Barry pushed Dean again, but this time Dean took a few steps back but didn't fall.

He marched up to Barry, and Lou Anne felt pride in seeing her boy so brave.

"I said to knock it off," warned Dean, "You ain't picking on me anymore."

"Who's gonna stop me?" asked Barry.

Barry went in for another push as Dean sidestepped around him. Barry lost his balance and with a quick shove from Dean, Barry tumbled. Lou Anne had to stop herself from cheering as Barry landed face first in the dirt. Her joy was short lived as she saw the rest of the Williams boys run around the corner.

"Now you're gonna get it," said an older Williams brother as he thrusted his fist into the palm of his hand.

"Ha, ha," laughed Barry. "You're gonna wish you'd just let me push you in the dirt by the time we get through with you."

Lou Anne was just getting ready to step in when she felt someone hurry by her. She was shocked to see it was Charlotte. Lou Anne quickly followed her.

"Boys!" yelled Charlotte, "That's enough."

"Oh, Ma, we're just getting to the good part," joked one of the older boys.

Charlotte marched over and grabbed the boy's ear and twisted it.

"Ow! Ma stop, that hurts," cried the boy.

"Oh, but we're just getting to the good part," Charlotte mocked as she let go of the boy's ear. She glared at her sons.

"Line up!" she ordered.

The boys stood for a moment, looking at their mother in confusion.

"Unless you boys want me to tan each and every one of your hides, you will line up immediately," ordered Charlotte. The boys remained put.

"Don't think I'll do it?" Charlotte's eyes narrowed. "Try me and see what happens. You boys think you're the meanest dogs on the ranch. Well, where do you think you got it from?"

She reached for another boy's ear, and they all scurried into a line.

"That's better," said Charlotte, her chin high. "Things are going to change from this moment on. You boys are done embarrassing me and your father with your bad manners. Acting like a bunch of coyotes around town, breaking stuff and treating others badly. Here we are at church, and you're getting ready to knock Dean senseless because he had the gumption to stand up to you. You oughta be ashamed of yourselves. I know I am."

She looked down the line of boys. "Now, we are gonna change a lot of things, so just you get ready. Not only are we gonna work on your manners, but you're gonna make amends to people you've done wrong. You'll help out at Johnson's Drug cleaning, and at the feed store. But first, when we get home, you're gonna clean up the yard you've spent years cluttering up with your junk. Then you all are having a bath and gettin' haircuts."

The boys groaned and whined. Charlotte shot them a look, and they shut their mouths. "You boys stink, and you look like orphans. I'll not have it any longer." She looked at Dean and softened her voice. "Dean, dear, would you come here please?"

Dean glanced at his mother with trepidation before walking to Charlotte.

"Barry, you need to apologize to Dean this instant. Shame on you for picking on a boy two years younger and a foot shorter. What? You can't pick on someone your own size?"

"But Ma," said Barry, "I was just foolin' around."

"Barry Williams, you apologize for being a big ape right this moment, or I'll have you mucking out the pig pens until you've grown a gray beard."

"I'm sorry," muttered Barry.

Charlotte looked at Dean. "So am I. I should've listened the first time your mother told me that Barry was being awful to you. They'll not bother you again."

She looked at her boys. "You could learn a lot from this young man. Takes a lot of courage to stand up to a bunch of boys twice your size. All right, sons, march to the truck, we're gonna get started on that lawn. I need y'all to clear me a space, then you can till up some yard for a garden. Might be a late start, but it'll be a start. After your baths, you can get started cleaning your rooms."

The boys groaned again but trudged to the truck as Charlotte walked with Dean to Lou Anne.

"Keep up the groaning and I'll make you do the laundry, too," Charlotte hollered at her children.

"I knew you could do it," said Lou Anne.

"Not sure how long this will last," said Charlotte.

"It'll last as long as you want it to," said Lou Anne, "Remember, you're the momma."

Charlotte gave her a grateful smile before following her boys.

Lou Anne looked at Dean. "I'm very proud of you."

"For what?" asked Dean.

"For starters, I saw you turn the other cheek when Barry pushed you the first time, and then, when it was clear he wasn't going to stop, you stood up for yourself. Charlotte was right, that was very brave," explained Lou Anne.

Dean kicked dirt. "It was nothing."

"It was just how your daddy would have acted," said Lou Anne with a smile.

"Really?" Dean's face lit up.

"Really," said Lou Anne. "Now, come on, we've got to get home and help with the twins."

"Are they in trouble again?" asked Dean.

"They are," said Lou Anne.

"I'll talk to them," said Dean, squaring his shoulders.

"Now, that is brave," laughed Lou Anne. "If they should look up to anyone, I do hope it's you."

Chapter Thirty

Walter walked from the house toward the barn. He had just gathered all the kitchen scraps and was making his way to feed the pigs when Jacob drove up with Leon.

Walter stopped, put down his bucket and wiped his brow with a handkerchief. He gave Jacob a wave as Jacob parked the truck. The sun was setting, but it was still sweltering outside.

"Hey there, Jacob," said Walter.

Jacob gave him a wave as he and Leon got out of the truck. "Hi, Walter, thought I'd take Leon to do some fishing. I was hoping it would have cooled off some, but it's hotter than a pan frying bacon out here."

"It is that," said Walter. He scratched his head. "Jacob, can I ask you something?"

Jacob nodded.

"How can you drive a truck while missing your right leg?" asked Walter. "I don't mean to be rude, I'm genuinely curious."

Jacob let out a chuckle. "I'd be curious, too. I have the fellas here at Quail Crossings to thank for that. Come take a look."

Jacob led Walter over to the truck and opened the driver side door. Walter peered inside and let out a low whistle as he saw a knob attached to a stick that lead down to a heavy block of angled wood attached to the gas pedal.

"I just press down on the knob when I want to go faster, then hook the stick into place to maintain pressure on the gas while I shift," explained Jacob.

"Snails move faster than he drives," joked Leon as he walked over.

Jacob laughed. "Well, I ain't in a hurry."

"That is amazing," said Walter. "Did it take you long to learn to drive it?"

"Probably not as long as it would have had I known how to drive before I lost my leg," said Jacob.

Walter looked at Jacob with wide eyes. "You didn't know how to drive before!"

"Not much of a reason for me to know," said Jacob. "Before the war, I could barely get a job, much less a car. Work was scarce in Sweetsville, the all-colored town where I lived, and no one outside of Sweetsville wanted to hire a colored boy."

"I never thought about that," said Walter.

Jacob gave him a smile. "Well, you probably never needed to."

"Can we go?" asked Leon, holding up the fishing pole. "Miss Dovie will have dinner ready before we've even cast a line at this rate."

"I've got to feed the pigs anyway," said Walter, pointing to his bucket. "Good luck with the fishing."

As he turned and went back to his bucket, Walter was secretly happy Leon had interrupted the conversation. As much as he tried to be open minded about a colored man being a part of the family, he always managed to say something awkward. He wanted to be just as natural around Jacob and Leon as the rest of the Quail Crossings clan. The honest truth was, the only coloreds he had been around were the extra help his family hired on occassion, and you just didn't talk to the help the same way as family.

Walter walked over to the pig pen, his mind still racing with thoughts on how to speak to Jacob like a normal man.

"But he's not a normal man," Walter muttered to himself as he shook his head. "He doesn't have the same rights as us, and Alice is sticking her head in the sand if she thinks he does."

Walter reached over the pig pen fence to pour the slop into the trough when he felt a hard pinch to his backside.

"Owww!" screamed Walter as the pinch got harder. He swirled around and knocked Norman with the slop bucket, losing half of the slop on his pants. "Dammit, Norman!"

"So it was you," accused Alice as she came around the corner.

"What?" asked Walter. He could feel his cheeks burning red.

"The twins," said Alice as she walked closer to Walter, "were saying that word a few weeks ago during the flour incident. We all assumed they had heard it from Nicholas, even though he swore it wasn't him. They heard it from you; didn't they?"

Walter rubbed his neck and looked at the ground, before looking up at Alice. "No, Alice, I rarely say that word. I only said it now because that evil goose bit my backside."

"And you're sure you didn't say it before?" quizzed Alice. "That Norman didn't do something to you that day to make you cuss at him like you did now?"

Again Walter rubbed his neck and glanced at the ground. "I'm sure."

"Walter Jefferson," Alice snapped as she pointed her finger at him, "I know when you're lying, and you are lying to me."

"No, I'm not," said Walter. He again rubbed his neck, feeling the sweat drip onto his back.

Alice folded her arms. "You rub your neck every time you lie. I've seen you do it with professors and friends at college, and now I'm seeing you do it here. I always knew that you occasionally lied to get out of trouble, I just never thought you'd do it with me."

She turned and marched to the house.

"Wait!" Walter called out. "I'm sorry."

He felt the frustration boil up from his stomach and desperately wanted Alice to turn around. He knew she didn't like lies, even the little ones he told to his professors and friends to get out of doing things he didn't want to do.

"Alice!" He called again, but Alice kept walking.

Robert stomped his boots free of mud and dirt on the back porch before stepping through the back door and into the kitchen. He heard the soft cries before he noticed Evalyn sitting on the floor sobbing in front of two banana cream pies, face down.

He rushed to his wife's side. "Evalyn, sweetie, what happened?"

"Those girls," snapped Evalyn, "Robert, I love them, but they are awful. They were supposed to be playing on the floor in the parlor while the pies were cooling. I was putting things away in the ice box when I heard the pies fall on the kitchen floor. My back was only turned for a second."

She let out another loud sob. "I warned the girls. I told them I had to get these pies to Ladies Circle bake sale today. The only reason we're even having a bake sale is because we have to raise money for new hymnals. Something we wouldn't have to be doing if they hadn't destroyed one. I don't have time to make more pies, not that the other ladies will be surprised. They just expect the girls to ruin everything, including my reputation."

She looked up at her husband. "Robert, they can't even go to the nursery at church any more. That's how much trouble they are. Susan can't get volunteers to watch the nursery if Bonnie and Beverly are in there. We've got a couple of heathens, and I'm at my wit's end trying to figure out what to do next."

Evalyn began to pick up the splattered pie from the floor and throw it back into the now empty pie pan. "I've tried lectures, making them sit in the corner, and taking toys away. I even paddled their behinds after the cookie incident, but nothing works."

Robert looked around the room. "Where are they now?"

"They are supposed to be cleaning their room," said Evalyn. She looked down at her broken pies. "Guess the pigs will enjoy the pie."

Robert stood and marched out of the kitchen to the door leading to the room the twins shared with Joy. As he walked into their room he saw all their dresser drawers open. The girls were throwing the shirts, pants, and underwear around the room.

"Daddy," cried Bonnie, "it's raining clothes!"

"Isn't it fun?" squealed Beverly.

"Bonnie! Beverly! You stop that this instant," boomed Robert.

The girls froze in their spots, and Robert knew it was because he had never gotten on to them before in their lives. He was busy with the pigs and the farm all day, so in the evenings, the last thing he wanted was to get onto his children. His heart sank as he thought of Evalyn crying on the floor, knowing he hadn't been any help at all over the last three years.

"In the parlor," he snapped. The girls quickly ran into the parlor. "Joy! Caleb! In the parlor now."

He didn't have to wait long. Joy and Caleb had already come to the parlor to see what their daddy was fussing about.

"Everyone sit," he ordered as he pointed to the sofa in front of the large rock fireplace. The kids did as they were told. He saw Evalyn standing in the doorway, wiping her hands with a dish towel, a curious look on her face.

"Let's get one thing clear," said Robert. "Your momma is the hardest working person I know. She deserves your love, respect and your help. We, and that includes me, have failed at being her family."

"What did I do?" asked Joy, folding her arms.

"Yeah," said five-year-old Caleb, following his sister's suit and folding his arms.

"Well, for starters, Joy weren't you focused on reading when you were supposed to be watching the girls and they got lost? Thankfully, we found them in the pig pen with the babies, but it could've been much worse. And Caleb, where were you just now when the twins were pulling pies off the counter? You knew your momma was busy, but did you offer to help by keeping an eye on them?"

Both Joy and Caleb bowed their heads. Robert turned his attention to Bonnie and Beverly. "Now for you two. I've had enough of your nonsense. You will stop all this mischief."

"What's meschauf?" asked Bonnie, mispronouncing mischief so badly that Robert had to bite back his smile.

"Getting into all this trouble," answered Robert, keeping his frown firmly planted on his face. "When your momma cooks, you will stay out of the kitchen. Any order your momma or I give you, you will follow. Things are going to change around here, and it starts with you two. You make any more messes, eat anything that doesn't belong to you, or cause any more trouble, you will answer to me." He looked at his children. "And that goes for all of you. Do you understand?"

The kids all nodded, their eyes wide.

"Now," said Robert, "Joy, go help your momma make some cookies for the bake sale. Those should be done in time, right?"

He looked at Evalyn who nodded slowly.

"Beverly and Bonnie, you will apologize to your mother, help her clean up the mess in the kitchen, and then go back to your room and clean up that mess. I don't want to see a single toy or piece of clothing on the floor and that includes under your bed. All those clothes better be folded and put up where they belong. Then go out and clean the chicken coop. From now on you two are in charge of feeding the chickens, cleaning the coop, and gathering the eggs. It's past time you two had some chores. You will also help your momma with the dishes after every meal, just like Joy does."

"But we don't know how to fold," said Beverly.

"Or clean the coop," said Bonnie.

"Caleb will teach you," said Robert.

"Why me?" asked Caleb with a whine. "I didn't do nothing."

"Exactly," said Robert. His voice softened a little. "None of us have done anything to help Momma. That stops now. Caleb, now that the girls are doing the chicken coop, you'll come help me with the pigs, once they've got the hang of things. We are family, and as a family, we need to look out for one another. That includes keeping each other out of trouble. Everyone understand?"

He was met with nods. "All right then, get busy."

Bonnie and Beverly walked to Evalyn and said they were sorry in their little three-year-old voices, heads bowed. Evalyn gave them both a hug, before the girls walked to the pie mess.

Caleb ran over and gave his mother a hug. "I'll make sure their room is tip top, just as soon as they're done in the kitchen."

He hurried after the twins as Joy approached her mom. "I'm sorry, Momma. I'll be more help from now on."

Evalyn gave her a hug as well. "You're a good girl, Joy, and I could definitely use your help. Start getting out the ingredients for sugar cookies. I'll be in there in a sec."

Evalyn walked over to Robert. "Thank you."

Robert shook his head. "Don't thank me for something way past due. I'm so sorry I wasn't looking out for you.

You're such a good mother, I just felt you had everything handled."

Evalyn kissed Robert. "We do now."

Chapter Thirty-one

Dovie walked across the hilltop that held the Knollwood Cemetery and tried to brush the hair from her face. The wind was howling as it often did on the Texas plains, and Dovie's bun could barely contain all her curls.

She walked past each headstone, knowing most of the people who lay in the graves. In a town the size of Knollwood, it was easy to know everyone, and the whole town mourned when it lost one of their own.

She walked to her momma's grave, knelt, and then put down a cluster of zinnias. "Sorry, it's not roses this time, Momma," Dovie said. "The rose bushes are not liking this heat." Dovie wiped her brow. "Of course, neither am I. We couldn't even have our 4th of July bonfire after the Independence Day picnic due to the lack of rain. One ember from that fire getting loose, and we'd have a mess of trouble."

She got back to her feet and walked to the next two headstones, the graves of her daughter and first husband. She placed a bouquet of daisies on Helen's grave and a dahlia on Simon's. She sat between the stones and visualized her family sitting across from her.

"The daisies don't seem to mind the heat this year, but that's probably the last dahlia we'll get." She sighed as she felt the tears coming. It never failed, every time she visited her family's graves on that old hilltop, she cried. "I'm sorry it's been so long since I've been out to see you all. I think about you both every day, you know that. Even though it's been sixteen years, I still wake each day with y'all in mind. Life has just gotten so busy, but as much as I love Gabe and the Brewers, I do wish you two were here. Gosh, I miss your hugs Helen. What I wouldn't do for one more hug. Oh and, Simon, just to feel you hold me, would be more than I could ever ask. I miss y'all so much."

She brushed the tears off her cheeks. "I need your advice, Simon. I'm not sure what to do about Nicholas, and you were always so smart about these things. Gabe tries, but as much as he loves Quail Crossings, that man has wings in his blood and isn't tied to the land the way you were. He just wants me to be happy and isn't interjecting too much of his thoughts on the matter. On one hand, I really respect that he's not trying to tell me what to do, but on the other hand, I wish he'd just tell me what to do."

She laughed at herself and looked at Helen's headstone. "Oh, Helen, you'd just love playing with all these babies. Of course, you'd be a full-grown woman by now either at university or having a family of your ..."

The words choked in her throat at the thought of the family Helen would never have. Helen would never know the joy of carrying her own children and raising them. The fact was Helen would never know the love of a good man nor the way one's heart races when they're truly in love.

As Dovie sobbed she felt someone sit behind her. She felt two large arms wrap around her and pull her close. She inhaled the scent of cloves with a hint of engine oil and knew it was Gabe. She leaned into him.

"I'm sorry," she cried.

"Don't you ever be sorry for loving your family so much it hurts," said Gabe and she could hear the crack in his own voice. "You can be sorry for a lot of things, but never that."

As Gabe tightened his hug around her, Dovie let her tears fall.

Elmer could smell the chicken frying as he stepped out of his truck. The smell made his mouth water and stomach growl, making him instantly regret skipping lunch. It had been a long time since he had come home to the smell of dinner on the stove. More often than not, he came home to every member of his family crying and had to calm them all down before going over to Dovie's to see if she had some dinner to spare, which she always did.

Not only was the smell of food wafting from the house foreign to him, so was the sound of laughing instead of crying. As Tiny's laugh danced on the air, he smiled. It had been too long since he had heard her laughing with her children.

Elmer walked inside and placed his hat on the peg by the door as he watched Tiny and Benny dancing to Bob Wills's *New Spanish Two Step* playing on the radio. Tiny twirled Benny around before turning to her pan on the stove and tending to the chicken.

"Daddy!" Benny cried as he ran to him, all smiles.

"Hey there, buddy," said Elmer picking up the little boy. "Looks like you and your momma are having fun."

"So much fun," said Benny. He scrambled down and ran back to his mother, who spun him around again.

Five month old Sophie laid on her stomach on a blanket in the corner of the kitchen and bobbed her head along to the music. Elmer knelt down and gave Sophie a kiss before making his way to Tiny and Benny. "May I cut in?"

"What?" asked Benny, scrunching his face.

"Can I dance with Momma for a minute?" Elmer clarified.

Benny nodded and sat in a chair. "I'm pooped anyway."

Elmer grabbed Tiny's hands and whirled her around the kitchen. Tiny's laugh grew louder and soon Benny was clapping along.

"Stop," said Tiny, between laughs. "I've got to turn to the chicken, and I'm sure the potatoes are ready to be mashed."

Elmer planted a kiss on Tiny's lips before giving her one final spin toward the stove.

"Whew," said Elmer as he walked over to the radio and turned it down. "Now I'm pooped. Dancing is hard work."

Benny climbed on his lap. "Sure is."

Elmer watched Tiny continue to make dinner and couldn't help but notice she still had pep in her step as she pulled the last of the chicken from the frying pan and mashed the potatoes.

"You're in a good mood," said Elmer.

"I am," said Tiny. "I talked to Dovie today."

"You did?" Elmer wondered how much he should broach the subject. He didn't want to ruin Tiny's good mood.

"Yes," said Tiny. She gave him a wink, "and as much as I hate to admit it, you were right. Not only did she not judge, she has some things for me to try."

"Well, it appears they are working," said Elmer.

"Actually, I haven't really started any of her suggestions," confessed Tiny. "Just knowing I'm not alone and there is help has put me in a great mood. Jeepers, Elm, I thought I was the only woman in the world who couldn't care for her kids. I thought I was broken. Dovie assured me I wasn't the first to feel this way after having a child, and I wouldn't be the last."

"So what do you need to do?" asked Elmer. "How can I help?"

"I'm glad you asked," said Tiny as she placed a platter of fried chicken on the table. "Dovie said rest is one of the biggest things, so she gave me some tea to drink at night to help me sleep. At first I told her I didn't need it because I sleep all the time. She said that sleeping all the time doesn't necessarily mean I was getting enough rest. But the tea is tricky, until I get the dose just right, I might not hear Sophie during the night, or I might be groggy in the morning. If you could help with Sophie and Benny, like you've been doing, until I figure out how much to drink that would help."

"I can do that," said Elmer. He looked at Benny. "Go wash up so we can eat."

Benny slid off his lap and ran to the back of the house where their bathroom was located. Elmer got up, helped Sophie lay on her back, and handed her a rag doll.

"What else?" Elmer asked.

"Mostly just be patient," said Tiny. "I have another tea to drink throughout the day to help with my emotions.

Jeepers, I'll probably be in the bathroom all day with all this tea I'll be drinking. Other than the teas, Dovie said it has a lot to do with routine. She said if I'm concentrating on my routine, it's harder to get bogged down. Just take one thing at a time, so in the mornings we'll get up, have breakfast, then after I clean up, we'll go to Quail Crossings. Dovie will watch the kids while I take a walk. She said getting some sun, moving around, and having a little peace and quiet during my walks will also help."

She put the potatoes on the table and then stopped. "Elm," she said softly.

"Yes?"

"Dovie also said this isn't a quick fix," confessed Tiny. "I may still have some bad days. The tea might not work for me, and we'll have to figure out something else."

Elmer walked over to Tiny and hugged her. "Don't you worry about that. I'm here as long as it takes."

Tiny burrowed her head into Elmer's chest. "I've been so awful. You'd have every right to run for the hills, but please don't ever leave me."

Elmer kissed the top of Tiny's head. "Never."

Chapter Thirty-two

July 29, 1950 – morning

Ellie shaded her eyes with her palm and looked around the pasture. She wanted to find some wild greens to make a salad for the big Saturday lunch, but the pasture held only dry, yellow grass that usually frequented their winters more than their summers.

She looked at the sky, hoping to see some rain clouds in the distance, but was met with only the light blue sky of the horizon.

Ellie dropped her hand and walked a couple of more steps, then froze. There, in the middle of the path, sat a large snake, sunning himself. Ellie's breath quickened, and she felt tightness squeeze her chest. She wanted to scream for someone to come help, but her lungs lacked air.

Flashbacks of looking down into the old water well full of rattlesnakes as the evil doctor held her over it, flooded her mind. She could see the doctor's wicked face sneering at her, as he called her the devil's child that needed to be cast down with the devil's serpent. She wanted to kick, bite, and hit the doctor so she could be free, but her arms and legs wouldn't move.

Ellie felt someone rush past her, snapping her out of her memory. It was Nicholas, and he was jogging right up to the snake. She wanted to warn him, but her body wouldn't follow her simple command to speak.

Nicholas slowed, then gently used his boot to pin the snake's head. Using very calculated moves, he reached down and picked up the snake right behind its head.

"You okay?" asked Nicholas, snake in hand. "It's just a bull snake. Bill taught me the difference on my first day at work. They're not harmful. Do you want to touch it?"

Nicholas held the snake out, and Ellie took a step back.

"All right," said Nicholas softly. "I'll go take it to the far pasture. Don't worry. You're okay now."

As Nicholas turned to take the snake farther into the pasture, Ellie felt her legs lose their shackles of fear. She couldn't believe Nicholas had saved her or figure out why. She hadn't been nice to him since he had come to Quail Crossings. As she was wondering if she should wait for him, a better idea flashed in her mind. Quickly she turned and hurried back toward the house.

Nicholas walked to the house after releasing the snake and knew he wasn't hiding his frustration very well. He could feel himself growing angrier with every step, but he couldn't figure out how to get Ellie to like him. Yes, he had stuck his foot in his mouth on more than one occasion and knew exactly why he was on her bad side. He couldn't figure out why he continued to stay there. She didn't even thank him after he took care of the snake.

"You okay?" asked Alice as she came out of the barn. "I swear I could hear you huffing from the orchard."

"I'm fine," snapped Nicholas.

Alice held up her hands in a peaceful gesture. "Fine, you don't want to talk about it. I get it. I'll go back to cleaning out the stalls."

"It's your sister," Nicholas blurted out.

"Evalyn?" Alice cocked her head. "What has she done?"

"No," said Nicholas. "Ellie."

"Ellie? She wouldn't hurt a fly," said Alice.

Nicholas walked closer to Alice and ran his hands through his hair. "Nothing really, it's just that I know I've said some stupid things around her and to her, but I've tried to make up for it. I can't seem to catch a break with her. Just now, I caught a bull snake in her path and took it to the far pasture because I could tell she was scared of it. I came back, and she was gone. She didn't even give me a nod of thanks. I don't think she'll ever forgive me."

"I don't think it's that," said Alice, biting her lip. She pulled Nicholas a little closer as if sharing a secret. "Five years ago, a doctor tried to throw her into an old water well full of rattlesnakes."

"A doctor?" Nicholas practically yelled.

"Shhh," said Alice. "Yes, and we don't talk about it because we almost lost Ellie. She stayed with the doctor's family for a time, and they accused her of being a child of the devil. His young child caught the house on fire, and even though Ellie saved both the child and the doctor's wife, the doctor and his brothers blamed Ellie beating her and putting her in the hospital. By sheer bad luck, he happened to move here as the county doctor. He tried to throw Ellie in the snake pit because he thought she was the spawn of Satan, but somehow the doctor fell in instead. While helping him out …:"

"Wait!" Nicholas shook his head. "She helped the man who beat her senseless and tried to kill her?"

"Yes," said Alice, "and she was bitten by a rattlesnake in the process."

"But you said Dovie saved Ellie from the mad man, the doctor, right?" said Nicholas looking very confused.

"She did," said Alice. "After Ellie pulled the doctor up, he tried to throw her into the well again. That's when Momma Dovie hit him with the butt of the shotgun."

"Wow," said Nicholas, again running his hands through his hair, "My Aunt Dovie did that? That's crazy …"

Before he could continue, Ellie propped open the front door with her hip and held out a very large basket of laundry. "Nicholas, is this all your laundry or is there more I need to wash?"

"If that's everything that was in the corner of my room, then that's all I have." Nicholas gave Alice a confused look.

Alice returned with a smile. "Looks like she's saying thank you in the only way Ellie knows how, working hard to make your life easier."

As Alice retreated to the barn, Nicholas jogged over to Ellie. "Here let me help you with that."

He took the large basket and carried it into the side room where the ladies did the laundry.

"I'm afraid I've gotten behind on my laundry. You really don't have to do this," said Nicholas eyeing all the dirty clothes.

"And you really didn't have to pick up that snake," said Ellie.

He sat the basket down, feeling guilt invade his body. He didn't know he had so many clothes, but he hadn't exactly been on top of the washing after Ellie went on strike.

"Alice told me why you're so afraid of snakes," confessed Nicholas as Ellie started to sort his laundry. "You are one brave and compassionate girl."

"I couldn't be like him," said Ellie flatly. "He would have left me to die down there." Her eyes glossed over, and Nicholas knew she was thinking about the pit. "I couldn't be like him," she repeated in a whisper.

He walked over and gently gave her a hug. "You are nothing like him."

He felt her shoulders relax into the hug, before she playfully pushed him away. "Stop getting sappy. I have work to do."

She continued to push him until he was out of the room and into the kitchen.

"Okay, okay," said Nicholas with a laugh. "Thank you."

"Nicholas," came James's voice from behind him. "What are you doing, son?"

Nicholas smiled at his grandpa. "Trying to convince Ellie not to do all my laundry. I'm quite embarrassed to say I've let it get away from me."

James looked into the room and smiled. "Well, it seems she's made up her mind. Have a seat, Nicholas. I want to talk to you before everyone gets here."

Nicholas did as he was told and began to get worried as James's earlier smile faded.

"Son, what I want to talk to you about is not an easy topic," James started. "I want to make sure you know I'm not trying to be mean but just wanting the truth. Regardless of what that truth may be, you will not be judged. You'll find no ill-will here."

"Okay," Nicholas said slowly.

James ran his hand through his gray hair. "Nicholas, why did you come to Quail Crossings?"

Nicholas relaxed a little. "I told you, Grandpa. I came because I want to run it someday. Of course, now I see it's a lot more than just bossing the hired hands around." Nicholas let out an awkward chuckle.

"Do you really want to run the farm, son? Or do you just want a portion of the profits?" asked James, bluntly.

"What?" Nicholas searched his grandfather's face for signs of a joke, but found no humor in James's light blue eyes.

"Look, Nicholas, if you're just here for what you feel is owed because you're family, I understand that. We can make arrangements," said James. "There's no reason you should have to stay here, doing work you don't want to do if that's the case."

Nicholas couldn't tell if he was more mad or hurt at James's statement. He knew he deserved the question. He drove onto Quail Crossings in his fancy car, ready to run the place. Anyone looking at the situation from the outside would think he was just a money-grubbing family member. Nicholas shook the thought away. He may have arrived that way, but he had done nothing but work hard, minus a few minor occasions, which he deeply regretted.

Dovie walked into the kitchen and stared at the two of them before releasing a huge sigh. "Oh Dad, you didn't. Everyone's pulling in the drive for our big Saturday lunch, and you choose now to ask him about his intentions."

Nicholas looked at his aunt. There was only one way she could have known what they were talking about, and it was because she, too, had questions about his intentions. "Do you feel this way too? That I just came here for money?"

Dovie hurried to Nicholas. "I'll admit, Dad and I have talked about it, but truthfully, neither of us knows. I thought we were going to give you until the end of summer to see if you liked it here before giving you an out."

"Well, I don't want out or your money," snarled Nicholas standing so quickly his chair fell over. He calmed his nerves and tried to steady his voice. "I've never wanted a hand-out, and I'll be the first to admit, I was an arrogant jerk when I arrived. But I thought I had proven myself since then. I thought I was finally becoming part of Quail Crossings, the way you all and the Brewers are."

Before Dovie or James could say anything else, Nicholas stormed out of the house and marched toward the barn.

Chapter Thirty-three

Alice hummed a little song as she mucked out Poppy's stall. The day was hot and she was glad to be inside the barn instead of out in the pasture in the full sun with Walter and Bill fixing the fence.

Nicholas stormed into the barn and kicked a bucket.

"Whoa," said Alice, coming out of the stall. "What in the world did Ellie do? Cut your shirts into shreds?"

"It's not Ellie," said Nicholas. He sat on a hay bale and put his head in his hands.

Alice walked over, sat beside him, and gently put her hand on his shoulder. She knew something big must've happened in the short time they had been apart, but she couldn't imagine what.

"What's wrong, Nicholas?" asked Alice.

"I've overstayed my welcome," said Nicholas. "I think it's time I left."

At his words, Alice's heart sank, and she felt panic creeping into her body. She grabbed his hand.

"What? Leave?" she shook her head. "Why?"

"My grandpa thinks I'm just here for money," said Nicholas. "He just offered me an out. Said we could make an arrangement. I don't even know what that means. Like I get a monthly allowance simply for being related?"

"Is that what you want?" asked Alice. Nicholas looked at her, pain written on his face. "Wait, what I mean is, do you enjoy working on the farm so much you want to make it your life's work? If you don't, then you *should* leave now."

Her heart panged at the words, "leave now" as her mind tried to sort out all her emotions. She wasn't supposed to like Nicholas, much less care if he was leaving, but she did. She liked him a lot more than she ever cared to admit.

"That's just it," said Nicholas, giving her hand a gentle squeeze before placing his other hand over hers. "I could see myself living here my entire life and never growing tired of it. I've grown to love it here."

"Then don't go," she whispered. "I know I don't want you to."

Alice found herself melting into his blue eyes just as she had done before after he fixed the tractor, but this time, she knew it was more than just respect for his initiative. Her heart raced, and she found herself leaning forward as Nicholas did the same.

Their lips met and fireworks erupted in her belly as lightening zipped through her body. She let go of Nicholas's hand and wrapped her arms around his neck as she leaned into him. He pulled her close, and Alice felt herself relaxing into his embrace.

Her mind raced. She was having her first kiss, and it was better than anything she had read in her novels and fairy tale books. As uncertain as she was about a lot of things regarding love, one thing was clear, she did not want the kiss to end.

"What's going on in here?" snapped Walter.

Alice quickly stood, letting go of Nicholas.

"Walter ... I ... um." Alice didn't know what to say. She didn't want to hurt Walter, but she knew she wanted to kiss Nicholas as much as Nicholas wanted to kiss her.

She felt Nicholas stand beside her. "Maybe we should all talk."

Walter balled his fists and rushed at Nicholas. "How dare you! How could you take advantage of Alice like that? Have you no decency?"

"No, Walter," was all Alice could say before he punched Nicholas in the jaw.

Nicholas stumbled back into the hay bales.

"Get up," demanded Walter.

Nicholas rose, rubbing his jaw. He held up his hands. "Okay, I understand you're upset, Walter and, in a way, I totally deserved that."

"You deserve a lot more than that," said Walter, punching Nicholas in the stomach.

"Walter, stop!" screamed Alice.

Walter didn't stop, and Alice was glad when Nicholas started fighting back. She didn't want them fighting at all, but she could hardly stand to see Nicholas taking all the punches. Nicholas landed a hard punch to Walter's face and matched it with another hard punch to Walter's side. Walter fell to one knee, and Nicholas took a few steps back and held up his hands.

"Stop it!" cried Alice. "Both of you cut it out right now!"

"I don't want to fight," said Nicholas, his lip bloody.

"Then you shouldn't have kissed my girl," snarled Walter as he got up and barreled his body into Nicholas's. The two men fell backwards, breaking through the wood that housed Bolt's stall. Alice let out a scream as the horse started to buck and kick. Bolt leapt over the men and ran right towards her.

Alice raised her hands, trying to get the frightened horse to stop, but it rammed her shoulder and knocked her to the ground.

In what felt like an instant, Lou Anne was kneeling beside Alice as Bill ran inside the barn. He grabbed a pail of water and threw it on Nicholas and Walter who were still rolling on the floor fighting.

"Knock it off, now!" demanded Bill. "Alice was almost trampled by Bolt due to your recklessness. Now get up. Y'all ought to be ashamed."

Nicholas got to his feet first and hurried to Alice.

"Are you okay?" he asked as he knelt beside her.

"I'm fine," said Alice as she rubbed her shoulder. She was sure there would be a bruise, but at least the horse hadn't dislocated it. She looked at Nicholas's face. His lip bled and he had a cut over one eye. The other eye looked like it would have a nice shiner. "Are you okay?"

"Stupid," answered Nicholas, "but okay."

Lou Anne and Nicholas helped Alice get to her feet as Walter exited the barn, also coming to her aid.

"Are you all right, Alice?" asked Walter. "Should I get Dovie?"

She could hear the edge in his voice but also his sincerity. Alice studied Walter. He had a cut on his cheek, chin, and arm, plus a busted lip. "Really, I'm okay. Thank you, Walter. Are you okay?"

Walter nodded but flinched as Alice tried to assess his cheek.

Nicholas stepped toward him and held out his hand. "I'm sorry I let it get that far, bygones?"

"Are you talking about the fight or kissing Alice?" snarled Walter.

"I'm sorry you saw that, and I'm sorry the fight happened...." Nicholas shook his head. "But I could never be sorry for kissing Alice."

Walter slapped Nicholas's hand away.

"I said knock it off, Walter," ordered Bill. "Or you're fired."

Nicholas took a step back. "I don't blame you for being mad. You should talk to Alice." He looked to Alice. "Whatever you decide, I'll respect."

Nicholas walked into the barn before coming out with a set of reins. He approached to Bill. "Bolt still have his halter on?"

Bill nodded.

"I'm gonna go see if I can track him down and clear my head in the process. I'm sorry for the damage to the barn. I'll help you fix it as soon as I get back, and I'll pay for any parts we need."

"He went that way," said Bill, pointing to the north. "I'll saddle up Pronto and start lookin' toward the northeast. Thankfully, Walter and I fixed the last of the fence today, so unless he jumps it, he should at least be on the property. Be careful, Nicholas, he's a lot tamer than he was, but he's far from broke."

Nicholas gave Bill a nod before jogging off toward the north.

"I had better go see to the kids. They saw Alice get hit, and I need to let them know she's okay," said Lou Anne as she eyed Walter. "Alice, do you want to come with me? Y'all could talk in the house."

Alice shook her head. She and Walter needed to speak privately. "Thanks, we're okay out here."

Lou Anne slowly turned and started toward the house. Alice was sure the rest of the clan was watching from the back screen door and the kitchen window. She was both relieved and embarrassed.

"Walter," Alice started slowly before her breath hitched. She had never meant to hurt him.

"It's okay, Alice," said Walter, the anger gone from his voice. "I'm sure you just got caught up in the moment. I forgive you."

"Forgive me?" Alice cocked her head.

"Yes," said Walter, "I'm sure Nicholas manipulated you in some way. That's all he's done since he's come to Quail Crossings. He can't be trusted. You must talk to James and have *him* sent back to New York City where his type belong. Once he's gone, we can be married."

"Married? Walter, I …," Alice started to protest but was distracted by Gabe, Elmer, and Robert hurrying outside. The men ignored Alice and Walter as they ran into the barn. She was sure Lou Anne had told them Bolt escaped and they were going to go help search for him.

"I love you, Alice," said Walter, taking advantage of her pause. He walked over and grabbed her hands. "I want to spend the rest of my life with you. Say you'll marry me, Alice. Say you love me too."

Alice looked into Walter's eyes and wanted to return his affection. He leaned down and kissed her, and she didn't back away. She wanted to feel the fireworks and lightning rushing through her body. She wanted desperately to tell Walter that she had romantic emotions for him, but as their kiss ended, Alice knew the truth. Her feelings for Walter did not go past friendship.

"Walter, I care about you an awful lot," said Alice, "but I'm afraid I don't love you in that way. I can't marry you. I'm so sorry."

Walter dropped her hands and paced before her. "It's Nicholas! He's turned you against me."

"No," said Alice, "Walter, I've never had romantic feelings for you. I've been clear about that from the beginning. This has nothing to do with Nicholas and everything to do with the fact that you refuse to listen to me. You keep saying you're waiting for me to have feelings for you, to see you in a romantic light, but no matter how many times I tell you I just want to be friends, you won't listen."

"I'm losing you to that Yankee?" Walter asked with disgust. "You're honestly going to pick him over me? You couldn't even stand him when he got here."

Alice shook her head. "No, Walter. I'm not picking you and I'm not picking Nicholas. I'm picking me."

"Fine," said Walter, the anger thick in his voice, "I think it's best if I leave on tomorrow's bus."

"You don't have to go," said Alice. "We can still be friends."

"No," said Walter, "I have never wanted to be just your friend, and I certainly won't stand by and watch you have feelings for another man." He cleared his throat. "Now, if you'll excuse me, I'm going to go see if I can help get Bolt back in before I pack my bags."

Alice felt her heart twist as Walter trudged toward the barn. Part of her wanted to call out and mend their broken friendship, but the other part of her knew she couldn't. She turned and started to walk toward the orchard, tears falling on her cheeks. She would never love Walter the way he needed her to. The kindest thing she could do was let him go.

Chapter Thirty-four

"What the devil is going on out there?" asked Dovie looking out the kitchen window towards the barn as Lou Anne entered the house. "Is everyone okay?"

"Alice is and that's all that matters. Walter and Nicholas were fighting," said Lou Anne, annoyance heavy in her voice. "They each have a few cuts and bruises, serves them right, but they're okay. Bolt got out when the boys rammed through his stall."

She walked to the doorway leading to the parlor. "Fellas, could you help Bill? Bolt got out and he could really use your help."

Gabe, Elmer and Robert hurried through the kitchen and out the back door.

"Leave Alice and Walter be, will ya?" Lou Anne hollered at the men.

"Jeepers," said Tiny.

"Lord, have mercy," said Dovie.

"You're kidding," said Evalyn. She turned to the children who were gathered in the kitchen deciding where to go and what to play. "Joy, you and the rest of the children go snap green beans in the parlor. Papa James had a big ol' bag in there. I bet if you help him he'll give you each a peppermint."

The kids rushed into the parlor, and as soon as they were all out of the room, the ladies rushed to the screen door to watch Alice talk with Walter.

"I can't hear anything," said Tiny.

"Should we go out there?" asked Evalyn.

"No," said Dovie, "let them have their privacy."

"You four looking out the screen door is letting them have their privacy?" Ellie teased from the sink, giving them a smile.

Dovie walked over and playfully hit her with a dish towel. "Like you aren't watching out this window?"

"Besides," said Lou Anne, still at the screen door with Evalyn and Tiny, "we've got to keep an eye out for Alice. This can't be easy on her."

"What started the fight?" asked Evalyn.

"Walter caught her and Nicholas kissing in the barn," said Lou Anne.

"What?" said Tiny with a gasp. "Our Alice was kissing a boy?"

"Ew," said Ellie. "Why would you want to kiss a boy?"

"Just you wait," said Dovie. "You might feel differently one day."

"Oh, and now she's kissing Walter," said Lou Anne with a bit of excitement.

"What has gotten into that girl?" said Dovie, marching back to the screen door. "I'm going out there to talk some sense into her. She can't be going around kissing both them boys."

"No, wait," said Evalyn. "Let them work things out."

"Jeepers, I've only ever kissed Elm in my entire life, and now here Alice is kissing two boys in one day," said Tiny. Dovie thought she heard a bit of awe in Tiny's voice.

The ladies watched as Alice broke away from the kiss. She and Walter exchanged a few more words before Walter turned to the barn and Alice headed to the orchard.

"I don't think that ended well," said Lou Anne. "They both look sad."

"Now, I'm going to go talk to her," said Dovie. "The roast is in the oven. Can you girls keep an eye on it and get started on the rest of the meal?"

"Of course," said Evalyn, "assuming Ellie hasn't already done it all."

She gave her sister a wink as Ellie stuck out her tongue.

Dovie stepped out on the stoop but stopped when she heard a car coming. It had to be Jacob and Leon since they were the only members of the family not yet there. She took another step and then stopped as Pastor Spaulding's car pulled into the drive instead of Jacob's truck. The pastor parked the car, then opened the door.

"Hi there, Dovie," said Pastor Spaulding with a huge smile. "You'll never guess who I found getting off the bus. Just about fell out of my loafers and had to give her a ride out here to see the look on your faces."

Dovie shaded her eyes from the sun and watched as the passenger door opened. The pastor hurried to the trunk to get something, momentarily obstructing Dovie's view. As he passed, Dovie let out a gasp. On the other side of Pastor Spaulding's car stood her one and only sister, June.

Walter lit a cigarette as he walked toward the north end of the pasture. He scanned the horizon, but he wasn't looking for Bolt like he had told Alice. He was looking for the only man who had ever taken anything from him.

He was hoping to find Nicholas before he teamed up with one of the other men. He wanted to talk to *him* alone.

His eyes narrowed as he spotted a figure over by the fence line fixing a wire and smiled when he realized it was Nicholas. Walter let out a puff of smoke as he looked around and felt relief when he didn't see another member of Quail Crossings nearby.

He picked up his pace and hurried to Nicholas. As if hearing him approach, Nicholas looked up and then stood firm. If Nicholas was intimidated by Walter's approach, he didn't show it.

"I bet you think you're something special," said Walter as he neared Nicholas. He took a large drag off his cigarette and ash floated to the ground.

"Walter, I don't want to fight again. It's up to Alice now. Please, be careful with that smoke," said Nicholas. "The pasture is really dry. You could light the whole place up."

"Shut up," snarled Walter. "I had the whole summer planned out to the letter. I'd come here and help Alice on Quail Crossings, and she would see how well I fit in. By the end of the summer, she'd finally look at me the way I've always wanted her to, and she'd agree to be my wife. From the moment I met her, I knew that I wanted her, but then you had to come along and take her."

"Walter," said Nicholas, "I'm sorry. I didn't mean for this to happen, but it did. I realize she's your friend. I know you care about her, so believe me when I say I love her. I'll treat her right ..."

"You love her?" laughed Walter wickedly. "You don't even know her! I'm the one who she should be with. Not you! She's mine."

Fury the likes Walter had never felt before took over his body. Rage coursed through his blood like a rabid animal. He could feel his heart pounding in his head as his hands curled into fists. He bit the end of his cigarette, barely aware it was even there, as he charged toward Nicholas.

"Walter, stop, your cigarette!" yelled Nicholas.

Walter didn't listen as he hurled his body at Nicholas for a second time that day. Nicholas caught Walter around the waist as Walter rammed into him. Nicholas let out a cry as his back slammed into the barbed wire fence.

Nicholas thrust his elbow up and connected with Walter's jaw. The two men froze and watched as the lit cigarette flew out of Walter's mouth and into the dry, thick weeds.

Chapter Thirty-five

Dovie's hand flew to her mouth as she took in the sight of her older sister. June's brown hair streaked with gray was cut short in a stylish bob that let her natural curls caress her face. She wore a navy blue, polka-dotted chiffon dress, shiny black low heels, and white gloves, looking as if she had just stepped out of the Sears catalog instead of off the bus.

June gave Dovie a wave as she took off her cat eye sunglasses. "You gonna just stand there on the stoop with your mouth agape, or are you going to come give your sister a hug?"

Dovie snapped her mouth shut and hurried down the steps to embrace the sister she hadn't seen in thirty-two years. They hugged each other tightly before June stepped back.

Pastor Spaulding hurried by with June's suitcase. "I'll just take this inside and then be on my way. Susan is waiting for me to go out to the Joel farm where they're having the big firehouse appreciation barbeque."

"Thank you, Pastor Spaulding," said Dovie.

"Let me look at you, little sister." June gave Dovie a big smile. "I swear you haven't changed a bit."

"Well, you have," said Dovie, "You're swankier than a T-bone on fine china. You look wonderful."

"Oh, this old thing," said June, swaying her skirt. "Now where is everyone? With all these cars parked here, you'd think you were having a party."

"Not a party," said Dovie, "just a big Saturday lunch with the whole family."

"You mean almost the whole family," corrected June, "since you couldn't have known I was coming."

"Oh gosh," said Dovie, stammering to find the right words, "I meant the Brewer bunch, all their kids, and Nicholas, of course."

"Where is that son of mine?" asked June with a frown. "I have a bone to pick with him."

"Is that why you're here?" asked Dovie. "Don't get me wrong, I'm so excited you've come. It's just that it's been a long time, and so much has happened that you didn't come home for."

"Of course it is," said June. "I've been worried sick. That little pup took off and didn't tell a soul where he was going. Nicholas's uncle was fit to be tied when he woke up and found his car missing. You don't want to know what I had to do to keep him from going to the police. Nicholas is a sweet, sweet boy, just wild and a bit lost." She eyed the red Packard convertible in the garage. "At least he's taken good care of it. I was glad to get your telegram. So quaint of you to send a telegram, by the way, when you could have just called."

"I didn't have your number," said Dovie.

"You didn't?" June started to take off her white gloves. "I was sure I gave it to you in the last Christmas letter. You know, Dovie dear, we should really correspond more than once a year. Now where is my boy?"

"He's out in the field. We had a horse get loose," said Dovie. "Don't you want to see Dad?"

June sighed. "Well, I guess it can't be helped since I'm here. It's not like I'll be able to avoid him."

"June," said Dovie, trying to bury her frustrations with her sister, "please give him a chance. He's always regretted giving you that ultimatum. It's been thirty-two years. Can't we let bygones be bygones?"

"Sister," June said flatly, "I'm not here to cause trouble. I just want my boy and the car. Until you've been asked to leave your home and never come back, don't you dare talk to me about letting bygones be bygones."

Dovie held up her hands in a peaceful gesture. "I don't want to fight. Come on in, there's a gaggle of people you need to meet."

"A gaggle of people." June laughed. "Dovie, you are just so cute. It's like you never stopped being eight-years-old."

Dovie wasn't sure if that was meant to be a compliment or an insult, but she decided to let it go. Big sisters teased little sisters; it was a way of life. All Dovie was concerned about was making sure June mended the bridge with their father, and if putting up with a little ribbing was the way to get the ball moving, she would put up with a hundred jabs.

As they turned and started toward the stoop, Dovie saw the girls scatter from the doorway. She was sure they were more curious than a cat near a mousetrap as to who June was. It would come as a surprise to everyone that the long lost sister had returned.

Walking up the stairs, Dovie wondered if her dad was strong enough for the reunion. He had a number of small strokes after his big one in 1945, and they were lucky that even though he moved and talked slower, he hadn't suffered more extensive damage. Dovie knew better than to lie to herself. James was not a young man anymore, and seeing June was going to be a shock to his system.

She opened the door to the kitchen and chuckled to herself as the girls looked busy. Ellie was stirring the beans on the stove, while Evalyn ran water over what looked to be a clean plate in the sink. Lou Anne and Tiny were sitting at the table, peeling potatoes and talking about the weather.

"Ladies," said Dovie, "I'd like you to meet my sister, June."

Everyone stopped and stared as Dovie rattled off all of their names.

"Nice to meet you," said June and the girls echoed with their own greetings. "Dovie, I had no idea you had such a houseful."

"Oh, just wait until their husbands and Alice get back inside," said Dovie. "It gets pretty cozy around here, so it's a good thing we like cozy. All the kids are in the parlor with Dad."

Before June could protest, Dovie lightly led, somewhat pushed, June through the kitchen into the parlor. James sat snapping green beans, the floor covered with eight children doing the same, while baby Sophie played on a blanket next to Joy.

"Cozy indeed," said June.

James looked up and lost his grip on the bowl of snapped beans causing it to roll off his lap and onto the floor.

"Papa James," the kids laughed and squealed as green beans scattered everywhere.

"June?" James asked as he struggled to stand.

"Yes, Dad, it's me." June held her arms open wide and with a big fake smile said, "I'm home."

Nicholas struggled to get out of Walter's grasp in order to stomp out the cigarette, but Walter wouldn't let go. Once again, Walter pushed Nicholas into the barbed wire, sending the sharp barbs into Nicholas's flesh. Warm blood trickled down his back as the fence broke under the weight of the two men.

Walter punched Nicholas twice before he was able to get his arms up to protect himself. He smelled the smoke and knew he had to act quickly. He grabbed Walter and threw his weight to the side, causing them both to roll over.

Now it was Walter's turn to cry out as the barbs tore into his back. Nicholas was thankful the wire hadn't rolled with him. Walter thrust up his hands as if to protect himself, but Nicholas didn't throw a punch. Instead, he quickly got off Walter and ran to the small fire the cigarette had started. He stomped at it with his boot.

"Help me stomp it out," yelled Nicholas to Walter, who was still on the ground. The fire was spreading quickly.

"It's too late," cried Walter as he got up and ran over, stomping fiercely. The fire quickly spread from one dry plant to the next. "We've got to get help."

Nicholas took off his bloody shirt, leaving only his white under shirt, and tried to beat down the fire. "No, we have to try and stop it. If we leave it'll grow out of control."

Walter started to cough. "We can't do it alone. I'm going for help."

"Okay. Go get help! I'll do what I can," yelled Nicholas, but it didn't matter. Walter was already running through the pasture and toward the house.

Nicholas continued to beat at the flames until his shirt caught fire. He let go of it quickly and again tried to stomp the fire out with his boot.

His feet grew hot and sweat poured from his body. A strong gust of wind blew in, fanning the flames and causing the fire to spread even faster. A deep fear arose in Nicholas as he looked up and saw the flames heading right towards the house.

Bill sat on Pronto and searched the pasture for Bolt, his heart trying not to sink at the thought of the stallion jumping over the fence. He had spent countless hours trying to tame the beast and had come to the sad conclusion that Bolt's last owner, had more than likely, been abusive.

The horse trusted no one, though he allowed Bill to get closer and Bill had even managed to get a blanket on him. Even if Bolt could never be ridden, Bill had already decided he wouldn't sell him. If nothing else, they could try studding him out. It might not work, but Bill knew if he sold the wild horse, no matter how beautiful he was, he'd end up in the slaughterhouse after being deemed un-rideable.

Bill turned to the north and saw a haze of white. At first he thought it was Bolt standing in the distance, but the more he looked, the more he realized, he was seeing smoke.

Bill turned Pronto toward the house and heeled him into a run. His heart raced. The sound of his heart beating quickly matched the thuds of Pronto's hooves hitting the ground. He prayed he was wrong and his eyes were playing tricks on him. He prayed that others were near the fire and could put it out quickly. But mostly, he prayed that Quail Crossings would still be standing come nightfall.

Chapter Thirty-six

Alice sat on the old bench in the orchard and let her tears fall. She hadn't meant to hurt Walter, but a part of her knew she had been letting him believe there could be a romantic relationship. He was her only friend in college, and she had been selfish in not wanting to lose him.

Norman waddled to the bench and let out a low honk. Alice patted the seat beside her, and as the old goose went to hop up, she helped by giving him a little boost. He sat beside her and laid his head in her lap.

"Oh, Norman," said Alice as she gently rubbed the goose's head. "I've really messed things up." Norman snuggled in closer. "I never once thought I'd have feelings for Nicholas. I wasn't lying to Walter when I told him I didn't want a romantic relationship. I really didn't think I did. There's just something about Nicholas that makes me feel …" Alice shook her head. "I don't know. It's like I've been looking for him my whole life but didn't realize it."

Alice looked at the ground. Hadn't that been what Walter wanted from her; for her to look at him and suddenly realize he was the thing she had always been looking for.

Norman raised his head quickly and let out a honk. He got to his feet and honked again, looking toward the north.

"What is …?" Alice didn't need to finish her question as the smell of smoke assaulted her nose. "Go, Norman, get in the barn."

Alice didn't wait to see if Norman followed her orders before she took off running toward the north pasture. As she broke through the trees of the orchard, she saw Walter running up the hill. He was breathing hard, his shirt was ripped, and he had traces of soot in his hair and below his nose. She looked past him and gasped as she saw smoke.

"Fire," Walter panted. He doubled over and placed his hands on his knees. Alice thought she could hear him wheezing. "Help."

"Come on," said Alice, putting her arm around Walter's waist and dropping his arm around her shoulder, so she could carry some of his weight. "We need to get the others. You okay?"

"I'm okay," said Walter, catching his breath, "but Nicholas is still out there."

"What?" asked Alice, standing tall.

"It spread too quickly," said Walter. "We couldn't put it out ourselves."

"Go! Ring the bell and get help!" Alice released Walter and took off running toward the north pasture, straight into the path of the fire.

"My June," James said again. A wide smile extended across his face as he stood in front of his chair in the parlor looking at his estranged daughter.

"Children, make room," said Dovie and the kids parted like the Red Sea, making room for James to walk through.

"Now, Dad, be careful," ordered June.

"I'm fine," said James as he finally made it to her, "I'm better than fine."

He wrapped his arms around her and squeezed her tightly. His heart did somersaults as tears formed in his eyes. James wanted nothing more than to be the strong father June had last seen, but he felt his strength crumble as his long, lost daughter embraced him. He started to sob.

As James reluctantly released June and took a step back, he pulled his handkerchief out of his pocket and dried his eyes. He noticed Dovie was ordering the children outside to play while Tiny was taking Sophie into Dovie's room, probably to lay her down for a nap.

"Sit, please," said James, feeling embarrassed as he noticed the green beans on the floor that the children hadn't picked up. "Sorry about the mess."

"Oh, don't worry about it," said June, looking around the parlor before sitting on the sofa. "Gosh, other than new curtains, the place hasn't changed at all. You would have thought Dovie would have modernized it a bit. I feel like I've stepped back to 1918."

Dovie clicked her tongue. "While I'm sure it's nothing like living in New York City, we have modernized. We added on a bathroom with indoor plumbing, not to mention, we have a telephone and an electric washing machine. Oh, yes, and we have a plane. Did I mention I went to Hawaii on my honeymoon? My husband, Gabe, he's a pilot, a bona fide war hero."

"A plane? Hawaii?" June cocked her head. "What do you mean?"

"Dovie, hon, can I speak with June alone please?" James asked as he sat by June on the sofa, purposefully interrupting. He didn't mean to be rude to Dovie, but the last thing he wanted was to have his girls debate who was more modern. He had been waiting thirty-two years for this moment.

"Of course, Dad," said Dovie. "I'll be in the kitchen if you need me."

James waited until Dovie left the parlor. He looked at June, sitting on the edge of the sofa with her shiny leather purse on her lap. His heart ached as he realized she looked more like a guest than a family member.

She turned and caught him staring at her. She fanned herself. "It's so hot. I forgot how hot it gets out here."

"I'm so glad you came," said James.

"I'm here for Nicholas," said June flatly. "He just left one morning. I thought he had gone out to get a job, but he never came back. I've been worried sick and probably still would be if Dovie hadn't sent me that telegram. Really, Dad, you ought to have phoned me the minute he arrived."

James nodded. "I'm sorry. I didn't mean for you to worry. I guess I hoped that you sent Nicholas."

"Why would I send Nicholas here?" asked June.

"To reclaim part of your home," James said more than asked.

"This isn't my home," said June, her voice soft. "This is the place where I grew up. New York City is my home."

James's eyes fell to the floor. "June, honey, I understand why you feel that way."

He looked up and thought he could see tears in June's eyes. He reached over and grabbed his daughter's hand. "Look at me, honey."

June slowly shifted so she was facing James. He confirmed she was, indeed, shedding soft tears. He squeezed her hand gently.

"I have one regret in life," he said. "That I can never take back those awful words I said to you before you went off to marry David Banner. The minute they flew out of my mouth, I regretted them, but I was a proud, stupid man back then and wouldn't let myself take them back. I am so sorry I said them. I can't imagine how hurtful they were to you. I was so wrong to say you could never come back here. I'm gonna say what I should've said thirty-two years ago. Our door is always open to you, no matter what. I love you, June. Your momma loved you, and I know Dovie loves you."

Tears were falling freely by both June and James. He reached up with his free hand and gently wiped a tear from her cheek. "I want you to be happy. I always did. Now I know that means even if you leave home with a boy I believe isn't good enough for you. If he makes you happy, then so be it. You are always welcome here, and our arms will be open wide. We love you."

"Oh Dad," said June as she wrapped her arms around him, "I'm sorry too. I should have never slammed that door in your face when you came to visit after Mom died." She pulled away so she could look at him. "I was so hurt, I didn't get to say goodbye to her, so I just pretended it didn't happen. If I had let you in, then I couldn't pretend any more. Then all that hurt would come rushing in. I couldn't bear it."

"Why didn't you come?" asked James. "We telegrammed when she got sick."

"David wouldn't let me." June looked at the floor. "Dad, you were right about him. I always knew I could come back, always knew you and Mom would love me just the same. It was David that made the ultimatum stick. I tried to come back when Mom got sick and then again when Dovie lost her family. He caught us. The first time he caught me, I couldn't get out of bed for a week, he hurt me so bad. The second time, he took it out on Nicholas, who was just eight at the time, because he looks like you." June choked back a sob. "He beat Nicholas so badly, I didn't think he was going to live, and David wouldn't let me take him to the hospital. I prayed to God if He let Nicholas live, I'd never try to leave again. I kept that promise."

"June, hon, why didn't you try to call us or write?" asked James. "I would have come to get you and my grandchildren."

"We didn't have a phone until after David passed in '46. He never gave me money of my own, so I couldn't even buy postage, much less send a telegram. Dad, he even went to the store with me, so I couldn't talk to anyone else. That was part of the reason I closed the door on you. I didn't want to accept that Mom was gone, but also I was afraid of what David would do if he found you there."

James gave June another hug, wishing he had sat on the stoop longer in New York City, even after the police told him to leave. Had he known what his daughter was going through, he would have shown David Banner a thing or two about how to treat June.

"So after he hurt Nicholas, and until David died," June continued. "I just did what he wanted so he didn't hurt me or the kids. We just pretended to be a perfect family." She gave James a small smile. "Nicholas had a lot of nightmares after his dad hurt him, and the only thing that would calm him down were the stories about Quail Crossings. I'm not surprised he came here. I'm glad he did."

"Me too," said James. "Are we okay now, June? Do you think you can forgive this stupid old man?"

"Oh, Daddy," June cried, "only if you can forgive this stubborn little girl."

"Always," said James.

June placed her head on James's shoulder as James wrapped his arms around his eldest daughter. As he cradled the daughter he thought he'd never see again, he looked to the ceiling and thanked God. His heart grew light having been relieved of his thirty plus year regret. He could feel joy pulse throughout his body.

Chapter Thirty-seven

"Fire!" came a voice from the kitchen.

June sat up. "What?"

Bill ran into the parlor followed by Dovie. Lou Anne grabbed the telephone and told the operator to send the fire department.

"There's a fire in the north pasture," said Bill. "I met up with the other fellas in the field, and they're loading up the truck with buckets, gunny sacks, and shovels."

June helped James to his feet.

"I'll drive the truck," said James.

"We're using Jacob's truck," said Bill, "so he can drive. Elmer and I will take the tractors out and plow a break. Lou Anne will be in Elm's truck, so we've got it handled right now. Evalyn's filling the old water trough and wash tub with water from the pond. That'll take a while, so we'll go on out there with smaller buckets, and everyone else will follow once the trough and tub are full."

Dovie hurried back into the kitchen spatting orders, "Ladies, grab every bucket, pot, pan, and bowl you can find."

June started towards Dovie's room.

"Where are you going?" asked James.

"To change," said June. "So I can help. Dovie, do you have some clothes I could use?"

"On the shelf in the closet," Dovie hollered from the kitchen. "Bandanas are in the top drawer of the bureau."

June hurried to change as Lou Anne hung up the telephone. "Bad news, the fire department is out at the Joel farm for the appreciation barbeque, and they don't have a telephone. Operator said it'll take a bit for someone to drive out there and get everyone."

"Momma Dovie," Ellie cried as she ran into Dovie's arms. James could see panic etched on her face as well as the burn scars on her hand and arm. The wildfire had to be bringing up very scary memories for her.

"It'll be okay, Ellie," said Dovie. She turned to Tiny. "Tiny, get the children in Evalyn's car and have Dean run to the orchard and get Alice. She's probably on the old bench." Dovie turned back to Ellie. "I want you to take the children to Rockwood. Okay? You'll be safe there. Can you do that? Can you watch the children for us?"

"What about you, Momma Dovie?" sobbed Ellie. "I'm scared. Come with us."

Dovie pulled Ellie in for a tight hug. "Ellie, honey, I have to stay here. I've got to start hosing off the house and barn, understand? I need you to be brave now and take care of the children. If the fire comes anywhere near here, I'll leave. I promise."

"Okay," Ellie said weakly. She wiped her eyes and stood taller. "Okay, I'll take the kids to Rockwood. I love you, Momma Dovie. I just need to grab something from my room."

"I love you, too, Ellie," said Dovie, as Ellie ran up the stairs to her room. "Hurry, okay?"

"I'll start calling around and see if anyone else can come help," said James.

"The operators is probably already doin' that," said Tiny as she ran through the kitchen with Sophie.

Ellie ran back down the stairs and thrust her rag doll into Dovie's hands. "Lovey will keep you safe, just as she did me for all those years."

James stood in the doorway leading to the parlor. He watched as Dovie looked down at the doll as if it were her most prized possession, and Ellie ran out the door to get the children to safety. He had never felt as helpless as he did now, watching his family gather all the supplies necessary to fight the fire. There was a time when he would have been the first one out the door, but now all he could do was pray.

"Alice, stop," yelled Walter.

Alice didn't stop. She couldn't. Nicholas was fighting a wildfire by himself. He was in danger and all she could think was … *Save him! Save him! Save him!*

A hand reached out and grabbed her shoulder, pulling her to an abrupt stop. The strong panhandle wind whipped through her hair, and she fought to keep it out of her face as she glared at Walter.

"What are you doing, Walter?" Alice cried. "Nicholas is out there!"

"I know," said Walter, as he pulled her close, "and I'm not going to let you run right into a fire to try and save him. You're not acting smart, Alice. You need to go back to the house, get help, and then stay put. I'll go back and help Nicholas, now that I know you'll alert the others."

Alice struggled to get free of Walter's grasp. "Let me go. I will not sit at home while everyone else is out fighting the fire."

"Oh for goodness sake, we're wasting time," said Walter. He swooped Alice up, threw her over his shoulder, and started walking back toward the house. "The only girl I know that thinks she can fight a fire bare handed wearing a dress and loafers."

Alice fought the urge to hit Walter on his back, but he was right. She had to get supplies. She couldn't run into a fire empty-handed and expect to help Nicholas. She would only be in the way.

"Okay, you're right. Put me down," she huffed, straightening herself up to wiggle out of Walter's grip.

"You won't run off?" asked Walter.

"No," said Alice. Walter put her down. "Like I said, you're right. It won't help Nicholas for me to go running in there without thinking. We'll get the others and then go back out there. But don't think for one second that I'm going to sit at the house and wait. It's gonna take everyone."

"Fine," said Walter.

Alice picked up her pace and started to run toward the house. She was glad to see Jacob had his truck full and was already headed out to the fire with Gabe and Robert. Bill and Elmer were following behind with the tractors and plows. She made a mental note to give Nicholas another big hug for fixing the old tractor. They would need it. Dovie and the ladies were busy filling Elmer's truck with pots and pans of water.

"Alice, honey," cried Dovie when she saw her run out of the orchard. "I'm so glad you're okay. We were so worried when we couldn't find you. Ellie just left with the kids, but take another car and go to Rockwood, would you?"

Alice noticed Lovey, Ellie's doll, in the pocket of Dovie's apron and considered how scared her sister must be knowing there was a wildfire so close to home. As much as she wanted to be with her sister, she wanted more to preserve the only real home Ellie had ever known ... that she had ever known.

"I will not," said Alice. "I'm going upstairs to change, and then I'm headed out to help Nicholas. He's out there alone."

"What? Oh, dear Lord, Nicholas!" A lady Alice didn't know hurried up behind Dovie, her face pale.

"Alice, this is June, Nicholas's mother," Dovie said quickly, then turned to June. "I'm sure he's fine. He's a smart, strong boy and the men are on their way out there."

"I'm gonna go change," said Alice. "Don't leave without me."

Alice hurried up the back stoop and into the house praying Nicholas was okay. She raced up the stairs and quickly changed into an old shirt and jeans. She grabbed a handful of bandanas out of her drawer and stuffed them in her pocket before sliding her feet into her boots. She ran downstairs, out the back door, and grabbed the last pile of gunny sacks as she jumped into the back of Elmer's truck with Walter and Tiny. Lou Anne was in the driver's seat with June and Evalyn sharing the cab of the truck.

"Y'all be careful out there," ordered Dovie. "I'll send out reinforcements when they get here and start watering down the house. God be with us all."

Nicholas continued to stomp at the fire. The ends of his blue jeans were singed off, and he wasn't sure how much longer his boots would last. His feet felt as if they were walking through boiling water. He had tried to pull the weeds in the path of the flames to make a break of some kind and slow the fire down, but it spread too quickly.

He backed from the fire as a coughing spasm took over his chest. His lungs burned and his throat ached. It felt as if his insides had been scorched. Taking his bandana out of his back pocket, he tied it around his nose and mouth and chastised himself for not thinking of doing it sooner. His mind had been focused on one thing, to get the fire out.

He heard the rumble of a truck and looked up to see Jacob driving over the prairie towards the fire. He could see Bill and Elmer on tractors behind the truck. Bill started off towards the far end of the fire as Elmer plowed towards him.

All the other men, except for James and Walter, seemed to be in the truck with Jacob. Nicholas let out a cheer as helped came closer. He wished Jacob would drive faster, but knew he was probably trying not to spill all the water out of the containers in the back.

As they approached, Gabe was the first to jump out of the back of the truck and run to Nicholas. "You okay?" he asked.

Nicholas nodded. "I'm sorry."

"Sorry?" Gabe cocked his head as Robert got out and started to beat the flames with a wet gunny sack.

"The fire," stammered Nicholas. "Walter had a cigarette. I tried to warn him, but he tackled me with it in his mouth, and I hit him in the chin causing it to hit the ground. I'm so sorry."

"We'll talk about it later," said Gabe. "Get in the back of the truck and keep those gunny sacks soaking. Get a drink, too. I'm not sure if you were brave or stupid for staying out here alone, but I'm glad you're okay."

"I'm not sure either," said Nicholas.

Nicholas ran to the truck. His body cramped and his legs felt as if they had turned to jelly. His whole body shook as the gravity of the situation hit him. The fire was headed straight south, toward Quail Crossings. It had spread to at least a mile in length eating up acre after acre of dry grass and weeds.

He scrambled into the back of Jacob's truck, as Jacob drove slowly to keep pace with the men and the fire. He grabbed a tin cup, filled it from one of the buckets, and then dumped it over his head, trying to clean his eyes of soot. He filled the cup again and drank. Even with his raw throat making it hard to swallow, water had never tasted so good. It was as if he hadn't had a drink in decades.

He filled his cup again as Robert came to get a fresh gunny sack. Nicholas spent the next half hour resting and handing out sacks. Then Robert jumped in to take a break, while Nicholas and Gabe tried to beat the fire back.

Soon Lou Anne showed up in Elmer's truck with Evalyn, Alice, Walter, Tiny, and … Nicholas blinked hard as his mom hurried out of the truck.

Chapter Thirty-eight

July 29, 1950 – early afternoon

Alice released a sigh of relief as she watched June run across the dry grass to Nicholas and engulf him in a hug. She fought the urge to do the same and felt some tension leave her body with the knowledge that Nicholas was all right.

She grabbed one of the gunny sacks soaking in the old tin wash tub, hopped to the ground, and ran straight toward the fire. Bill and Elmer were making good time on the break, but it was still far from being completed.

The gunny sack was heavy with water. Alice wondered if she had made a mistake by not going to Rockwood. She shook the thought away as she approached the flames. She felt as if she were walking on the sun. She started to beat at the flames and heard the fire pop and sizzle in protest. Soon Walter was beside her, also with a wet gunny sack.

They beat the fire with all their might for what felt like an eternity before retreating back to Jacob's truck to resoak the sacks. June headed back to the house in Elm's truck to refill the trough and washtub. Alice jumped in the back of Jacob's truck with Nicholas and Gabe, who were drinking water.

"Alice and Walter, take a break. Drink plenty of water, we've got the clean bucket in the corner," ordered Gabe, grabbing a shovel and handing another to Nicholas. "Then here in a bit, give Robert and Evalyn a break. Keep alternating so no one gets too worn out."

Alice didn't argue as Nicholas and Gabe jumped out of the truck. Her arms felt heavier than lead, and her lungs started to burn. She handed a fresh gunny sack to Evalyn. Walter sat in the bed of the truck with his head in his hands as Alice handed a bucket of water to Robert.

"Walter, get up and help," Alice commanded, as she handed a gunny sack to Tiny. "We need you."

"I can't move," said Walter. "The fire's too hot. We can't stop it."

"We don't have any other choice but to try," said Alice, "If we don't, Quail Crossings and everything around will burn."

"Walter!" Robert ordered from the side of the truck. "Get off your rear and fill the buckets."

Evalyn jumped into the back of the truck, holding her wrist. Walter wiped his eyes, pushed himself up from the bed of the truck, and filled a bucket to hand to Robert.

"Evalyn, are you okay?" asked Robert, concern plastered on his face.

"Evie," cried Alice as she scurried to Evalyn.

"The fire just got my wrist a bit." She looked at her husband. "Really, I'm fine. Do what you need to do."

Robert reluctantly returned his attention to the fire.

"Let me see," said Alice.

Evalyn uncovered her wrist and revealed a nasty red burn. "It's nothing. I've had worse frying chicken."

"Liar," said Alice. "You should go to the house and have Dovie look at it."

"I will when the fire is out," said Evalyn.

"Fine," Alice said with a huff, knowing she'd say the same thing if their places were reversed. "Then at least clean it. I'll go help on the line."

"Be careful," said Evalyn.

"Always," said Alice, giving her sister a quick peck on her cheek.

Alice grabbed a wet gunny sack and ran beside Nicholas who was shoveling dirt on top of the fire with all his might. He had been fighting the fire longer than any of them, but Alice knew he wasn't holding back.

"Are you holding up okay?" asked Alice.

He gave her a weak smile. "What? You think we city boys can't handle a little heat?"

Alice tried to return his smile. He was exhausted, and she knew it. They all were. Even with his joking, Alice could tell Nicholas wouldn't stop. His brow was furrowed with determination, and Alice was sure, no matter how futile the task seemed, he'd fight to the end for Quail Crossings.

She looked back to Jacob's truck to check on Walter, and her heart swelled with disappointment as she saw him sitting once again with his head in his hands.

Knollwood's two fire trucks raced down the back driveway, and Dovie felt her heart leap at the sight. George and Ben Wheaton were right behind them with their tractor and a half-dozen farm hands. Behind them a line of cars, tractors, and pickup trucks trailed. They were filled with people willing to help, and Dovie figured the whole town of Knollwood was pulling into her drive.

She directed the firemen toward the fire line, and turned to see Kathleen Wheaton and a slew of women setting up food and water stations on the picnic tables. Dovie could only imagine how hungry her family was as they hadn't eaten since early morning.

Dovie hurried inside and grabbed the roast from the oven. She took it outside. "We can make sandwiches with this. I also have some baked beans ready."

"Oh, Dovie, sweetie, are you okay?" asked Kathleen, placing a basket of bread on the table.

"I will be once this fire is out," said Dovie. "Can you tend to things here? I want to hose off the barn."

"Of course," said Kathleen.

"Thanks, just help yourself to anything you need in the house," Dovie said to the women.

She ran toward the barn and grabbed the long hose, thankful it was already hooked to the faucet. She pulled the handle of the faucet all the way up to get the most water pressure available and started to hose off the back side of the barn. Soon, Pastor Spaulding was beside her holding another hose, helping to wet the barn. Dovie wasn't sure where the other hose came from, but she was sure thankful for it.

"Didn't think you'd see me so soon again, did you?" he said with a smile.

"On any other occasion I'd say it was delightful to see you again," said Dovie. She glanced at the fire. It was so close now, she could see the flames licking the air as everyone worked hard to put it out. She could make out each one of her family members as they either beat, watered down, or tried to snuff the fire out. A sense of pride engulfed her as she watched how hard everyone was working. One thing was certain, Quail Crossings wasn't going down without a fight.

Nicholas heard Gabe and Robert let out a cheer as the fire trucks rolled in front of the fire. Instantly, the trucks started to spray the fire with their large hoses. He heard a tractor coming from his right and saw George Wheaton plowing near the far end of the fire. A half dozen men jumped out of the back of the Wheaton truck, driven by George's son, Ben. They started shoveling dirt onto the flames. Truck after truck kept coming, and Nicholas couldn't help but feel hopeful the whole ordeal would soon be over.

He wondered if his arms would fall plum off if he let himself stop and think about how tired he was. Every muscle in his body ached as he continued to try and snuff out the fire with dirt.

As he stepped backward, he found his boots sinking into freshly plowed dirt and knew he was at the fire break Bill and Elmer had plowed. He looked up to see Bill starting to plow another fire line about fifty yards away and Elmer starting to plow by the fence line heading toward the barn. Even though he knew another fire line was a smart move, he hoped they wouldn't need it.

Something white moving in the distance caught Nicholas's eye as he continued shoveling dirt on the fire. He squinted through the smoke and ash. His eyes were dry and burned like crazy, but he was sure he wasn't seeing things.

Bolt stood on a small hill just to the east. The white horse reared and bucked. Nicholas ran in the horses' direction. He stopped short as he realized Bolt was bucking, not because he was a wild horse, but because he was surrounded by flames.

Nicholas picked up his pace and ran toward the horse. He hurried along the fire line passing men as they shoveled the freshly plowed dirt on top of the fire.

"What's the rush?" yelled Ben from his truck.

Nicholas stopped and jogged back to Ben. "Do you have a lead rope and a blanket? We've got a horse trapped in the field."

"You're in luck. I just happen to have both," said Ben, "Hop in."

Nicholas jumped into the bed of the truck as it picked up speed.

"Where's he at?" hollered Ben.

"Over by the draw," said Nicholas.

As they neared Bolt, Ben stopped the truck, and Nicholas jumped out. Ben handed him the rope and blanket through the window. "How do you reckon you'll get over there?"

Nicholas studied the fire and terrain. It was a miracle Bolt had found a spot the fire left untouched. There were no breaks in the fire that surrounded the horse, that much was certain.

Nicholas tucked the rope under his arm and threw the blanket over his shoulders. "Guess I'm going through it."

"Look," said Pastor Spaulding, "the fire's at the plow break. I think it's stopped."

Dovie shielded her eyes from the sun to look but kept her hose pointed firmly at the barn. The water pressure was faltering around the house, which made her even more thankful for the help. She could see the firemen spray their hoses as countless people, including her family, either beat at the flames with wet sacks, shoveled dirt, or poured water onto the flames. Pastor Spaulding was right, it looked like they had the upper hand.

Just as Dovie's heart started to leap with joy and a smile began to creep on her face, the wind blew hard and she watched in terror as the fire stirred high up in the air. It danced in the wind like a small flaming tornado, and then landed on the other side of the fire break.

The gusts continued, and the flames picked up speed, racing straight toward the barn with the entire firefighting team of men and women stuck in-between the two fires.

"Oh, dear Lord," cried Dovie.

"They'll be okay," said Pastor Spaulding as the wall of fire rushed toward them.

"My family ...," Dovie cried, looking at Pastor Spaulding, "... just about everyone I love is out there in the middle of those two fires."

The pastor put down his hose and grabbed Dovie's hand. "I know you're scared, but right now we've got to get all these people out of here. The fire is headed straight for us."

Dovie nodded and the two of them ran toward the house.

"Kathleen," Dovie cried, "get the women and James and get out of here. The fire's headed toward the house. It jumped the break."

"Oh no," cried Kathleen and Dovie knew she was also worried because Kathleen's husband and son were both fighting the fire.

"Ladies," Dovie hollered toward the women setting up food for the fire fighters, "the fire is headed this way and fast. Y'all need to get on out of here. It's not safe."

"Kathleen," Dovie gently grabbed her friend's hand, "you have to listen to me. I know you're scared. So am I, but I need you to get Dad out of here. I'm going to stay and get the animals out of the barn and then start hosing down the house."

"I'm not going anywhere," said James as he gingerly walked down the back stoop.

"Neither am I," said Kathleen squaring her shoulders.

Dovie stared at her father and friend in disbelief. "You have to. The fire, it's coming."

"You can't do it alone," said Kathleen.

"Kathleen's right," said Pastor Spaulding. "I've sent the other ladies to the Two Dot Ranch. They should be out of the path of the fire there."

Dovie placed her hands on her hips, ready to tell the lot of them to get going, but couldn't. She knew they were right. She couldn't hose down the barn and the house alone. She gave them a nod. "All right, let's get busy then."

Chapter Thirty-nine

Alice watched in horror as the fire jumped the break line. Half the pickups and one of the fire trucks immediately sped forward to get ahead of the new fire. The others kept working on the original fire. Alice wiped the sweat from her brow. If she had felt she was in an oven before when fighting just the single fire, standing between the two made her feel as if she had stepped into Hell itself.

She handed June the gunny sack to soak and grabbed a cup full of water from the back of Jacob's truck. Her throat ached, and her chest burned. She wished the drink would put out the fire in her lungs, but she still felt the pain even after the cold water.

"Have you seen Nicholas?" June asked.

"Yes," said Alice as she looked in the direction of where she had been fighting before, but Nicholas was gone. "Well, he was just over there. He must have gone with the other men to fight the new fire."

June gave her a nod as Alice grabbed a bucket of water and rushed back to the fire line. She threw her water on the fire and felt as if she were trying to catch the wind. No matter what they did, the fire still raged on.

Running back to the truck, Alice handed her empty bucket to June and grabbed a full bucket. As she threw her bucket of water on the fire, she heard a loud pop and crack that was different than the sound of grass burning. She looked over just in time to see flames run up the side of a tree in the orchard.

Alice visualized the old bench that James had built for his wife, Sylvia, and then her thoughts turned to Norman. She had left Norman sitting on the bench. She looked over her shoulder. Jacob's truck was already a few yards ahead. Alice thought about running and getting help, then shook her head.

She cupped her hands around her mouth and yelled. "I'm going to the orchard to get Norman!"

She tossed the empty bucket down and ran for the trees. She wasn't planning on fighting the fire in the orchard, just seeing to it that Norman was in a safe place. She ran hard, picking her knees up so she wouldn't trip in the freshly plowed dirt.

She ducked between the rails of the wooden fence and ran into the orchard.

"Norman!" she hollered. "Norman!"

She ran deeper into the orchard until she had reached the bench. Norman was lying under the bench, head tucked under his wing. Alice ran to the bird.

"Norman, you silly goose, there's a fire coming," Alice nudged the bird, but he didn't move.

"Norman?" Alice felt her heart sink as she nudged her feather friend again, and again he didn't stir.

Ben handed Nicholas a shirt. "Here, you'll need all the protection you can get."

Nicholas looked down and realized he was still only in his undershirt. He'd been so focused on fighting the fire, he hadn't given a second thought to the shirt he'd lost while trying to beat out the fire when it first began. He shrugged on Ben's shirt but was unable to button it up.

Wrapping the blanket over his head and shoulders, Nicholas readied himself for the jump. He really wished he had thought to soak the blanket before rushing out to save the horse, but there wasn't time for that now.

Nicholas looked to the sky. "Dear Lord, don't let me die being stupid," he muttered before taking a deep breath and went half running-half leaping through the flames. He felt the fire lick his pant legs. The intense heat made him feel as if he might pass out. His boots hit the ground hard, and he somersaulted to a stop.

He looked at his jeans and was relieved to see they hadn't caught fire. He stumbled to his feet, not wanting to get trounced on by Bolt who was still bucking and rearing.

He tucked the blanket under his arm, held Ben's lead rope in his other hand, and slowly approached the horse.

"Whoa there, Bolt," said Nicholas in a soothing voice, holding up his hands. "I'm here to help, but I can't do that if you keep bucking. Whoa now, I know you're scared buddy, so am I. Whoa now."

The horse still danced but had stopped his rearing and bucking.

"That's it, boy," said Nicholas walking slowly to the stallion. "Let me just get this rope on your halter, and we'll get you out of here."

Bolt steadied as Nicholas gently clipped the lead rope to his halter. Nicholas made a mental note to thank Bill for all the hard work he had put into green breaking the horse.

A month ago and Bolt would have stomped him to death for even attempting to clip on a lead rope.

The fire inched toward them as the wind stirred, and again, the horse reared.

"Whoa," hollered Nicholas as he grabbed the lead rope with both hands. The blanket dropped to the ground and Nicholas knew what he had to do. As Bolt steadied again, Nicholas carefully reached down and picked up the blanket. Walking slowly, but deliberately, Nicholas went to Bolt's side, shook the blanket gently, releasing it of its folds, and then slowly tossed the blanket over the horse's head, using it as blinders.

Bolt's dance slowed, and the horse calmed.

"That's it, boy," said Nicholas. He looked around, trying to find a spot where the fire had died down enough to allow passage through. He knew he wouldn't have the protection of the blanket now. Spotting a place where the flames looked low enough to jump, Nicholas ran towards it. Bolt hesitated, causing Nicholas to pull harder on the lead rope.

The horse followed, and Nicholas picked up his pace. As he approached the fire line, he closed his eyes, threw his arm over his face, and leapt through the flames. He could feel the rope grow taught as Bolt reared, then jumped over the fire. Nicholas kept running until he felt the force of something hit him. He opened his eyes to see Ben slapping the flames out of his shirt. He could feel the burn on his right arm.

"That was about the dumbest thing I've ever seen," said Ben.

"Ahh, you're just mad I ruined your shirt," joked Nicholas. "Come on, let's get this guy back to the barn."

James held onto the stoop railing as he hosed down the backyard of Quail Crossings. The area was muddy and pretty much saturated, but James kept the hose moving. He walked a few steps past the stoop and sprayed the hose near the garage until he got tired. Then went back to the stoop to rest. He knew he wasn't covering much ground and his hose was down to a trickle, but he wasn't just going to sit around and watch as everyone else fought the fire.

He looked at the barn as Pastor Spaulding and Kathleen hosed down the barn and corrals. Elmer plowed near the barn, making an additional fire break as Dovie tried to saddle Pronto. The horse danced as the fire neared, but good ol' Tex, whom Dovie had already saddled, stood still and alert. This wasn't Tex's first fire, and he was trained not to panic.

Poppy and Marigold, the milk cows, were tied to a nearby tree as the chickens roamed the yard freely. A couple of ranch hands from the Two Dot Ranch had loaded up the pigs to take them to safety and were headed to check on the cattle herd next to make sure they stayed out of the path of the fire. They already had permission from James to cut the fence and herd them into the next pasture if they needed. James hoped they wouldn't need to.

James caught movement out of the corner of his eye and looked over in time to see Walter stumble out from behind the garage.

James dropped the hose and hurried as fast as he could to Walter. "You okay, son?"

"I'm fine," said Walter making his way to the cars parked behind the garage.

"If you're fine, you need to be out there fighting the fire," said James as he followed Walter. "You need me to get Dovie? Has the heat gotten to you?"

"Look out!" yelled Dovie.

James and Walter looked over to see another gust of wind stir up the fire high in the sky. The flames blew right past the pastor and ignited the barn's roof. Pastor Spaulding and Kathleen pointed their hoses up to the roof, but no matter how hard they tried, their water could not reach the flames. They just didn't have enough pressure.

"Walter, run and go get a fire truck," demanded James, starting toward the barn as fast as he could.

"James, I'm sorry," answered Walter.

James turned just in time to see Walter get into Dovie's car, back up, and peel out down the driveway.

Chapter Forty

Alice coughed hard and shook Norman again.

"Get up! Mr. Norman, you have to wake up!" she cried.

Hot tears ran down her face as the goose remained motionless in his curled up position. Alice got on her hands and knees and crawled under the bench. She gently placed her head on Norman's chest, and let out a cry of relief when she felt a subtle rise and fall.

Alice coughed again. "I bet it's the smoke," she whispered. "He can't wake up because he's inhaled too much smoke."

She scooped Norman up in her arms and pulled him out. She stood and patted the goose's back. "Don't worry, Mr. Norman. I'll get us out of here."

Just as she said the words the branches above her started to crack as the fire spread through them. Burning leaves fell to the ground, igniting the dry grass around her. Alice turned, looking for a way out of the orchard, but the flames surrounded her.

She held Norman tighter as she kept searching, looking for any kind of opening. She spotted a small area of unburned ground. It wouldn't take long for the fire to spread there as well, so Alice made a run for it. Her lungs burned, and she coughed hard. Her legs felt as if they had lead weights attached to her ankles, and Norman's weight made her arms feel even weaker than before. She pushed harder, determined to break through the fire.

Just as she came to the spot a large flaming branch fell to the ground and landed at her feet. She let out a scream as she fell backwards.

Dovie threw another bucket of water on the barn. She handed the empty bucket to James who handed her a full bucket. She glanced at her father. "Dad, you need to get out of here. Go to Two Dots Ranch and rest. Take my car."

"Dovie, hon, I'm not leaving without you, and you know I'll fight for this place until I fall plum down. Besides, Walter took off in your car about twenty minutes ago."

"He did what?" Dovie looked over at the garage to confirm her car was missing. "Where did he go?"

She threw another bucket of water on the barn.

"I don't know," said James. "He just said he was sorry and then took off."

Dovie froze. "In my car?"

"Hun, we have bigger things to worry about," James huffed.

Dovie shook away her shock, grabbed another bucket, threw it on the fire and hurried back. She couldn't imagine why Walter would just leave while everyone else was trying so hard to fight the fire. She wondered if he was so upset over Alice kissing Nicholas, he just couldn't stay, but she couldn't shake the feeling he was just being a coward. If he was going to be that way when a crisis struck, it was better that he left. Alice needed a man she could count on.

Her heart pounding with anger, Dovie kicked the hose when she came back to find the trickle had turned into a drip. Now they had fire on their doorstep with no way to fight it and they were a man short. She grabbed a hoe, ready to start snuffing the fire out if it came any closer.

Dovie sighed as her heart grew tired with anger. It took too much energy to be mad at Walter. She said a little prayer asking for forgiveness. It was easy to be angry at him, but she had no right to think of him as a coward. He could be hurt or delirious from the heat. He might even be searching for help. She wished he would have sought her out for treatment before leaving if he was feeling bad. He could be in a lot of danger driving around without a clear head.

She caught movement toward the pasture gate and was surprised to see Nicholas coming through it with Bolt.

He hurried over to her and eyed the barn. "Where should I put him?"

"See if you can tie him to the tree over by Pronto and Tex. Maybe the other horses can keep him calm. I can't believe you found him," answered Dovie.

"I can't believe I did either," said Nicholas with a smile that spoke only of relief. "I'll get him secure and help with the barn."

Dovie nodded as he started to the old cottonwood where the other horses were tied up. Birds of all kinds start to squeak and cackle in the trees above the house as a large crack and pop thundered through the air.

"Oh my," gasped Kathleen, reaching for a bucket. "What was that?"

"It came from the orchard," said James, looking in that direction. "It's on fire."

"Oh, dear Lord, help us," said Dovie, "Pastor Spaulding we need those fire trucks out of the field and over here now."

"I'm going," said Pastor Spaulding. He untied Pronto's reins from the tree and hurried into the saddle, giving the horse a nudge. Pronto didn't waste any time going into a full gallop.

"I can't believe we didn't notice the fire had spread to the orchard," said Kathleen, wiping her brow. "What should we do? Keep on the house or head off the fire at the orchard?"

"How can I help?" asked Nicholas.

"Grab a hoe," said James. "The barn's a loss. We need to concentrate on saving the house. Start building the biggest fire break you can."

Nicholas nodded as he ran towards the shed to grab another hoe.

"Dad, you have to go!" cried Dovie.

James hobbled toward the orchard, walking as far as the hose allowed. "I'm not going anywhere."

Dovie gave Kathleen a look, and Kathleen ran to the front part of the house. Dovie suspected Kathleen was going for the old rocker that sat on the front porch. As Kathleen went for the chair, Dovie took one last look at the barn. Flames poured out the loft window, and Dovie felt a tear drip on her cheek. She remembered how her daughter Helen, then Alice, and finally Ellie, had found solace in the hay stack in the loft. She wondered if Helen's old roller skates were still hidden within the straw, or Alice's old books, but she was really glad Ellie had stopped hiding her beloved rag doll Lovey there. Instinctively, she fingered the doll in her apron pocket and hoped it would protect her and Quail Crossings as Ellie believed it would.

She turned, unable to look at the barn any longer, and hurried to help her dad. She wrapped her arm around his back to give him additional support. Nicholas ran by with the hoe, and Kathleen arrived with the old rocker.

A scream pierced through the air, and everyone froze.

"Someone's in the orchard," James yelled.

A hand flew to Dovie's face. "Dad, it sounded like Alice."

"Alice?" Nicholas dropped the hoe.

Before anyone could say another word. Nicholas had jumped on James's trusted horse, Tex, and was barreling toward the flaming orchard.

Gabe looked up in time to see the tops of the dry orchard trees ignite. "Get the trucks to the house! Everyone, back to Quail Crossings!"

"Do you think our house will be okay?" asked Lou Anne as she looked across the field toward the house she shared with Bill.

Gabe looked in the same direction. So far the fire was staying to the south and west, but there were no guarantees that a shift in the wind wouldn't move the fire east. Bill was already plowing a fire line in front of the property.

"Take a dozen men and try to steer the fire away from your place," said Gabe. "Everyone else needs to go to Quail Crossings, or we'll lose everything."

Lou Anne nodded and hopped into Elmer's truck. She hollered at some men with gunny sacks as she drove by, and they hopped in as the rest of the men started to retreat to the main house. Gabe was glad the originally plowed fire break was just enough to lead all the men and trucks safely to Quail Crossings.

"Jacob," he hollered as he ran towards Jacob's truck, "we've got to get to the orchard."

Jacob nodded. "We'll have to go around. There's no gate in the fence line this far north."

Gabe let out a loud whistle, gaining the attention of the fire fighters on his side of the line. "Follow us!"

Gabe got in Jacob's truck. "Jacob, we don't have time to go around the fence, you're gonna have to drive through it."

"Through it?" Jacob swallowed hard.

"Yep," confirmed Gabe, "you're gonna have to go fast. Can you do it?"

Jacob nodded slowly. "For Quail Crossings, I'd do just about anything."

Jacob revved the engine as he threw it in gear. Gabe gripped onto the door and the seat, trying to brace himself. Jacob's tires peeled out in the mud before the truck launched forward.

"Steady now, Jacob," said Gabe. "Don't kill it."

Jacob switched gears and pushed the truck harder. Jacob shifted again. Gabe looked over and saw the speedometer at 60 mph and a large smile on Jacob's face as the truck rammed through the wood fence. Gabe threw his hands up to protect his face as the fence splintered around the truck and windshield.

Laughing loudly, Jacob steered the truck around the trees and slowed it to a stop about fifty yards from the flaming orchard. "Whew! I've never gone that fast before!"

Gabe smiled as he got out of the truck. "Just don't make a habit out of it."

Hopping into the back of the truck, Gabe was pleased to see that most of the water buckets remained upright. He grabbed a soaking gunny sack and hopped back out of the truck bed, running for the orchard. Other trucks were now coming through the makeshift gate Jacob had made.

A scream filled the air, and Gabe felt his blood run cold. Someone was in the orchard.

Chapter Forty-one

Nicholas watched as Jacob broke through the fence with his truck. He was glad to see one of the fire trucks pulled through the gap, and was now focusing its hose on the orchard.

"Look out!" he yelled to the men as they made a line to beat off the fire before it could reach the Quail Crossings homestead.

The men parted, giving Tex plenty of room to run through.

"All right, Tex," said Nicholas as they approached the flaming orchard, "don't fail me now. Let's show those young horses how it's done."

Tex picked up speed and leapt over a burning log as they entered the orchard. The heat licked at Nicholas's arms and legs, but Tex landed gracefully in a clear patch of ground. Nicholas pulled on the reins, slowing Tex so he could look for Alice. The smoke was thick and burned his eyes. Tex danced a little, but stayed steady. Nicholas hopped off and started to walk, pulling Texas along by the reins.

"Alice!" Nicholas cried. "Where are you?"

Again Nicholas turned in a circle trying to get his bearings. Where would she be? Why would she even be in the orchard during the fire? His thoughts turned to the bench James had made for Sylvia. Maybe she was trying to save it.

He led Tex in the direction of the bench and tried to shield his eyes from all the smoke. He pulled his bandana over his mouth and nose. He coughed hard as his eyes began to water and burn. It was hot in the orchard, and Nicholas was sure if he didn't find Alice soon, they'd be baked alive.

His heart dropped as the orchard seemed to be alive with nothing but smoke and fire. He and Tex seemed to be the only things left that weren't burning. His body shuddered as he remembered the scream. Was he too late?

He caught movement and hurried toward it. It was just a shadow of blue and a speck of white, but it was definitely moving and had to be Alice.

He pulled Tex's reins harder as he tried to hurry to the shadow. Alice came barreling through the smoke, Norman tucked safely in her arms.

"Oh, Nicholas," she cried as she ran into his free arm, "I thought I was dead, and Mr. Norman won't wake up."

Nicholas pulled her to him as tightly as he could. All he wanted to do was kiss her and never let her go, but he knew what they had to do; get out of there and fast. The fire continued to spread and the smoke was thicker than it had been in the pasture.

"Can you manage to get on Tex?" Nicholas asked. "Hand me Norman, then I'll hand him back to you and get myself on."

Alice nodded and grabbed Tex's reins with one hand as Nicholas took Norman. She hurried onto the saddle and reached down for the goose. Nicholas handed him up before he jumped behind Alice and, once again, took hold of the reins.

"Hold on," he ordered to Alice.

He gave Tex a heel and leaned over Alice, trying to protect her from the debris that was falling from the trees.

The horse spun in a circle as if looking for an escape route.

"Come on, Tex," hollered Nicholas. "Come on, boy!"

Tex hopped and danced, backing away from the flames. Then as if he had seen an opening, the horse took off towards the west, gliding over flaming branches and zigzagging his way through the burning trees. Nicholas wrapped his arms around Alice and Norman, and grabbed onto the saddle horn, trying to keep everyone on Tex as the horse ran wild. He knew he wasn't an experienced enough rider and prayed Tex didn't throw them all to the fiery ground. With a sudden bolt to the south, Tex made another amazing leap and jumped out of the orchard. The horse kept running, and Nicholas fought to pull the reins back.

"Whoa!"

Nicholas heard James before he saw him. The old man stood up from his rocker and put both hands up. "Whoa now, Tex, you're okay. Whoa."

The horse stopped, danced for a second, and then dropped his head to drink the cool water puddled on the ground.

Dovie and Kathleen were by Tex's side in an instant. Nicholas slid off Tex first. His legs were shaking violently, but he forced himself to stand as Alice handed Norman down to him.

"Mr. Norman won't wake up," said Alice.

"Give him here," said Dovie.

Nicholas passed Norman to Dovie, and, just as his hands were free, Alice limply slid into his arms.

Alice awoke with a start. She rose quickly and her head spun, her stomach threatening to lose all its contents. She slowly laid back down and closed her eyes.

"It's okay, you're in my room and safe and sound," came Dovie's voice. Alice could feel a cool washcloth being placed on her forehead. "You took in a lot of smoke. Just take a few deep breaths."

Alice inhaled and exhaled deeply before opening her eyes. "The fire?"

Her throat ached, and her voice came out raspy.

"It's almost out," said Dovie. "The trucks moved in just in time, and we had some fire trucks come in from Tuckett and Perry to help."

Alice felt tears drip from the corners of her eyes. "Mr. Norman?"

Part of her didn't want to ask. His body had been so limp when she handed him down to Nicholas. No one had to tell her he was an old goose. She knew already that his time was limited. She had just always pictured Norman laying down under his favorite cottonwood by the pond and just drifting away, not choking to death on smoke.

Before Dovie could answer there was a soft knock on the door.

"Come in," said Dovie as Alice looked up to see Nicholas walking in with a large bundle.

Alice sat up as Nicholas placed Norman in her arms. Alice could see the goose was breathing fine, even though his eyes were still closed.

"Has he woken up?" Alice asked.

"Yes," said Nicholas. "I gave him a bath, and he honked at me the whole time. I think he's just worn out from yelling at me."

Alice looked at Nicholas. She could tell he had washed his face, but his hair was still full of dirt and soot. He looked so young, yet so much older than when he had first arrived at Quail Crossings.

"I'm gonna go check on Dad," said Dovie, giving Nicholas a little pat on the shoulder. "Make sure he's resting."

Alice gently rubbed Norman's soft back. Her heart both ached from the thought of how close she came to losing him and leapt for joy knowing he was okay. She gave him a little kiss on the head. "You'll always be my bestest friend," she whispered.

"I can't believe I'm jealous of a goose," Nicholas said with a laugh.

Alice grabbed his hand. "Oh Nicholas, how can I ever thank you for saving us? We would have died had you not rushed in."

Nicholas gave her a half smile. "You should really be thanking Tex. He did all the work and got us out of there. I was terrified."

She gave his hand a squeeze. "You were very brave. I can't believe you'd run into a fire for me."

"Seems I do crazy things for the people I love," he said, his blue eyes gazing at her.

"You love me?" Alice felt a smile tugging at her lips as her heart danced.

He leaned down and brushed his lips against hers. As he leaned back, ever so slightly, Alice smiled. "I love you too."

Chapter Forty-two

July 29, 1950 – evening

Alice and Nicholas walked onto the back stoop with Norman. The whole Quail Crossings gang and most of the town gathered around the wooden picnic tables in the backyard eating roast beef sandwiches, baked beans, corn on the cob and the other fixin's the town's women had brought. Kids weaved around the adults, splashing in the mud and laughing as if their whole world hadn't been on fire just hours before. The sun was setting which surprised Alice. It seemed like just moments before, it had been morning.

"Here, let me take Norman," said Evalyn. "You two get something to eat and drink. It's been a long day."

"How's your arm?" asked Alice, pointing to Evalyn's bandaged wrist.

Evalyn smiled. "Like I said, I've had worse frying chicken. Dovie says it'll heal nicely and probably won't even leave a scar."

Ellie brought over two plates filled with food and handed them to Alice and Nicholas. They sat down on the stoop and balanced their heaping plates on their laps.

"We've got pies, cookies, and cakes for dessert. Once I got all the kids to Rockwood, I just couldn't stop baking. Seemed to calm all of us down. Let me know when you're ready for it."

"Thank you, Ellie," said Alice.

Bonnie and Beverly ran up begging to pet Norman. They jumped up and down at Evalyn's feet splashing mud.

"Girls, calm down," commanded Evalyn, and the girls stopped jumping. "Come on over here, and you can pet Norman. Just let your Aunt Alice and Mr. Nicholas eat without a side of mud, will ya?"

Alice laughed as Evalyn, Ellie, and the girls walked towards a bench by the garage. She scanned the large group of people and was thankful the air was cooling down a bit as the sun set. She smiled at James who stood nearby talking with George Wheaton. As she looked through the crowd, she studied each face before looking at Nicholas. "Where's Walter?"

Nicholas swallowed hard. "Umm... I'm not sure how to tell you this."

A lump grew in the pit of Alice's stomach. "What happened? Tell me he's okay."

James walked over. "Alice, honey, Walter is okay as far as we know."

"As far as we know?" Alice cocked her head.

"He took off in Dovie's car during the fire," said James.

Dovie brought over the old rocking chair, and James sat. Dovie took a seat on the stoop by Alice.

"What do you mean?" Alice could tell the pit in her stomach was changing from fear to doubt. "Walter wouldn't just leave."

"Dad saw him," said Dovie, putting an arm around Alice. "He just said he was sorry and left."

"We need to go find him," said Alice. She started to stand, but Dovie applied the slightest of pressure to Alice's shoulders telling her she should remain sitting.

"Alice, hon, it appears he got scared and left," said Dovie. "He didn't even take his stuff."

Alice shook her head. "No, that doesn't sound like Walter, and why would he say he was sorry? Sorry about what?"

Nicholas cleared his throat. "I know what he's sorry about." He placed his plate behind him on the stoop, then stood. "Can I have everyone's attention?"

"What are you doing?" asked Alice. She was confused and couldn't stand the thought that Nicholas was about to tell everyone Walter had turned coward. Walter was still her friend.

Once everyone was looking in their direction, Nicholas cleared his throat again. "I just wanted to say thank you to everyone who came out and saved Quail Crossings. I know y'all don't know much about me, but my mom used to tell me about this place when times were tough with my dad. I always dreamt of this place, but my dreams paled in comparison to the reality. Quail Crossings is more than a plot of land, it's the people that live here and folks that surround it. There's a sense of heart here you don't see many places. Watching everyone come together, stepping into harm's way to save their neighbor, well, that's incredibly humbling."

Nicholas swallowed hard, and Alice wondered if he was on the verge of tears.

"Because of that," Nicholas continued, his voice cracking a bit, "I'm so very sorry. It was I who started the fire."

Alice felt her mouth fall open as shock raced through the crowd in the shape of murmurs and gasps.

"I didn't mean to," said Nicholas, "Walter's cigarette fell to the ground as we were fighting in the pasture. The fire was an accident, but my actions of fighting with Walter weren't. At the time, I thought I was defending myself, but, in hindsight, I realize I could have gone about the whole situation differently and avoided not only the fire, but hurting another person. If my time at Quail Crossings has shown me anything, it's that we help rather than hurt. So, I'm sincerely sorry."

He looked at James. "I'll rebuild the barn and fence and replant the orchard, whatever you need me to do, Grandpa. Please forgive me."

Nicholas melted back down to the stoop, covering his face. Alice's heart broke for him and she placed a hand on his back. She had never heard a more sincere apology and could tell Nicholas felt the weight of Quail Crossings sitting on his shoulders.

James slowly stood and put a hand on Nicholas's shoulder as Dovie moved over and crouched in front of Nicholas.

"Oh, Nicholas," said Dovie, "you sweet boy."

"Son," said James, "there's nothing to forgive."

"That's right," said Gabe coming over to stand behind Dovie. "You fought that fire harder than anyone else."

Bill and Lou Anne walked over, followed by Evalyn, Robert, Elmer, Tiny, and Ellie. They all gathered around Nicholas as he sat on the stoop, his head in his hands.

"You saved Bolt," said Bill.

"And me," whispered Alice.

Mr. Norman let out a loud honk as if to have himself included. Everyone laughed.

"And Mr. Norman," said Alice. "You saved my bestest friend."

Nicholas looked up, his eyes red. "None of that would have needed saving had I controlled myself. I could have cost you everything. How can you forgive me?"

June walked over, and Dovie scooted to the side so she could face her son. She gently cupped her son's chin. "This is the heart you were talking about son, this is family."

Chapter Forty-three

Alice woke to the smell of bacon frying and the sounds of wood falling to the ground. She was surprised at how sore she was after fighting the fire. Her lungs still ached, and her throat still felt raw. Through her discomfort, she quickly got dressed and hurried downstairs. Ellie stood over the stove frying bacon as Dovie washed some dishes in the sink.

"What's going on?" asked Alice looking out the back screen door. "What time is it?"

"Quarter past nine," answered Dovie. "Ellie's making some fresh breakfast. Just about everyone else has already been in to eat. Tiny's in the parlor with the kids, and all the others are cleaning up outside. Bill, Robert, and Nicholas are salvaging what they can of the barn. Gabe took his plane up early to survey how much pasture we lost, and Lou Anne and Evalyn are doing a check of the fence line in the truck so we can buy supplies."

"Why didn't you wake me?" asked Alice. "I practically slept the whole day away."

Dovie laughed. "There's still plenty of day, and truth be told, I wanted you to rest. You inhaled a lot of smoke yesterday."

"No more than Nicholas," countered Alice as she pointed to the barn where Nicholas was helping Bill and Robert dismantle the remaining wall.

"He was up before dawn," said Ellie as she forked the bacon onto a plate. "Thankfully, I already had the biscuits made, or he would have run out of here without breakfast."

Dovie nodded. "When I got up he had already milked Poppy, silly old cow was standing by the stoop, just waiting to be milked. I guess we left one of the pails sitting there, and she figured that was the new milking station."

"Best milk cow in the county," said Ellie with a smile.

"Best milk cow in the country," corrected James as he walked into the kitchen and took a seat at the table. He motioned to Alice. "Come sit down and eat with me, Alice. An old man hates to eat alone."

"You just getting up, Mr. James?" asked Alice as she sat next to him.

"This is his second breakfast," teased Dovie. She kissed her dad on the forehead. "But I'm glad to see his appetite picking up."

There was a quick rap on the back door as Pastor Spaulding let himself and his wife, Susan, in. "Good morning folks."

"Good morning, Pastor Spaulding, Susan," said Dovie, taking the pastor's hat. "Y'all didn't get enough of us yesterday?"

"Just bringing your car back," said Pastor Spaulding. He eyed the bacon. "Any chance you've got some extra grub. I'm starving."

"Pastor Spaulding," gasped Susan, "you had a full breakfast this morning."

"Never mind," said Dovie, "Dad is on his second breakfast as well, and Alice hasn't eaten yet. There's plenty for everyone, so please sit down."

Dovie headed to the cabinet, then stopped short. "Did you say you brought my car back?"

Susan nodded. "It was parked in front of Annette's Café."

She reached into her handbag and pulled out a folded sheet of paper. "Alice, there was a letter left in it for you."

Alice reached for it as her heart pounded in her chest.

"I opened it," confessed Susan. "Once I realized it was for you, I stopped reading."

"She wouldn't let me read it either," teased Pastor Spaulding as he helped himself to a piece of bacon.

Alice looked around the room as everyone stared at her and the letter. "I think I'll go upstairs and read this."

She thought she heard a collective sigh as she got up and walked back upstairs. Alice knew they were all curious about the letter and had hoped she would read it out loud. She knew she probably would, but she wanted to read it alone first. She closed her bedroom door and sat on the edge of the bed. Her hand trembled. She wasn't sure she wanted to open the letter at all. There was no question it was from Walter, but she doubted she was ready to hear what he had to say. He had been her friend for a year, and she had valued that friendship. Her heart ached as she remembered their kiss and how badly she wanted to feel something for him, but didn't.

Taking a deep breath she unfolded the letter:

Dearest Alice,

I'm sorry to be writing this letter instead of telling you in person, but I couldn't stay. As I sit in Mrs. Pearce's car and write this, I realize everyone probably thinks of me as a coward, and they're right. I am one. Part of me wants to turn the car around and go back to Quail Crossings, but a larger part of me is too ashamed. I'm ashamed of how I acted. It was my cigarette that started the fire, and I couldn't even be brave enough to help put it out, much less own up to it face to face.

Please tell everyone I am sorry. When I get back to Amarillo, I will be sending money to help rebuild Quail Crossings. I know it seems like an easy way out, but I hope you'll encourage Mr. Murphy to use what I send. It's not a perfect solution, but I hope to make some amends.

I will not be returning to West Texas State College in the fall. I've decided to work for my father instead of continuing an education in agriculture. Farming isn't in my nature, this summer has definitely taught me that.

Alice, I wanted you from the minute I saw you, and I don't fault you for not feeling the same way. I'd be lying if I said writing that last bit didn't hurt a little. I will probably always wonder what Nicholas had that I didn't, but I will never wonder about how you felt regarding me. You loved me as a friend, and even though that is not what my heart longed for, I will never forget your kindness.

I don't regret meeting you, but the sad truth is, I regret coming to Quail Crossings. Seems the place you love most in the world, took you away from me. You will never be happy any place else, and I would never be happy there. With that knowledge and knowing your heart lies with Nicholas, I believe we will never see each other again.

Sincerely,

Walter

Alice felt the tears drop on her hands before she realized she was crying. Her heart stung as she gasped for breath. She didn't want to say goodbye to Walter but knew he was right. As much as she loved her friend, it would only hurt him to see her with Nicholas.

Alice fell back on her bed and looked to the ceiling. She thought of Walter's smiling face and forced her own smile as she whispered, "Good-bye, Walter."

Alice sat against an old cottonwood tree and rubbed her shoulders. She was still sore from fighting the fire and the clean-up duty hadn't done anything to help ease the pain. She knew very well that part of her soreness was sadness. Even though she had accepted what Walter had to say in his letter, she was still upset by how hurt he had been.

"Mind if I sit?" asked Nicholas.

"Please," said Alice, her heart racing a little. They hadn't had much time to talk since his confession and the clean-up efforts.

"I heard you got a letter from Walter," said Nicholas.

"I did," answered Alice, leaning her head back against the tree and closing her eyes. She wasn't entirely sure she wanted to talk about it, as guilt intruded her excitement of having Nicholas close.

"I feel I owe him a huge apology," said Nicholas.

Alice opened her eyes and raised an eyebrow.

He shrugged. "I feel guilty."

"You do?" Feeling some relief that she wasn't alone in her guilt.

Nicholas nodded and grabbed Alice's hand. "You're an easy person to love, Alice Brewer, and I have no doubt that Walter loved you. I know exactly how he felt because I fell for you so hard, my heart would have shattered had you only wanted to be friends. So although I feel guilt, I also feel extremely lucky. For some crazy reason, you decided to love me back. I intend to spend every moment of my life proving to you exactly how lucky I feel and showing you how much I love you."

"So, does that mean you're going to stay?" asked Alice. "I heard your mother talking about you driving home together."

Nicholas nodded. "I am going back to New York."

Alice felt her breath hitch and tried to take her hand away from Nicholas's, but he held her tightly.

"Alice, it's not like that," explained Nicholas. "I'll be back as soon as I can. Gabe has even offered to fly me back when I'm ready, but I do have to go home. I have to get my uncle's car back to him, and it's not fair to have my mom drive back alone. Mom thinks my uncle might want me to work a couple of months for him for using his car. I have to make things right with him, but then I'll be back."

"When are you leaving?" whispered Alice.

"After the barn is built and the new fence is up. Mom wants to stick around and spend time with Grandpa. They have a lot of catching up to do. She called my uncle today, and he's willing to wait on the car now that he knows it's in one piece."

Alice's smile returned. "Promise you'll come back?"

Nicholas caressed her cheek before putting his arms around her and giving her a soft kiss on her lips. As he parted slightly from their kiss, he smiled. "Wild horses couldn't keep me away."

Alice leaned forward and kissed Nicholas again.

"There is one more thing I'd like to do for Grandpa before I go, but I need your help," said Nicholas as they released their embrace.

"Anything," Alice said with a smile.

Chapter Forty-four

September 9, 1950

James traced the etching on the bench and felt his eyes grow misty. Nicholas had done a wonderful job replicating the old bench that had been destroyed in the fire. Just below the etched flower, Nicholas had added a single word, "Heart."

"He did a good job, didn't he, Norman?" James said as he sat on the bench.

Norman let out a honk that James took as agreement. The goose waddled next to the bench, and James gingerly bent down and picked him up, setting Norman next to him.

"We've had some good years, haven't we, Norman? Seems like yesterday I was building the bench for Sylvia and you were just a gosling, getting into all kinds of trouble. Now she's been gone a long time. It's funny, even though I'm surrounded by family, I still miss her every day. I wonder what she would think of how things are now."

He laughed. "She would probably hate the telephone but love the new barn. Got to tell you, the boys did a fine job replacing it. Poppy has never had such a fancy stall, and

I'm so glad they were able to make a door from the old barn wood, a little of the old with a little of the new seems like a nice mix to me."

He sniffed a little. "I wish Sylvia were here to see June and Nicholas, but she'd cry when they left, even knowing Nicholas will be back. I wish she would have gotten to know him. He's such a fine young man, and I can't say I hate that he and Alice are smitten. Sylvia would love that they are taking their time, with Alice going back to school to become a teacher. I really like the idea of Alice continuing her education before they get married. Sylvia would think that was very progressive of me, but if their love is as strong as I think it is, it'll hold until she graduates."

Norman laid his head on James's knee. "Sylvia would love that Dovie and June are getting along so well. Although I'm not sure how she'd feel about Dovie taking flying lessons with Gabe. I'm sure she would trust him, but if man were meant to fly, he would have given us wings."

Norman let out another honk in agreement. "I know Dovie worries about being gone too much, but I told her to take to the skies and not to worry about this old man, especially now that Tiny's feeling better. She seems to have gotten her old pep back. She's even taken Leon under her wing. Jacob has found a nice little house not too far from the butcher shop, and the women of Quail Crossings have seen to it that it's more than a house, but a home. I sure am glad Jacob let Leon read all those letters he wrote to Blu. It seems it has made them closer than ever."

James pulled Norman a little closer and patted him on the back. "We've been through so much, haven't we? Dust storms, tornados, and fires ... faced hatred, illness, and war. But we've also shared so much love. We've watched this family bounce back time after time because we simply won't quit on one another. I'm sure we'll all face more trials in life, but I'm surer than ever our family will pull through whatever is thrown at us. I've never felt so much love at Quail Crossings as I do now. We've lived a good life, Norman ... a really good life."

James felt his tears roll down his cheeks and reached up to brush them off. Norman looked up and let out a concerning low honk.

James gave the goose a smile. "Don't worry, Mr. Norman, these are happy tears."

Author's Note

The question I get asked most frequently is if this is the last book in the *Quail Crossings* series. The short answer is … it is not.

The *Quail Crossings* family is a part of my life now. I've grown to love and cherish them just as much as you have.

Originally, this was going to be the last book in the series, but then the children started to tell me their stories. So, I will be continuing the series with *Quail Crossings Generations,* starting with Joy's story.

Now for the long answer to the above question. Where I will continue the series, I have a lot of other stories and characters that I would love to introduce to you that do not live at Quail Crossings. I hope you'll journey with me as I branch out genres and wander into new stories, with exciting characters and amazing adventures.

So even though I cannot tell you how often I'll produce a *Quail Crossings* book, I can tell you that I plan on writing a few "lost years" novellas so you can continue to read about the family you love.

I'll produce them as fast as I can, along with new novels, but I won't skimp on my quality control. You might like to see books from me come out faster, but without that quality control I guarantee you, they won't be as good.

Thank you for all your love, friendship, and support. You all are the key holders to my dream. Without you the door would have never been opened.

Thank you, from the bottom of my heart, for not only supporting this crazy dream I have of telling stories, but for falling in love with Quail Crossings.

Don't worry readers, these are happy tears.

Sincerely,
Jennifer McMurrain

The Brewer Family

Abe Brewer
b. April 5, 1899

m. June 10, 1916

Eva (Wicker) Brewer
b. Aug. 30, 1901

Bill Brewer
b. Oct. 23, 1917

Evalyn (Brewer) Smith
b. Nov. 26, 1921

Elmer Brewer
b. Dec. 3, 1925

Alice Brewer
b. Mar. 12, 1929

Ellie Brewer
b. Jan. 31, 1932

Bill and Lou Anne Brewer

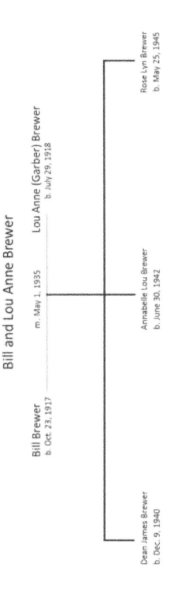

Bill Brewer
b. Oct. 23, 1917

m. May 1, 1935

Lou Anne (Garber) Brewer
b. July 29, 1918

Dean James Brewer
b. Dec. 9, 1940

Annabelle Lou Brewer
b. June 30, 1942

Rose Lyn Brewer
b. May 25, 1945

Robert and Evalyn Smith

Robert Lee Smith
b. Sept. 18, 1919

m. March 23, 1930

Evalyn (Brewer) Smith
b. Nov. 26, 1921

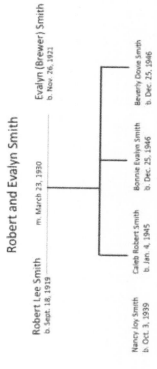

Nancy Joy Smith
b. Oct. 3, 1939

Caleb Robert Smith
b. Jan. 4, 1945

Bonnie Evalyn Smith
b. Dec. 25, 1946

Beverly Dovie Smith
b. Dec. 25, 1946

Elmer and Mary "Tiny" Brewer

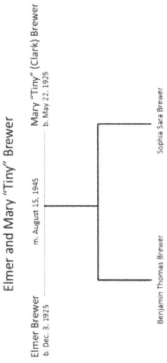

Elmer Brewer   m. August 15, 1945   Mary "Tiny" (Clark) Brewer
b. Dec. 3, 1925   b. May 22, 1925

Benjamin Thomas Brewer   Sophia Sara Brewer
b. June 1, 1946   b. Feb. 28, 1950

The Murphy Family

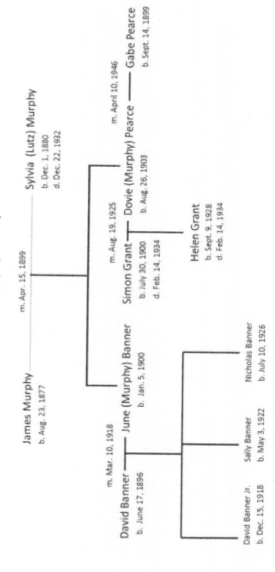

James Murphy
b. Aug. 23, 1877

Sylvia (Lutz) Murphy
b. Dec. 1, 1880
d. Dec. 22, 1932

m. Apr. 15, 1899

Simon Grant
b. July 30, 1900
d. Feb. 14, 1934

Dowie (Murphy) Pearce
b. Aug. 26, 1903

Gabe Pearce
b. Sept. 14, 1899

m. April 10, 1946

m. Aug. 19, 1925

Helen Grant
b. Sept. 9, 1928
d. Feb. 14, 1934

David Banner
b. June 17, 1696

June (Murphy) Banner
b. Jan. 5, 1900

m. Mar. 10, 1918

David Banner Jr.
b. Dec. 15, 1918

Sally Banner
b. May 3, 1922

Nicholas Banner
b. July 10, 1926

If you enjoyed *Forever Quail Crossings*
watch for *Before Quail Crossings*
coming to ebook in early 2018

Enjoy an Excerpt from
Before Quail Crossings

Chapter One

July 12, 1932 ~ Tuckett, Texas

Evalyn Brewer threw herself at her mother's leg and latched on. "Please, Momma, you can't do this."

"Evalyn, you let go this instant," snapped Eva Brewer as she picked up the infant from the bottom drawer of the dresser that had served as a crib for Baby Ellie. "You're eleven-years-old, for crying out loud, stop acting like a child."

The girl remained latched onto her mother. "You can't leave Ellie there. You just can't! She's family. She belongs here with us."

Ellie coughed and wheezed as she tried to catch her breath. The sound reminded Evalyn of a small dog that had barked so much it had become hoarse. She knew Ellie needed a doctor, that wasn't the problem.

She looked toward the corner where her older brother, Bill, and younger siblings, Elmer and Alice stood watching the scene unfold. She could tell Bill wanted to intervene, but he being only fifteen, she was sure he didn't know how. A plan quickly started to develop in Evalyn's mind. She could control the situation and would make sure that Ellie got the help she needed and stayed with her family.

Evalyn let go of her mother's leg and stood tall. She dusted herself off and then raised her chin to her mother. "You're right, Momma. I'm no longer a child, and I can take care of Ellie. I'll take her to the doctor and then bring her home. You won't have to do anythin'. I'll see to all her needs."

She reached out for the infant. She had taken care of Ellie since the child's birth, now shouldn't be any different. With five kids in the house, three of which were under the age of seven, her mother had basically thrown Ellie to Evalyn after the child was born. Evalyn hadn't minded. She loved taking care of the baby.

She changed Ellie's dirty diapers and did all her laundry. She put the baby to bed and got up with her when she stirred. The only thing her mother did was the one thing Evalyn couldn't do ... nurse. Evalyn cringed every time she had to ask her mother to feed the baby. Eva acted like feeding her child was a filthy chore.

Evalyn had felt like everything was going well, even with the feedings, until the first duster after Ellie was born, blew in. Ellie had started to cough the second the storm had hit and hadn't stopped. The duster had been almost a week ago.

Ellie coughed again.

"This child can't stay here, Evalyn," snarled her mother. "She'll infect us all with her nasty cough and then we'll all be laid up. Is that what you want? Do you want your father and me to cough ourselves to death? What about Alice? Do you think your four-year-old sister deserves to die, too?"

Alice started to wail. "I don't wanna die, but I don't want Ellie to go."

Bill put a gentle hand on Alice's shoulder. "You're not going to die. Everything will be all right."

Evalyn tried to keep her temper from spilling out her mouth. Her blood boiled and she wanted nothing more than to grab Ellie and run away with the rest of her siblings, "I don't want anyone to die, but Momma, the dust pneumonia ain't catching."

She should have been prepared for the backhand, since it happened often, but her mother's hand caught her off guard and she stumbled backwards. Bill stepped forward, but didn't approach their momma.

"Don't you sass," screamed her mother. "You ungrateful child!"

Charging at her mother, Evalyn clawed for Ellie. "You're not going to take her! I won't let you. She's mine!"

Evalyn heard the door burst open, right before she felt two large hands grab her around her waist. Fear replaced what had been rage as she flew backwards and landed hard into the side of the bedframe where she and Alice slept. She instinctively raised her arms as her father loomed over her and started to hit her with his belt.

The belt stung her arms and sides and Evalyn couldn't help but cry out.

"That's enough, Pa," Bill said firmly, standing in front of Evalyn. "Evalyn's done causing trouble."

Evalyn peeked between her arms to see her father put his belt away. Alice ran to her and hugged her with scrawny arms. She was still crying, but now Alice was repeating the nickname that her siblings called her. "Evie. Evie. Evie."

Their mother's lip turned up in disgust. "Don't call her that, Alice. Her name is Evalyn. She's named after her mother and should be proud to be my name sake. Ungrateful children, all of you."

Their father, Abe, pointed his finger at Bill. "Son, don't you ever get in-between me and my discipline again, or you'll be the one receiving the blows."

Abe sneered at all his children. "Now, we're going to the doctor to see about Ellie. You children ought to be ashamed of yourselves giving your mother so much trouble. I expect all the chores to be done and this house to be in top shape when we come back, with dinner on the table if it takes us that long."

Putting his arm around his wife, Abe guided her to the door.

"Ellie," Evalyn cried softly. She felt as if her parents were leaving with her very heart instead of her baby sister. Tears flooded her cheeks and her arms and sides burned.

"You're bleedin'," said Alice.

Evalyn looked at her forearm and sure enough the belt at left a long gash.

"Bill, Evie's bleeding," Alice said again, this time looking at her big brother.

Bill bent over and helped Evalyn off the floor and to the edge of the bed.

"Elmer," said Bill to his seven-year-old brother, "get the kit, please. Alice, will you get me a clean rag with water from the pump?"

Elmer hurried to the cabinet where the medical kit was kept as Alice grabbed a fresh rag from the finished laundry pile and ran outside to the pump.

"You've got to learn to keep your temper, Evie," Bill said tenderly. "It never ends well when you lose it."

"Don't you care that they took Ellie?" Evalyn narrowed her eyes at her brother.

Bill nodded. "I hate that they took her, and I realize we'll probably never see her again. But I hope that Ellie will get better and then find a good home where someone loves her just as much as you have done." He sat beside her and rubbed her back gently. "Ellie was lucky to have you Evie, but you're only eleven and a baby needs her ma. You know that."

After tending to Evalyn's arm, Bill gave each child a list of chores that needed to be done before their parents got back. Evalyn hoped Bill was wrong and that they'd come back with Ellie and some medicine. She also prayed for a miracle. That when they found out Ellie was going to be okay, her parents would have a change of heart and be more loving towards all their children.

She shook the thought away as she swept the uneven planked floor. The floor was in bad need of repair and all the children knew they needed to wear shoes at all time, or they might stub their toe on a warped plank or get splinters. Whenever it rained, although those moments were few and far between during the drought, the water leaked right through the roof and onto the floor. They didn't have enough pots and pans to catch all the leaks and at some point her parents had just stopped trying.

She imagined Ellie learning to crawl on the treacherous floor and literally cringed at the thought. There was no way Ellie could learn how to crawl on such a rough surface.

Alice came in the door, two eggs tucked in her small pockets and big tears falling from her eyes.

Evalyn put the broom down and went to her sister, who was gently putting the eggs in a basket. "What's wrong, Alice?"

"Clucks died last night," stated Alice.

Evalyn wrapped Alice up in a hug. Clucks had been Alice's favorite chicken. Bill had warned Alice not to get attached to the chickens, that they'd be family meals if they ever stopped laying eggs. Unfortunately for all the children, Clucks was a chicken that loved to be hugged, and they all soon grew attached to the lovable hen.

"Elmer's plucking her now," said Alice.

"I'm sorry, Alice," said Evalyn.

As sorry as Evalyn was, she hoped a good meal of chicken would raise everyone's spirits when her parents brought Ellie back from the doctor. They were living on mostly beans, her father stating they needed to keep the chickens for laying eggs. They were down to four chickens now that Clucks had died, with the prospect of no more since their rooster had perished during the last duster.

She glanced over at the egg basket, just five eggs. Most likely, her parents would eat the eggs on biscuits while the kids ate porridge. Evalyn's stomach rumbled and she considered frying an egg for her and Alice to share, but then thought better of it. If her parents suspected an egg missing they'd tan all their hides. Plus, it wouldn't be fair to just cook an egg for her and Alice, when Evalyn knew her brothers were equally as hungry.

"Okay, Alice," said Evalyn as she stood. "You need to go finish your chores. We don't want Pa being angry at us because we cried over a chicken all day."

Alice wiped her eyes and then her nose on her sleeve as she nodded. Evalyn picked the broom back up as Alice ran out the door to start watering the garden. Watering the garden was one of the hardest jobs on the farm. Alice couldn't carry the large bucket from the faucet to the garden full, so she had to make a lot of trips. Evalyn swept faster so she could help her little sister, insuring the job would get done before her parents returned.

She heard the rumble of her father's truck and stepped to the open door. Bill came around the house and hurried to Evalyn's side. She felt her brother's firm hand on her arm as a lump grew in her throat. Her parents sat in the truck for a minute, speaking to each other, before getting out.

"No!" cried Evalyn as her mother walked around the truck with her arms empty. "Where's Ellie? You go back and get her! You go back and get her now!"

Bill tightened his grip on Evalyn's arm, reminding her to keep her temper.

"Ellie died," stated Abe. "We can't afford a burial, so that's that. We'll not speak of it again."

"No," she cried as she shook her head and looked to Bill. "It can't be. I won't believe it. No. No. No."

"I'm so sorry, Evie," Bill whispered.

Evalyn's heart throbbed with pain as grief rose from her belly. Her legs turned to jelly as she fell into her brother's strong arms and wept.

Acknowledgments

Writing is often thought of as a solitary occupation, but the truth is it takes a lot of people to put a book together. I absolutely couldn't do it without these people: *LilyBear House staff and author family, Alyssa Foresman, C.D. Jarmola, Heather Davis, Marilyn Boone, Cindy Molder, Brandy Walker, Randy and Cathy Collar, Anna Collar, Theresa Messner, Claressa Carter, Rubina Ahmed, Linda Boulanger, Darlene Shortridge, Lynn Endres, Christina Laurie, Cheryl Trenfield, WordWeavers, Linda Derkez* (who has helped me with a number of flap copies), *The Minions, Family, Annaley, Mike McMurrain,* and most importantly *My Readers,* I am thankful for each and every one of you who have taken the time to read my books and an extra thank you for those who have become my friends due to them.

About the Author

Having a great deal of wanderlust, author Jennifer McMurrain traveled the countryside working odd jobs before giving into her muse and becoming a full time writer. She's been everything from a "Potty Princess" in the wilds of Yellowstone National Park to a bear researcher in the mountains of New Mexico. After finally settling down, she received a Bachelor's Degree in Applied Arts and Science from Midwestern State University in Wichita Falls, Texas. She has won numerous awards for her short stories and novels. She lives in Bartlesville, Oklahoma, with her husband, daughter, two spoiled cats, and two goofy dogs.

Author photograph by Sister Sparrow Photography

Other works by

Jennifer McMurrain

Quail Crossings Series

Quail Crossings
Return to Quail Crossings
Missing Quail Crossings

Spirit of Love Series

Winter Song
Summer's End

Novellas

The Divine Heart
Birdsong
Heart of an Angel

Anthologies & Collaborations

Whispered Beginnings
Seasons Remembered
Amore
Chicken Soup for the Soul: The Dog Did What?
Seasons of Life
A Weekend with Effie
Seasons to Celebrate

Short Stories

Thesis Revised
Emma's Walk
Footprints in the Snow
Finding Hope
Jar of Pickles
The Looking Glass